SINS OF YESTERDAY

BOOK ONE OF THE ARIZONA SERIES

ROMEO PREMINGER

CONTENTS

BOOKS IN THE SERIES

THE ARIZONA SERIES

Sins of Yesterday
Daddy's Boy
Ties That Bind
Promises We Keep
When Fallen Angels Fly

1

PEOPLE SAY I lived an extraordinary life. Funny thing is, it never felt like that to me. Maybe your life is extraordinary, and you don't even know it. I guess it all depends on who's doing the looking, and if they're looking from the inside out or the outside in.

All I can say, from the inside looking out, my life sure never seemed extraordinary. Especially as I got bigger and the whole world got bigger, and I could see plenty of folks who were a lot more extraordinary than me.

I grew up in Le Moyne Parish, Louisiana, one of them what they call Acadiana parishes in the southwestern part of the state. You had your poor folks like my family who lived on John's Island, your rich folks who lived in Franklin Acres, and the little city of Le Moyne in the middle where everybody did their business whether it was shopping at the Piggly Wiggly, dropping off their mail at the post office, or going to church. On Sundays, my brothers, sister, and me would watch the well-dressed Franklin Acres families coming out of the big, white stone, stained glass Our Lady of Grace cathedral while we was pulling our wagon of groceries on the other side of the street. Walking home from school on the shoulder of Parish Road 108, we'd see them folks speed by in shiny sedans and sports cars. Sometimes a group of boys from Saint

Augustine's Academy would slow down in a Pontiac hot rod, and they'd shout mean things and toss junk at us from their cars.

We were John's Island trash, low down swamp rats, and worst of all, Fanning freaks, which made us the lowest of the low. Folks said we was cursed on account of my great granddaddy. I didn't know the whole story back then. My grandma would only say Luke Fanning done a terrible thing what lost his big house, his acres of farmland, and everything else.

But in 1984, when I was fifteen years old, I wouldn't have said my life was more bad than good nor good than bad. It's true, we didn't have much but a rickety old house and a bad reputation. The house could've used a new roof, and it was something other folks would call an eyesore on its half acre of weedy land. But we had each other, us four kids, and we didn't know any better than to say our lives was just about the way they was supposed to be.

Us four is my younger brother Duke, my younger sister Dolly, Little Douglas who was just four years old, and me. Plus we had Grandma Tilly and Grandpa George who lived next door at the very end of our sleepy dead end street. My daddy drove an eighteen-wheeler coast to coast, so he wasn't home most of the time. That was best for everyone concerned.

You likely noticed I didn't mention my mama. That's because Louisa Fanning drove off an icy highway into Lake Verret coming home from church two Christmas Eve's past. She was only twenty-nine years old. That went down as another chapter in the cursed Fanning history.

I shed some tears, but with me being the older brother, some survival instinct I never knew I had kicked in, helping me stay strong. Someone had to pull us through. We'd be fooling ourselves to think we could count on Daddy. He started drinking himself to sleep even worse than he'd been drinking himself to sleep before. As for my mama's family, we couldn't count on them, neither.

Even before the funeral, we'd never seen much of the DuChamps. My grandpa and grandma on that side hadn't approved of Mama marrying a Fanning. They say folks in Acadiana invented stubbornness, and that's the truth. We didn't even get an invitation to their house after the burial, and we had to take two busses and walk a mile and a half to visit Mama in the DuChamps family plot all the way in Evangeline Parish. By rights, my daddy could've had her buried in the cemetery in town, but he never fought the DuChamps over the issue. We all knew the reason. If you told my daddy he could save a dollar, you didn't have to tell him twice.

I'd been taking care of next to everything around the house. Little Douglas needed to be washed and fed. Duke and Dolly needed their three square meals and someone to make sure they kept up with school and did their chores around the house. Daddy never did more than leave us a few dollars when he left out on one of his three week hauls. When he was home, he expected his clothes washed and dinner on the table, so that was up to me as well.

We did have Grandma Tilly to keep an eye on us. She and Grandpa didn't have much money since Grandpa splintered his skull in an accident at the sawmill up in Oakdale before I was born. I'd only known Grandpa George as a pasty old man who could lose his way from one house to the other if he didn't have Grandma to help him along. Mostly, he just stayed home getting paler and thinner yet somehow staying alive. But Grandma took care of Little Douglas while Duke, Dolly, and me went to school, and she'd make us pies and the most delicious bread pudding you ever tasted. Best of all, she gave us love, and I can tell you we were starved for that after Mama died.

I'd just finished my sophomore year of high school when a new storm blew into our lives. I remember that last day of school. On the way home, Duke and I had picked up branches from the side of the country highway, and we were sparring like Jedi knights with light sabers while Dolly gathered black-eyed Susans from the thatches.

Duke is just one year younger than me. He had Daddy's curly blond hair and his sights set on being a major league baseball player, along with getting into some mischief with a cheerleader in the nearer future. My brother Duke was all boy.

Dolly was twelve and a flaxen-haired girly-girl like our Mama. I'd always felt like I was something in-between, and with my dark brown hair and snub nose, I didn't need folks to remind me I stuck out in the Fanning clan. But I could hold my own in play fights with Duke and turn around and braid Dolly's hair the way she liked. Looking back, it's funny people never remarked I had the best of both worlds. Then again, it was 1984 which meant it was more like 1954 in Le Moyne Parish. Folks liked their worlds kept simple and if not that, they liked them separate.

I spotted the trouble that day when we were halfway down the road to our house. Daddy's pickup was in the drive. He wasn't due back until the following Friday, never mind Dolly had graduated from grade school earlier that week. It was one of many milestones in our lives he missed. I pointed out his truck to Duke and Dolly. Duke and I tossed aside our sticks, and we all three drew up together to walk to the house.

I could hear some conversation between Daddy and Grandma Tilly when we stepped up to the porch, but when I opened the screen door and walked in with my siblings, the two stopped talking. I set my eyes on Daddy. He was wearing an unbuttoned shirt and his dusty work pants. His slate blue eyes flashed fiercely at the sight of me. I had no idea why.

Dolly skipped over to give him a hug, and Duke followed along. Daddy didn't give hugs. You was lucky to get a nod out of him, and that day he definitely didn't look like he was in the mood. I'll give Gus Fanning this: he was a good-looking man back then. Even with his curly blond hair damp and greasy, he had a hardened kind of handsomeness. He must've recently taken off his trucker cap, and his thick chest and forearms glistened. A half-emptied bottle of bourbon sat on the kitchen table.

Dolly and Duke attacked him with questions, wanting to know how long he'd be home, and if he would take them to this place and that. Dolly asked if he wanted to see her diploma. Duke wanted to know if he'd drive him out to the batting range. I don't know why, but my brother and sister never could learn their lesson with Daddy.

"I ain't taking any of youse nowhere," he growled.

Grandma Tilly gathered Duke and Dolly and told them to run off until supper.

While they shuffled out the door, Daddy fixed on me with a smirk. "What's for supper, Arizona? You getting good at being the *lady* of the house."

He always made me feel small. I'd planned on making franks with beans. The shameful truth was that was all we had in the larder.

Grandma Tilly eyed me warmly. "Arizona's been taking good care of his brothers and sister. I'm sure he'll come up with some-thin' special."

"Franks and beans," I said.

Daddy swaggered up in front of me. He stunk of booze. "Franks and beans? What kind of supper is that on the day your daddy come home?"

He towered over me. Six foot one and one hundred and eighty pounds of ropey muscle in comparison to my slim five foot eight. And what did he expect? He never left us enough money to buy anything special.

"We didn't know you was coming home." My heart was in my throat, but I swore to myself I wouldn't cower from him.

Grandma Tilly stepped in. "Franks and beans'll do just fine. I'll make a nice pecan pie to go wit' 'em. Won't take mo' than an hour."

Daddy stared me down like I had shit smeared on my face. I didn't know if mean words were coming out of his mouth, but he could speak his mind with just a look. As far back as I can remem-ber, he let me know where I stood. I was an embarrassment, and I'd never be man enough for him. I spent the better part of my life shrinking away from my daddy, but I was getting to the age when I didn't shrink so much. Maybe I wasn't the kind of son he wanted, but I sure knew I didn't want to be the kind of man he was. Truth is, he didn't treat Duke much better, and Duke was his spitting image and just as rough and tumble as any son Daddy could wish for.

I went to the kitchen to check on the beans I'd left out on the counter soaking in a ham hock.

After dinner, Dolly and I cleaned up the pots and pans and dishes in the kitchen. We were both on pins and needles. Daddy had come home in one of his moods, and it was the worst I'd seen in some time. He drained his bourbon over dinner and sent Duke to fetch a second from his truck. When Grandma brought out Little Douglas, Daddy roughhoused him so hard, he sent him tumbling to the floor and wailing.

Grandma scooped up Douglas to console him. Daddy sneered and said the boy was a sissy while pointing his gaze at me. Some grudge was burning inside him. It reminded me of the nights he put hands on Mama, and Duke and I had to get between them to protect her.

Daddy swayed out to the front porch to drink his bourbon and smoke his pipe. Duke followed to try to get him interested in tossing a baseball with him. I listened to Daddy curse him out and tell Duke to leave him alone.

I would've gone out to the yard to play with Duke myself, but I had a promise to keep that night. Grandma had stuck around to keep an eye on things, so when Dolly and I finished with the dishes, I cleaned up in the bathroom, pulled on a clean shirt, and stole out the back door to sneak through the woods.

The woods behind our house was our playground growing up. During the day, I mean. At night, them pine woods seemed haunted when banks of fog drifted in and you heard sounds you could swear didn't come from anything in nature, or at least nothing you wanted to meet. But in the daylight, Duke, Dolly, and me loved to play hide-and-seek back there, and Duke and I found a creek where you could catch little frogs and crayfish if you was quick handed about it. I knew the trails through the winnowy pine trees like I knew my backhand, and that night I followed the way to a special place where my best friend Preston Montclair and I liked to meet up.

Preston lived on the other side of John's Island, straight through the pine woods. Everyone called that the Cajun side of the island since that's where the French-speaking families lived. I don't mean the Broussards or the Granvilles who sent their kids to Saint Augustine's for school. But even on John's Island where everyone was just scraping by, people kept to their own kin. West was Cajun and East was Irish, and if you know your Louisiana history, the Irish who came over to the Mississippi Valley had to make their living working jobs the French folks wouldn't give their African slaves. Us Fannings came from generations of ditch diggers and railway grunts.

To get back to my story, I went trekking through the woods that night for a secret rendezvous. One summer, when Preston and me was twelve, we'd found a weathered stone house hidden back there. It wasn't much bigger than a shed and scarcely a shelter no more. Its two windows had shattered, the wood door had rotted and come off its hinges, and the roof had caved in and become a nest for finches. Still, Preston and I thought it was just about the greatest discovery known to man. We found an old, rusty musket back there, which looked like it went back to the Civil War. We figured the house had been home to a hermit or maybe some minor way station for soldiers in some past age. Back then it was all ours.

The ancient house was dark and still as I approached. At school that day, Preston and I said we'd meet up after supper, and usually that meant Preston would get there first with all the chores I had to do after feeding my brothers and sister. That night, however, I thought I must've beat Preston, which was none too comforting in the night-shrouded forest.

I was old enough to be cynical about the stories people told about bigfoot and cannibals and swamp creatures lurking in John's

Island woods. But I was also old enough to have heard about prison fugitives and serial killers.

The cicadas had started their early summertime clamor, swelling and ebbing in a nocturnal tide. Little flocks of creatures which I knew had to be bats flapped overhead. I was wishing I hadn't run out of the house without my big yellow Eveready flashlight. I kept my eyes peeled on the house's shadowy interior and stepped toward the doorway, looking for Preston.

Out of nowhere, somebody grabbed me around my sides, and I shrieked and shook away, nearly tripping over myself. A familiar chuckle burst out, and a flashlight clicked on. Good ol' Preston. Giving me a heart attack just for kicks.

"You too easy to fool, Arizona."

"Dammit Preston." I scowled at him. But once my heart slowed down, I thawed from the sight of him. Preston had a wavy shag of fawn-brown hair and big brown friendly eyes. He eased up close and gently wove his hands behind my hips.

"How's this? Now don't be sore at me. I had to grab you. I been dreaming about you all day long."

He smothered my mouth with his. No doubt about it, I'd been dreaming about Preston all day as well. We'd been sweethearts since seventh grade, and I can tell you that's not an easy thing in Le Moyne Parish where boys like us got beatdowns or worse if people found out.

The most notorious story was Howard Hobbs. He was two grades ahead of me and had the gentlest soul. He'd never done as much as say a bad word about anybody. Howard had just been born with the misfortune of having a high voice and effeminate ways, which made him a target for cruelty by the dumb hicks at our school.

Last Halloween, a gang of kids grabbed Howard off the street, tied him to the back of their truck, and dragged him through town. They left him dead in front of his house. The police never arrested the devils who did it, though the good ol' boys boasted about it far and wide. The law just took their word it had been an accident, and I suppose Howard's family was too ashamed to ask for justice. I'll be haunted by that story until my dying day.

Preston and I were careful, though. We never spoke a word about our relationship to anybody, and we minded not walking too close to one another at school. As far as anyone knew, we were just friends, and that didn't draw any attention so long as Preston kept up with the Cajun boys in our class.

I won't lie. It was hard. Not just the fear of being caught, but the way our relationship sometimes made me feel on the inside. I'd prayed about it, asking God to turn me right, though the sad truth was I'd never been taught how to pray. Daddy's family were Baptist, and Mama's were Catholic, but Daddy didn't want us kids going to any kind of church. I'd only been to a Catholic church once with my mama when I was little. I didn't follow anything that was going on, but I remember how beautiful it was with all the stained glass and the steepled roof of the altar that looked high enough to reach up to heaven. I thought some-times about going back there and confessing about me and Preston to a priest in one of their private booths. I guess I was too chicken to do it. Besides, when Preston held me in his arms, I couldn't see how the feelings we had for each other couldn't be right.

We kissed that night until we were breathless and aching for each other. Preston smelled so nice, fresh from the shower, all clean and fragrant from his Old Spice deodorant. He was my slice of heaven, maybe all I'd ever get from the stingy world. It took all my willpower to slow him down.

"My daddy's home," I told him.

Preston frowned. Then he gave me a sharp look. "And he'll leave again. You can be sure of that."

I shifted away from him a bit. Horseflies fluttered in my stomach thinking about Little Douglas, Dolly, and Duke on their own back at the house. Meanwhile, Preston pulled me close again.

"How you gonna run off on me after you got me all warmed up?" That smile of his was like a lasso. It made me want to follow him wherever he cared to lead, probably even off the railway bridge over Atchafalaya River if he asked me to take the dive with him.

"I can't be gone long." I faced Preston glumly. "He's on a tear. Grandma Tilly's with Little Douglas, but she won't be much help if Daddy start acting up."

Preston took my hand in his. "You want me to come home with you?"

It was nice of him to say, but it was just about the last thing that would make Daddy behave.

"I'm serious, Arizona. I been practicing my hooks and upper-cuts since my Pere put up the boxing bag in the basement. I named it Gus Fanning. I got fists of steel to lay him out cold. You just say the word."

I smirked. Preston bowed his head, got a grim look on his face, and play-jabbed me in the tummy, grinding his fist into my flesh to tickle me.

"You saying I ain't got what it takes?"

I caught his hand to stop him from tickling me.

"Now that ain't nice, Arizona. Making fun of me when I trying to stand up for you." He attacked me with his hands, squeezing my sides, poking my armpits, making me squirm and laugh.

I wrangled to quiet his hands, and his flashlight tumbled to the ground. "Cease fire, you damn fool." I knew Preston was just trying to cheer me up. Could be he'd been practicing with his boxing bag in the basement, but he was no bigger than me and hardly a match for my daddy, unless he was seeing double from all the bourbon marinating his brain.

Preston got both his arms high around my back and hugged me. It felt so warm and good with both our bodies hot from wran-gling and wanting each other.

"There ain't nothing I wouldn't do for you. You my moon and stars, Arizona Fanning. I'll never let nobody hurt you, including Gus Fanning who never did one thing right besides making you."

The moonlight traced his beautiful face. Preston had a way of putting things that made it hard to not believe him. Though sometimes I wondered if I deserved so much love and kindness. Sometimes I wondered if we were blazing a trail to hell.

He nuzzled his nose against mine. "Two years," he said. "Don't you forget. Then we can run off to New Orleans, Atlanta, or even New York City. You take your pick of places where we can be together and never worry 'bout what nobody thinks."

I sighed. "Two years is a long time."

"C'est la vie, cher. You think we oughta run off sooner? I got my working papers. My uncle Merle say he can get me a job at his garage and bait and tackle store in town. Save up some money to buy us bus tickets and some extra to get us settled somewhere."

I ran my hand along his hard shoulder and down his upper arm. Sometimes all I wanted was to run away with Preston. But even if there was someplace where the two of us could be together without worrying about getting tied to a pickup in the middle of the night, I had Duke, Dolly, and Little Douglas to think about.

"You're sweet. But we should finish high school, don't you think?"

Preston held me firmly by the hips. "If you say so. The waiting's hard. Why you gotta be so good, Arizona? I can't help wanting you all the time."

We kissed again, and Preston led me into the musty house. The place sure wasn't grand, but it felt luxurious to me. Preston joked it was our five-star hotel, and sure as eggs were eggs, he'd take me to a five-star hotel some day, and we'd make love proper on silk sheets. To hear him tell it, we'd be drinking champagne and eating caviar like Prince Charles and Princess Diana.

That crumbling house in the woods was fine with me. Just being with Preston anywhere made me feel like I had anything a man could need. The thing about love is it's the one thing in the world that comes for free, which is not to say it's an easy thing to find. I was learning it's the rarest, most precious thing in the world. I loved Preston. Maybe it was wrong in the eyes of God, but it was hard to reckon God paid any mind to a poor country boy like me. And Preston and I found each other in a tiny speck of the world where boys like us hid from one another in fear for their lives. If that's not a miracle, I don't know what is.

We kissed and hugged and nuzzled and got our hands down each other's shorts, doing grown-up things we'd only discovered were possible a few months back. They wouldn't call it a sin if the devil didn't make it feel so good. I'd heard that somewhere. Maybe from a preacher on the radio. Anyway, it's the truth.

Afterward, we tucked up in a corner of the house, bathed in darkness and the musty fug of the stone-walled house. I played idly with the pad of Preston's hand. As nice of an escape it was seeing him, I still had heavy things on my mind.

"Is it wrong to hate my daddy?"

Preston snorted. "You say the funniest things, Arizona."

I wrung his hand. "Really. I been puzzling over it since he came home. I think I hate him, and I don't know if that makes both of us wrong. He's my daddy, and I'm his son."

"A daddy's a man who raises you. Gus Fanning never done nothing for you and yours 'cept give you grief. You ask me, you don't owe him nothin' 'less he turns around and starts treatin' you right. And I wouldn't hold your breath for that to happen. My uncle Beau's the same way, but he did my aunt and cousins the favor of packing up and moving out. My cousin Jean-Marie just calls him a sperm donor."

Preston knew all about what my daddy had put my family through, and I supposed that way of thinking made sense for him. Preston's father, Richard Montclair, was a good man. He always looked you in the eye, said comment ça va, which is how do you do in French, and he always shook your hand. He had a steady job at a chemical plant, volunteered at the firehouse, and made sure Preston and his brothers and sisters had all the latest clothes and bicycles and Walkman radios. When my daddy was away for weeks and hadn't left us enough money for food, Preston's father even made groceries so the four of us had something to eat.

I only had Gus Fanning to raise me.

Thinking about those things made me antsy, and I had to beg

Preston to let me go. We'd stolen happiness for a spell, but an hour or so every few nights was all we could steal. Then Preston dug something out of his shorts pocket and pressed it into my hand.

It was tiny, square-edged and hard like metal. Preston clicked his flashlight on.

"They gave us these today in woodworking class."

I examined it closer. It was a pin, some kind of graduation award. Preston was in the vocational track at school. He was good at things like carpentry and metalwork.

Preston grinned at me. "Soon as the teacher handed 'em out, I knew I wanted to give it to you. You don't have to wear it. Just keep it. So even when we apart, it won't be like we apart 'cause you'll always have something of me."

My eyes grew wide. That little pin would be the most precious thing I'd ever owned.

"You sure?"

"If I'm lying, I'm dying, Arizona."

I pulled up my shorts and tucked the pin into my pocket. Preston hopped up and embraced me from behind.

"I love you. Don't forget it."

I gripped his hand, tearing up a bit. "I love you, too."

2

I RACED HOME feeling light as a feather. Preston Montclair loved me. Happy fool that I was, I wanted to shout it to the moon. The stars in the sky seemed brighter, the world felt easier, and everything seemed right.

Two years was a long time to wait to make a life together, but we'd managed keeping things secret for near three years already. I hadn't seen the world outside of Le Moyne Parish, but I'd heard in big cities like New Orleans there was lots of men who was gay, come from all over Louisiana.

In a place like that, maybe Preston and I could be free. I could go to college and get a part-time job while Preston worked. I'd done well at school. I'd thought about studying to be a teacher. Or maybe, since I liked writing, I could become a journalist. Everything felt possible that night.

That easy feeling turned on a dime and scattered when I crept out of the woods into our backyard.

Lights were on. I could see that through the kitchen window. I didn't dare take a peek around the front to see if my daddy was still out there on the porch, but I prayed he was. The back door led into the kitchen, and then I'd have to pass by the living room on my way to the bedroom I shared with my brothers. I'd just be quick about it, I told myself. I carefully opened the creaky back door and stepped inside like I was creeping over a minefield.

The house was quiet. The hallway to the bedrooms was dark. I thought I'd caught some luck that night, and I'd sneak into my room with no one to the wise.

I made it a few steps out of the kitchen. Then my damn nosy eyes wouldn't behave. I glanced into the living room. Daddy was sitting in his armchair. Our gazes crossed, and I froze. His lip curled up in an ugly sneer.

"You think you can come and go as you please?"

I watched him twisting his bottle of bourbon in his hand. Not more than a couple of drops left. His face was puffy and glazed, but the sight of me had him looking scary and alert.

"You the big man now, huh? King of the roost. How old are you?"

I wasn't sure if he was taunting me with that question or if he'd just lost track.

"Fifteen."

"Fifteen," he repeated in a mocking way. His eyes dug into mine. "So, you know what's what?"

I knew no good could come from talking to him. I can't explain why I didn't just go on my way. As much as I detested my daddy, his menacing stare still held power over me.

"What's a fifteen-year-old fella like you sneaking out of the house at night for?" He coughed out a laugh. "You don't look drunk." He put on an enlivened face. "You got a girly you been getting in trouble with?"

My head was helplessly blank. He'd twist around and make fun of anything I had to say anyway.

Daddy set down his bottle and pushed up from his chair. He looked unsteady and thirsting for a row.

"You gonna answer me, Arizona?" He swayed over, bare chested, stinking of alcohol and tobacco. I stood wooden all the while he placed his big hand on the back of my neck, catching himself on wobbly legs and bobbing his head.

He forced a bloodshot look into my eyes. "You gonna tell your Daddy? You got a girl?"

My insides curdled, but I willed myself not to flinch from him. He threw back his head in a boozy laugh and came back at me, flushed and mean. "'Course not. I know what you are. You a no-good faggot."

He turned his shoulder for a half second and launched his fist with surprising speed. The room throbbed light and dark, and then pain scorched white hot on my face. I tripped back on my bottom, clutching my nose. Warm blood flooded my hand.

I tried to scoot away from him on my backside. Daddy righted himself after nearly falling from that thrown punch. He staggered in my direction and lorded over me.

"Can't take a punch, fag boy?"

He kicked my leg with his steel-toed boot. It stung, but it could've been worse. He teetered above me, clumsy from all the alcohol.

"You ain't better than me," he mumbled blearily. "Don't you forget it." He stabbed a shaky finger at me. "I see what's stirring in your head."

Tears stung my eyes. I dug my heels into the floor to slide away from him.

He foundered on to his knees and craned over me with his hands pressed into my shoulders. His weight pinned me to the floor.

"I look at you and see your mama. Pretty boy." He grabbed me hard between the legs. "You like that, don't you?"

I howled. "Daddy, stop."

"You always was an uppity bitch just like her."

I shoved and thrashed to get out from under him, then he collapsed on top of me. I felt like I was suffocating, like we were both being dragged to hell. After all the pain my daddy had inflicted, he nuzzled his alcohol-stinking lips against my neck. It was worse than when he had struck me, my rotten, drunken father forcing on me things he ought never do to his son.

"You make me do this," he whimpered. "You know I love you, Pip. I didn't mean to hurt you. It's only 'cause I's in love with you."

I did the only thing I could do. I hollered bloody murder. He got off of me, and gradually I realized Duke and Dolly had run out from their rooms to pull Daddy away.

I scrambled to my hands and knees and pushed up from the floor. Daddy lay on his back, covering his face and sobbing. Duke and Dolly stared at me for explanations. I was so ashamed, I couldn't say a word to them.

I staggered to the bathroom, locked the door, turned on the sink and washed my face. Blood stained the porcelain like I was rinsing a brush coated with bright scarlet latex paint.

I HAD A whopper of a swollen nose the next morning, and it was ugly like rotten meat. It stung so bad, it hurt just to think. I felt like burying myself in my bed all day with the shutters drawn over the windows.

But Little Douglas was up and needed looking after, and all us kids needed breakfast. Luckily, Grandma had put Little Douglas to bed in a diaper. He was still wetting himself at night sometimes, especially when Daddy was home.

I got Little Douglas cleaned up and dressed, woke Duke and told him to keep our little brother in our room until I gave the okay to come out. Then I went to the bathroom. I pulled out the wadded toilet paper I'd stuck up my nostrils last night, stuffed clean ones up there and padded to the kitchen in my pajamas.

Sometime last night, Daddy got up and made it to his bed. That spot on the living room floor where he had collapsed on top of me felt like it was circled like a crime scene chalked for evidence. I knew that was all in my head, but it made me sick just looking in that room. I had no idea why he'd called me Pip. Mama's name was Louise, and everyone called her Lou. Daddy had been so far out of his mind, I supposed there was no use trying to make sense of anything he'd said.

While I was at the stove making Little Douglas's farina, Grandma Tilly showed up at the house. I tried to hide my face from her, but she caught one glimpse and swooped over.

She clicked off the stove, sat me down at the kitchen table, and went to the freezer to empty a tray of ice cubes into a plastic bag. She handed me the ice bag, and I placed it tenderly, high up on my nose. The cold hurt at first, but then it numbed the pain a little. I sat there while she finished what I'd started and set the kids up in the living room to eat their breakfast in front of the TV.

I heard her travel to my daddy's room, and then she came into the kitchen and sat down across from me. I stared down at the table. I didn't want to talk about what happened. For a while, it seemed like she didn't either, just sitting there in silence.

Then she muttered, "I never shoulda left you kids last night."

I peeked at her. Her aged face was grim.

"He hurt you anywhere else?"

I rolled up one leg of my pajama bottoms to show her where a big yellow-purple bruise had bloomed on the outside of my thigh. That was hardly anything though compared to the pain in my nose.

She sighed and got up from the table. "This what we gonna do. The kids are spending the day with Grandpa, and I taking you out for breakfast."

I gaped at her. "Looking like this?"

"How many times you been invited out for breakfast? Now go on and get dressed. They seen worse at Waffle House." She came around and cocked an eye at me. "No fussin', young man. We'll get one of them booths for privacy."

I marched back to my room to change, and by the time I came back out in a clean T-shirt and jeans, Grandma had Dolly and Duke lined up at the door with their backpacks and Little Douglas's hand in hers to head out.

I HAD A fierce appetite once I saw all the plates of waffles and flapjacks and tasted the delicious aromas in my mouth. The hard part was the eating. I had to cut up my flapjacks and sausages real small, and it still hurt like blazes to stretch open my mouth and chew.

My stomach was determined, however. I worked out a method of getting small forkfuls into my mouth, sipping some coffee to soften things up, and swallowing my breakfast down. Grandma gave me a couple of her prescription Tylenols she had left over from her hysterectomy, and that helped some once they kicked in.

She sat across from me at our booth with just a cup of tea and a wedge of lemon. True to her word, she'd asked the hostess for a booth in the far corner of the restaurant where I wouldn't get nosy looks. She watched me eat without saying anything. I was grateful for that. I wasn't sure how well I'd do trying to talk when it was so uncomfortable eating.

When I finished my plate and wiped my mouth with my napkin, she pushed some words out.

"Arizona, I ain't saying what your daddy done was right, but there's a reason, and I think you old enough to know."

My eyes grew big, then that stung too, and I winced. Grandma scowled and knit her hands together tightly on the table. She had a way of comforting, which I called hugging with her eyes. That's how she looked at me. My mama could do that too. I'd gotten a lot of those hugging looks from both of them like they knew I needed some extra kindness.

"Your daddy...well, he's who he is. We could pray morning, noon, and night for him to change and love you kids proper, and it wouldn't make a lick of difference." She gave me a sharp nod. "Don't think I ain't tried. I been praying for a miracle since before you was born. But at some point, you just have to accept things for what they is. Even a preacher will tell you that, 'less he's one of them holy roller frauds you see on TV. Anyway, I know that now."

She sniffed, holding back tears. "I ain't never going to let him hurt you again, Arizona, and not your brothers or sister neither."

Tears burned in my sinuses. I bowed my head, and that delicate feeling passed. I think my sore head wouldn't let me go through the agony of crying.

"He never treated you right," Grandma went on. "I'm sure you know that better than me. He never treated your mama right, neither. And now I'm gonna tell you the reason, though they both made me swear not to say."

I peeked up at her.

"Your mama, the one who birthed you, she's not your mama who raised you." Grandma put her hand to her mouth. I stared at her, not wanting to believe.

She trembled and forced the words out. "Your daddy, he was with another woman he thought he was going to marry before Lou. She left you something of hers. Made me promise to give it to you, and I kept it 'til the day came to tell you the truth."

She dug into the pocket of her skirt and brought out a little blue velvet jewelry box. She placed it on the table and pushed it toward me.

I didn't want to even touch it at first. That pretty little box seemed poisonous. It would erase everything I'd known about myself, everything I'd known about the world. I didn't want a different mama.

But Grandma nudged me, giving me some courage. I took the velvet box in my hand. It was small enough to wrap my fist around. I split it open and saw a gold cross pendant on a gold chain. The initials on the cross were P.B. It looked far more expensive than any jewelry anyone in my family owned. Something people would laugh at if they saw me wearing it.

"It was a gift from her stepdaddy for her first communion," Grandma told me. "Phillipa Bondurant. That's your mama, Arizona."

I left the jewelry box on the table and looked away from Grandma. I didn't want the fancy necklace. I didn't want some mother I'd never known. Daddy had just beat me up and worse. Why was she telling me this?

"Pipa, or Pip, your daddy called her."

Hairs shot up on the back of my neck.

"She would've loved you, Arizona. Which is not to say your Mama Lou didn't love you as her own. She did. You know that, don't you? But you're becoming a man now, and a man oughta know where he comes from."

I scowled at her. "What's the point? My mama's dead. This woman wants to claim me now? Where she been?"

Grandma wrung her hands, shifted her gaze. "She passed, baby. It was a hard labor. The doctors saved you, but they couldn't save Philippa."

I scuffed my sneaker on the floor. I felt like vomiting. I wanted to storm away, but a weight pressed down on me, and I couldn't move.

"It's the truth, Arizona. And ain't you deserve the truth?"

I tucked my face into my elbow and hiccupped tears.

"Oh, darlin'. I know you just been through an ordeal, but there was no right time to tell you. It wouldn't have done no good while your Mama Lou was alive. Wouldn't have done you no good so soon after she died. But it don't change nothing. Don't make a speck of difference. Grandpa and I still love you. Duke, Dolly, and Little Douglas, they'll always love you too. You got two mamas looking out for you from heaven. That's more than most people have."

The truth of that sank in, which is not to say I felt more special. If what she said was true, I'd killed my birth mama coming into the world. Then the mama who raised me was stolen from us. I never felt more sure the Fanning curse was real. Both my mamas left me to be raised by a man who hated me.

"Your daddy loved your mama," Grandma said. "It could be the one good thing he ever done, taking you in when Phillipa passed and her family wanted none of it. He took up with Lou soon after, and your brother Duke came along. Your mama Lou,

she had so much love in her heart, it was nothing to her raising
you as her own."

I savored every word she said. Things shifted in my mind. I'd
always felt like I didn't belong. Now I knew the reason for it. It was
something, well, normal, I guess you'd say rather than ugly and
wrong.

Grandma's bearing hardened a bit. "As much as your daddy
needed someone to mother you, that was when he start to change.
It happen with men. Some more than others." She bit down on her
finger. "I can't explain your daddy. I never did give him nothing
but love, but he was always looking for something more. Maybe it
something he supposed to be born with. Maybe it something that
just plain don't exist in the world, but he got it in his head he
deserve it, and he won't treat anyone with kindness until he get it."

She patted her misty eyes with a napkin and put on an ironic
grin. "Mothers don't know everything about their children. We say
we do, and we do understand a lot, but I ain't figured out your
daddy in all these years. I know this, though. It got nothing to do
with you. You nod your head and lemme know you understand
that, Arizona. It's *his* shame, *his* burden he been carrying ever since
he was a child."

When Grandma gives you that look and asks you to do something, you do. I'd say I believed what she said seventy-five percent,
but I gave her a one hundred percent nod.

"Good. Now here's as much as I figured out about you and
your daddy. Some knowledge you can put to use. I was saying your
daddy turned when Lou had Duke. What you need to understand
is men get jealous when their wives have babies. Some more than
others like I always say, but if there's a bad habit to pick up, you
can bet your daddy's first in line wherever they're giving it out."

I grinned at that.

"They say women is weaker and more emotional than men."
Grandma hooted. "You just spend some time with a father who's
used to getting all his wife's attention, and now it's portioned out
to this child and the other, and not because she has a choice, mind

you. A child require time and care a grown man don't need. But your daddy start to resent it. He resented your mama, and he resented you. Mama Lou, I should say. Your grandpa went through that streak while I was home with your daddy and your uncle Benjamin, with the moping and the complaining and the short temper and all."

She smiled to herself. "Until I set him right. That's what mamas do. We got to raise the children and raise the husbands again after the children come. Nobody around to raise us." She clucked and looked at me squarely. "Now you tell me that's fair. Well, for most fathers it just a phase. I said this was information you could put to use, Arizona, so pay attention. When the time comes you have a wife and babies, spare a little patience for the woman. It'll save you both some grief."

She laughed, and I smiled along. I couldn't tell her I didn't see a wife and babies in my future. Maybe someday I would. I didn't know. The thought of telling her about Preston made me squirm inside. Instead I asked her a question.

"You saying Daddy resents me because Mama Lou had to take care of me in addition to Duke, Dolly and Little Douglas?"

It didn't make sense to me why he'd hold onto that grudge now that I was grown and taking care of everyone in the house, not to mention the fact Mama was gone now and not doling out her attention to anybody.

Grandma sealed her lips in a tight frown. "It's more than that, darlin'. Why, he resents all of you for having to share Lou. I tol' you I ain't figured it all out, and I had my talks with your daddy. He's getting another one soon as he wake up from that bender he put on last night. Not all men know how to treat the people they love. Your daddy loves you, and he's giving it to you, showing it as much as he can. It ain't much. Lord knows he just lousy at it. It's his struggle, Arizona, and maybe you catch it the worst because he lost your mama Philippa, and then he saw Lou take so strong to you." She shook her head. "I could see his rage burning inside him when you was little and I came around the house." She glanced at me. "I know you seen it, too. You seen things no child should see."

I had, and what frightened me the most was remembering him lying on top of me on the living room floor, that horrible whimpering voice of his, him clutching at me like I was some long-lost love who I now knew was my birth mother. I still felt his hand between my legs, his lips on my neck, all parts of me dirty and spoiled. I was scared that feeling would never go away.

"Baby, I ain't telling you any of this to say you gotta forgive what he done. That's up to him to make right, and up to you to decide."

I'd never forgive him. Any ounce of love for my daddy he hadn't already killed before last night died right then and there sitting with my grandma in Waffle House. All my life he wanted me to feel small and useless. He held back the truth about my mama just to hurt me.

"There gonna be changes," Grandma went on. "I ain't trusting him with any of youse. I always feared this would happen. I made him promise last night he'd leave you be. You might as well know this, too. Your daddy lost his job yesterday. That's why he was drownin' his sorrows in the bottle."

My eyes shot up. "How'd he lose his job?"

Grandma was careful at first. I stared at her. I deserved to know. The one thing the bastard was good for, the one thing he did I couldn't do was make money to pay the bills. We were two months overdue on the oil bill already. Now Daddy had gone and lost his job?

"Your daddy dug himself in some deep problems, darlin'. He got caught selling some of the furniture off his truck."

The worry on her face was troubling. Grandma already had a face that was a patchwork of wrinkles, but she looked even older and more fragile as her eyes trembled. Then she set a palm down on the table with finality.

"Well, he lucky the company's not taking it up in court. Ten years he had that job. It counts for something."

"How we gonna live?"

"He'll find another job. Get his butt over to the workforce commission in Lafayette to sign up for unemployment checks till he finds one."

Grandma raised her hand to get the waitress's attention and settle up. The conversation had me pulled and twisted up like taffy. I eyed the gold cross necklace my mama had left for me. I probably sound like a fool, but it made me feel special. I closed up the box and snuck it into the pocket of my jeans.

GRANDMA SAID NONE of us was staying with Daddy till he cleaned up his act. When we got back to her house, Duke was in the yard trying but not succeeding to teach Little Douglas how to swing a junior-sized wiffle bat. Dolly was sitting in the shade of the old mulberry tree, stringing together daisies. Grandpa was just as we had left him, nodding off in his rocking chair on the porch.

I took a good look next door before I followed Grandma into the house. Daddy hadn't come out of bed as far as I could tell. The mailbox flag was still turned up, and the blue, plastic-wrapped Thrifty Nickel was still on the doorstep. Maybe we'd have some luck, and Daddy would sleep straight through to next morning.

A few days later, I was helping Grandma gather laundry around the house while the other kids were outside playing. Her house was smaller than Daddy's. She and Grandpa slept in one bedroom, and there was just one other with a full-size bed. We decided it would do for Duke, Little Douglas, and me. Grandma had fetched my sleeping bag from Daddy's place, and I was sleeping on the floor while Duke and Douglas doubled up on the bed. Meantime, Dolly slept on the living room couch. Grandma and I were picking up my brothers' clothes strewn around our bedroom.

The front door creaked open, and slow shuffling steps groaned down the hall. Grandma's nose twitched, and she shot a glance that way. I looked over and saw Grandpa putter by the bedroom. Grandma dropped her laundry bag and tore out to the hall.

"Now what you doing, George? You supposed to be watching the kids."

"I have to use the bathroom."

Grandma gasped, and then she muttered, "It too late for that."

I drifted over to the bedroom door. Grandpa was grimacing like a little kid. The leg of his trouser was darkened with urine.

I'm ashamed to say Grandpa George terrified me. He was old and sickly looking, and you could see in his vacant eyes he'd lost comprehension of just about everything around him. I hated having to hug him on his birthday and Christmas. He pressed his cold, dribbly lips against my face, and he stunk like a dirty fanny. I knew it wasn't his fault. That head injury made him the way he was. But I couldn't help feeling I might catch what he got from being too close to him. We kids would be in better hands if Grandma put up a scarecrow in the yard to watch us.

She helped him along to the bedroom and shut the door to get him out of his wet clothes. I went back to finish gathering the laundry, and I hauled the big bag to the back of the house where Grandma had a washer.

Then Dolly shrieked from the yard, and I hustled out to see what in kingdom come was going on.

She was standing in the middle of the yard, staring next door. It didn't look like nothing was physically wrong with her, but I knew something wasn't right.

Dolly pointed to our house. "Daddy got Little Douglas."

Daddy was carrying our little brother, headed toward the front door stoop with Duke running after him. A wood paneled station wagon I'd never seen was parked out front. I charged toward the house.

I became a different man that day. I'd murder Daddy for grabbing my little brother even if I died doing it. I overtook Duke to get to the bastard.

Grandma came out to the porch and whistled as loud as a policeman breaking up a bar fight. We all three froze.

"Augustus Harrison Fanning, you put that boy down. It take but one phone call, and I'll have Social Services on the way."

Daddy bowed his head for a moment. He must've been making mental calculations. Grandma's voice had been loud enough to rouse the neighbors' curiosity. But then, he quickly stole into the house with Little Douglas and shut the door.

I ran. I tried the doorknob, but it wouldn't budge. I beat on the door with all my might, and Duke joined me, hollering for Daddy to open up.

Grandma bustled over quicker than I'd ever seen her move. She jangled out her ring of keys from her skirt pocket and fit the house key into the doorknob. She turned to me and Duke.

"Y'all wait out here."

We both stood back. Grandma turned the knob, pushed her way into the house, and closed the door behind her.

A lot of shouting went back and forth, though it was muffled, and I could only make out bits and pieces. The door opened up again, and a woman and a man stepped out. They were neatly dressed and looked to be around my daddy's age. They shied away from Duke and me, walked briskly to their car like they were dodging TV reporters, and the car revved up, made a three-point turn, and shot off down the street.

I had no idea what to make of that. Then Grandma came out with Little Douglas holding her hand, and I breathed in a lungful of air. She pulled Little Douglas toward her house. I looked to Duke, and we followed her. Then Daddy shot out to the front stoop, hollering at Grandma.

"You got no right taking the boy away from me. I'll call the police myself. See what they say about taking a father's children away from him."

Grandma plowed ahead, up the stairs to the porch and into the house. Dolly scampered after her.

I glanced at Daddy. He wore an ugly sneer, staring at Grandma's house. If he had looked my way, that was all it would have took for me to swagger over to him and try out my fists.

But that day, he paid me no heed. He just shut himself up in the house.

LATER, AFTER LITTLE Douglas, Dolly, and Duke had gone to sleep, I sat with Grandma on the porch, and she told me what had happened.

"Your daddy done lost his mind. He found an adoption service and thinks he gonna sell Little Douglas to pay off his debts."

My jaw dropped. It still hurt a little, but my face was mending.

"I'll have to call Social Services," she said. "Get things settled proper." She eyed me carefully. "They gonna want to talk to you, Arizona. About the other night. You gonna have to be brave, baby. Tell 'em what happened exactly as it did. For the sake of your little brother, you hear?"

She teared up and covered her face in her hands. I'd never seen her fall apart like that. It was like a knife to my heart.

Grandma rocked a little and steadied herself. I leaned over from my chair and took her arm.

"I'll do whatever you say."

She looked at me kindly. "I'm not gonna let him sell off Little Douglas or any of you kids."

She was quiet for a moment, minding her thoughts. It sunk in what an evil thing Daddy tried to do. What kind of man sells his baby boy? What price could you put on a child? I hadn't thought my daddy could be *that* evil, but it seemed like every day, layers were peeling away and showing me how ugly he was on the inside.

That night all three of us boys slept in the bed, Little Douglas between me and Duke. Neither Duke or me was sleepy, and I knew he was itching to know what was going on. Little Douglas was sound asleep, so I told Duke quietly what Grandma had said.

I'd been through a lot of firsts in just a few days, and that night I saw Duke sob worse than any child I'd seen before. I had to get him out of the bed and sit him down in the corner of the room because he was going to wake Little Douglas with his heaving and moaning.

I put my arm around him. "Grandma's not gonna let Daddy do it. Look here." I made him turn his head to face me, and I stared straight into his eyes and nodded.

"W-we g-gonna live here now?"

"Mm-hmm. So long as Daddy's not well." I gave Duke's shoulder a squeeze. "We gonna be all right. I'm your older brother. I'll always look out for you. And Dolly and Little Douglas."

I remembered we were technically half-brothers. Back at Waffle House talking to Grandma, I'd worried that would change how Duke and Dolly thought about me and wondered if it meant we weren't so close after all. But comforting Duke straightened all that out in my head. Like she said, it didn't make a speck of difference. We were blood and always would be. I loved all my siblings, and I'd fight like a tiger if anyone tried to hurt them.

THE NEXT FEW days were jittery for sure. Grandma didn't want any of us even stepping out of the house, and we were all three entirely copacetic about that. I was so caught up with keeping a watch on Daddy, I didn't even think about calling Preston. Then when I did, I got jittery even more wondering if he'd be angry I hadn't called, or if he'd be a fool and run over to try to give Daddy a beat down for hurting me.

I couldn't risk it. I'd call Preston when things cooled down, I decided. Meantime, I listened and peeked out the kitchen window that looked toward Daddy's house.

He didn't come out often. Just one day I saw him hop in his

pickup and come back with groceries and a box from the liquor store. He never made good on his threat to call the police and never tried coming over to the house. If he did, Grandma was ready for him. She brought down Grandpa's rifle from the gun rack and kept it at the ready in her bedroom.

We loosened up a bit after four days, though I still had a feeling Daddy was plotting something while he holed up in the house. Grandma was more optimistic. She said she'd give him a week, and then go over there and have a talk. That meant she wasn't calling Social Services, which I was plenty happy about. I didn't want a stranger asking me questions and deciding where me and my brothers and sister ought to live.

Then one night, just after dinner, I heard a car pull up on our street. I raced to the living room window and Duke followed me.

A brown Chevrolet taxicab idled in front of Daddy's house. Then he came out in a buttoned checkered shirt, jeans, and a pair of boots he must've just shined. His hair was groomed and still slick from the shower, and he'd shaved. He got into the back seat of the cab, and it drove off.

What a relief. I knew exactly where he was going. The one lick of sense he had was not to drive when he was tying one on. He had to be going to the bar for the night. There was a divey place in Le Moyne he hung out at when he was home for a stretch. If I knew the old drunk, he'd be out until closing time.

I explained all this to Duke and Dolly, and we danced around like fools. Grandma got her set of keys, and we each made lists of what we'd been missing. For me, my clothes, my record albums, my notebooks, and Preston's pin, which was socked away in the pocket of the shorts I wore the night Daddy belted me. For Duke, his baseball, mitt, and bat and sneakers, and his baseball cards. For Dolly, her games, dresses, and stuffed animals. We shouted over each other reciting it all. It felt like Christmas Day.

We grabbed big garbage bags for packing the stuff and snuck over next door with Grandma. The four of us filled all eight bags, and then we dragged our belongings back to Grandma's.

That was when it hit me, I should call Preston. It was still early, and my nose was looking less puffy and gruesome and the purple bags under my eyes had faded. I couldn't meet up with him at our special place in the woods. That was too far to stray in case Daddy came home. But I could ask him to meet me in front of the house so we could see each other and talk. Preston's mom answered and put Preston on.

He said he'd have to sneak out late that night. His aunt, uncle, and cousins had come over for dinner, and everyone was staying to play cards. I told him that was fine, and we said we'd meet around midnight. I brushed my lips against the phone receiver, pining for him.

Grandma was so happy we had our freedom, she said Duke and me should get her old charcoal grill fired up out back, and we'd roast weenies and make s'mores. She worked out a plan for one of us to keep a stakeout on the front porch every half hour, while the rest of us ate, played, and gazed up at the night stars. Funny, she even brought out Grandpa's box of cigarillos and let him smoke. We could all keep an eye on him in case he dropped a burning ash on his shirt.

We put Little Douglas to bed at ten, and at eleven, Grandma and Grandpa turned in. I stepped out to the porch while Dolly and Duke fought over who got to take their nightly bath last. I prayed Preston would make it over before Daddy came home.

When I saw Preston emerge from the shadows down the street, I glowed inside. I ran out to meet him by the street curb out front, and we shook hands though I sure wished it could've been a kiss and a hug.

Preston's eyes sparked from the sight of my face. I turned my head.

"I'll kill him."

"It ain't that bad. 'Sides, you can't kill him. He ain't home."

I tried out a smile to lighten his mood. Preston shook his head grimly. I glanced up and down the street. The house next door was dark, but the one across the street had lights in the windows. I drew Preston over to a spot beyond the lights from the porch, and we sat down on the lawn and held hands hidden in the narrow space between us.

"I missed you like crazy." Preston hung his head glumly.

"I missed you, too. I would've called sooner." I told him everything that had happened. Preston kept glancing at Daddy's house, and I sure was thankful he wasn't home because Preston had a reckless look in his eyes.

After a while, he spoke. "Well, I know what I gonna do. I'm coming back with my tent and sleeping bag. Gonna set up camp right here for when your Daddy shows up."

I scowled at him.

"He can't get away with treating you like that."

"Nothing good's gonna come from you trying to fight him." I squeezed his hand. "My Grandma's got a whole lot of stuff to work out so the three of us can keep living with her. It's not that I don't appreciate you standing up for me, but you gotta understand: This is *our* problem to fix. It ain't just about me."

I hadn't planned on it, but what Grandma told me about my Mama Philippa spilled out. I guess I couldn't keep it cooped up any longer. I even showed Preston the pretty necklace Mama Philippa had left me. I found myself carrying it around in my pocket, even in my pajama bottoms at night.

"Good ol' Gus Fanning." Preston shook his head. "You say your mama's name was Bondurant? Turns out you got some French in you, just like me."

We glanced at each other and chuckled. I hadn't even thought about that. Sitting so close to Preston, I was dying to lean over and give him a kiss. The street was deserted. If we were quick about it, nobody would see.

Preston's nose twitched. He shifted around. "You smell smoke?"

I hadn't till he mentioned it. I looked back at Grandma's house. In an instant, flames surged in the side window of Grandma's bedroom. I jumped up and barreled to the house. Preston raced after me.

The stench of smoke was thick in the front hall. I ran to the living room first, got Dolly off the couch and sent her outside with Preston. Then I staggered deeper into the house.

Smoke billowed from Grandma and Grandpa's room, and I could feel a furnace of heat beyond their door. I looked to the bedroom where my brothers were sleeping. I had to get Duke and Little Douglas out first.

I shoved open their door and shouted to Duke. The fire crackled and smoked against the adjoining wall to Grandma's bedroom. Duke gathered Little Douglas in his arms, and I hurried them down the hall out the front door.

The burning fumes were nearly suffocating me. I stared at the smoldering door to their bedroom and hollered for Grandma and Grandpa. Flames seeped out to the walls of the hallway. I'd never felt such heat. I warred inside between the panic of being burnt to death and the terror of leaving Grandma and Grandpa to die.

Hands grabbed me. It took me a moment to reckon what was happening, then I realized my legs had given out. Preston was dragging me down the hall.

He got me to my feet on the porch, and I stumbled along with him, retching out smoke while my lungs clenched for precious air. I fell down again on the lawn, and everything thereafter felt distant like I was witnessing it from some place beyond my body. Dolly and Duke screaming for Grandma. The house lit up like a tinder-box. Police sirens and firetrucks lighting up the street. My daddy bursting out of a taxicab and collapsing to his knees.

4

WE BURIED GRANDMA and Grandpa four days later. None of it seemed real until they lowered the caskets into the ground. Then a sob burst out of me, and I felt like my insides had been tore out. When my mama passed, I had Grandma to console me. I had no one to hold my hand and rub my back to say everything was going to be all right. How could anything be right ever again?

The firemen said the fire had started from one of Grandpa's cigarillos in the bedroom. An ember must've fallen on the carpet and caught fire that fed up the window drapes. I knew it wasn't my fault Grandma and Grandpa was gone, but it felt like my fault. If I hadn't been outside with Preston, I might've smelled the smoldering carpet and gotten Grandpa and Grandma out of the house in time. Grandma always looked out for me, and I couldn't look out for her the one time she needed it.

I had no one to confess that to. My guilt would be locked up in my head forever.

Everything was gone. The fire had razed the house to a plot of blackened wood and steel. The greatest loss of course was my grandparents, but Duke, Dolly, Little Douglas, and me had also lost a safe home and our most beloved possessions. A few days after the burial, we dug through piles of burnt wood and cinders and couldn't find a single thing to remember Grandma by. The old scrapbook she kept with all our family photos was no more than black ash. Her jewelry box, which she said she'd leave to Dolly some day, fell apart in my sister's hands.

We went back to living with Daddy. The four of us never talked about it, but we had no place else to go. I was just plain numb. Nothing seemed to matter with Grandma gone. I would've wandered into the woods and made my home in that ancient stone house out there for the rest of my days, but I guess I had enough sense to realize that wouldn't do no good for my younger brothers and sister.

As for Daddy, we all just stepped around him like he wasn't there. It wasn't so hard while Uncle Benjamin, Aunt Gracie, and my little cousins Doris and Robbie stayed at the house. With the place cramped with kids and cots, Daddy kept on his best behavior. For days, Grandma's friends and neighbors stopped by with casseroles, baked hams, cakes, and well wishes for us, so he had to put on appearances.

But once Uncle Benjamin and his family packed up to drive back to Florida, I dreaded what we'd face. Sure enough, no sooner than we'd seen them off in Uncle Benjamin's Chrysler minivan, Daddy went into the house to scrounge through the kitchen for a bottle of bourbon.

Duke and I sent Dolly out back with Little Douglas and went to keep an eye on Daddy.

He sat down on his easy chair with his bottle in hand, and he kicked off his boots. Duke and I drew up together and watched him from the hallway. He didn't seem to mind nor did he acknowledge us at first while he took gulps of his precious liquor.

Eventually, he frowned and cocked his gaze at the ceiling. "That settles it. I'm putting the house on the market, and I'm splitting youse up. Duke, you can come with me. Arizona, well, you too old and fruity for anybody's interest, but we'll find some wayward home for boys to take you in."

I pointed my finger at him. "You'll do nothing of the sort, you lousy, drunken piece of shit. Try taking a swing at me now. I want you to try."

My veins were flooded with hatred for that man. I'd kept it bottled up, but nothing stopped me from speaking my mind to Daddy now. Duke held me by the arm. "Daddy, what you talking 'bout?"

"I'm talkin' 'bout moving on, son. Starting over. A fella I met down at the bar works for one of them carny shows. Say he can get me a job. It's seasonal work for the most part, but it pays alright. They give you room and board. You save up the money and buy a trailer for the winter." He scratched his scruffy chin. "They ain't supposed to hire boys younger than sixteen, but they ain't sticklers for the rules. I'll leave it up to you, son. You come along and make some money or see what kind of people pay a thousand dollars for a fourteen-year-old boy." He chuckled and pointed his bottle at Duke. "There's some. I can tell you that."

I looked at Duke, pleading with him to let me go and make Daddy eat his words.

"Why would you do that?" Duke said. "Grandma didn't want us split up."

Daddy kept staring at the ceiling. "Grandma left us, you might've noticed son. Just like all women leave us." He took a slug of his bourbon. "You remember that. Ain't one good woman in the world." He smirked. "Well, lookie there. Your brother Arizona might have the right idea after all. Maybe we all should be fairy cocksuckers like him."

Cold-blooded rage rose up in me. I saw black, and before I knew what I was doing, I pulled away from Duke, grabbed the bottle from Daddy's hands, and I clubbed him across the head. It didn't smash like in the movies. That wallop sent him bowed over his easy chair, one leg twitching faintly, drool hanging from his mouth.

Duke shouted. I dropped the bottle and cringed from the sight of what I'd done. I'd seen it in my head. The bottle was supposed to shatter, just shutting Daddy up, making him think twice about talking to me like that. I shook my head and whimpered. I hadn't meant to. It hadn't happened. The world needed to rewind so I could take it back.

Distantly, I was aware of Dolly coming into the house with Little Douglas, and Duke talking frantically on the phone with a 911 operator. All I could do was pace around the living room and cover my face with my hands.

DADDY GOT TAKEN to the hospital, and I got taken to the police station in handcuffs while child welfare workers took my brothers and sister away. Don't ever say your life can't get worse. Mine was gone to shit when I woke up that morning, and then the ground opened up so I was swallowed into a deeper pit of hell.

I spent a night in jail, and then, on account of my age, Social Services took over. The social workers decided to transfer me to a hospital in Baton Rouge where I was locked up in a psychiatric ward for kids. That was only slightly different than being in jail. I had to give up the clothes off my back to wear a hospital gown and a cheap pair of socks. I was indoors all day long. There were bars on the windows, and all the furniture was fastened to the floor like they were afraid somebody would steal it. I slept in a hospital bed and shared a room with a shifty-eyed kid with a scar across his lips and a palsied hand. He never spoke one word to me, and I didn't care to ask him how he'd ended up in such a place. The nurses fed me pills that kept me groggy day and night anyway.

I met with a social worker, a doctor, and a lawyer who'd been assigned to me by the state. None of them would tell me what happened to my siblings, though I asked each of them several times. They just wanted to know if I had hallucinations or voices talking to me in my head. The lawyer explained I had an arraignment hearing with a judge later in the month. I'd been charged with assault and battery, and if my daddy died, I'd be charged with murder.

Apparently, the demon was still alive, and no one would say what kind of shape he was in. I hadn't wanted to kill him, and I told everyone that. The lawyer said it was best for me to plead guilty, and she'd tell the judge I hadn't been in my right mind since I'd just lost my grandparents in the fire. She said in most cases that would be enough for me to be kept in Social Services' custody up until my sentencing. After that, I'd likely get probation though there was a chance I'd be sent to a juvenile detention facility for a few months.

I cried myself to sleep at night, worrying about Little Douglas, Dolly, and Duke and hating myself for being the cause of breaking up our family. Maybe Daddy would've done it one way or the other, but I sure hurried up that situation and put them through another fright when the ambulance workers carried Daddy out of the house on a stretcher.

I made a collect call from the hospital to Preston, and his mother answered. Mrs. Montclair told me not to call the house and hung up. After that, I was pretty sure the best thing for me to do was to end it all. I was no use to anybody. No one cared about me. I thought about stockpiling the pills the nurses gave me and taking them all at once. I thought about using my bedsheets to make a noose to hang myself.

I can say now I'm thankful I was too chicken to do either, though at the time I felt like a failure for not having the guts to do it.

Things got a little better when the social worker brought me letters from Duke and Dolly. They'd been taken into a foster home just a few towns over from Le Moyne along with Little Douglas. They said everyone was doing fine, and they both told me they loved me and to stay strong. Duke mentioned he'd visited Daddy in the hospital, and Daddy was making a good recovery, getting better by the day.

Then one day, Uncle Benjamin came to visit. I prayed he had some good news. He was our only kin.

We'd never spent much time together, just a few Thanksgivings and Christmases at Grandma's house over the years. But I'd always thought of Uncle Benjamin as a righteous man. He never got hot-headed like my daddy. He was younger by two years, and Grandma always said Benjamin had made a good home for his family. He was a welder for NASA, working on space shuttles in Cape Canaveral.

I suppose I thought he'd say he and Aunt Gracie were taking in Duke, Dolly, and Little Douglas. But Uncle Benjamin was careful all through the fifteen minutes of our visit at the hospital.

He assured me my brothers and sister were in good hands with their foster family, the Petersons. The family had a farm, and they was good people and had lots of room and cornfields and chickens. He asked how I was doing, and I told him I was getting by, and I was anxious to get out and see my family again. Uncle Benjamin nodded and changed the subject, talking about my cousin Robbie's football league and how my aunt Gracie's mother was moving in with them because she had some kind of problem with her knees.

He left me with two impressions. The first was he was scared of me, thinking I had gone and lost my marbles. The second was, he was headed back to Florida straightaway. Besides taking care of his mother-in-law, my aunt Gracie was pregnant, he'd explained. They had plenty on their hands without taking in four more kids. Uncle Benjamin said we'd do just fine whether or not my daddy came out of his rehabilitation able to care for us or if we needed some other family to take us in. He and Aunt Gracie would gladly welcome us to the house for holidays. He'd given the court a deposition to say I'd never been violent or delinquent.

And that was that.

AFTER TWO WEEKS in the psychiatric ward, a caseworker came by to say he'd found a foster family to take me in through my arraignment and sentencing. I wasn't suicidal anymore, and I was glad to get out of that dull hospital where all you did was bide time. I'd played so many games of dominoes and crazy eights, I think I might have truly gone bonkers if I had to spend another day just sitting around in there.

Of course, I had no say in where to live, and while my caseworker, Mr. Applewhite, drove me out of Baton Rouge in his Datsun, he explained the family lived east of the city, some place called Livingston. I'd be two hours away from my siblings, and that was by car. God only knew how long it would take me by bus, not that I even had any money for bus fare.

The Slaughter family had a white-sided ranch style house on an acre of land. I could hardly complain, but it was right on a country highway with cars and trucks speeding by. Four cars were parked in the driveway, though only one of them looked like it was in operating condition. One had no tires and was propped up on cinder blocks. The rolling lawn was weedy and had a big plastic rooster and one of those cutouts of a farmer's wife bending over by the flower bed in the front.

A Native American girl who looked like she was a little younger than me answered the door, let us in, and said she'd find Mama Slaughter. Mr. Applewhite had told me her name was Darlene. Inside, they kept a big gold portrait of Jesus in the foyer, and it smelled like diapers and vinegar. I counted six kids in the living room on one side of the house. They were all grade school age and looked pretty grubby. Everyone was barefoot, and the boys sat around without shirts. On the other side of the house, there was a den that had been turned into a bedroom. I saw three cots in there. One of them was occupied by a bored-looking girl paging through a *Life* magazine that might've been older than her.

A sturdy woman with a beehive of bleached blonde hair waddled down the hall carrying a twelve-month-old girl in a diaper. She went straightaway to chatting with my caseworker. It seemed they knew each other pretty well. Then she glanced at me.

"You must be Arizona. That's a name I won't forget." She turned back to Mr. Applewhite. "He's up to date on all his shots? No lice or bedbugs?"

Mr. Applewhite assured her I was healthy as could be. I felt like I'd been brought in from a kennel.

He told me he'd be by the following Tuesday morning to bring me back to Baton Rouge for my arraignment. Then he handed me a shopping bag with some clothes they'd set aside for me at the Salvation Army, and he left.

"All the boys sleep in the back room." Darlene Slaughter looked me over. "My husband and I don't usually take in children as old as you. But I tol' Mr. Applewhite we'd make an exception since it was just two weeks. This is a *Christian* household, Arizona. No cussin', no fightin', no stealin', no drinkin', no smokin', and you best believe you keep your hands to yourself when it comes to the girls. We know about the kind what comes from John's Island." She raised one hand dramatically and shut her eyes. "But in Jesus' name we pray he wards over you and keeps you on the righteous path."

Darlene glanced into the living room and fixed on a dark-skinned boy who looked to be the oldest. "Petey. You show Arizona where y'all sleep."

She turned around and stomped back down the hall. Petey and I exchanged tentative grins, and I followed him to the boys' room. Two twin sized bunk beds, two sleeping bags rolled up neatly at the foot of each.

Petey climbed up to one of the top bunks and gathered Matchbox cars and action figures into his skinny arms. He brought them over to a crawl space where a dingy little mattress had been laid out. That cubby wasn't more than three feet high, four feet wide and five feet long.

"What're you doing?" I asked him.

He pointed to the bunk. "That your bed now. Older boys get the top bunks."

I stopped him. "I'm not gonna take your bed. I just got here." I looked to the crawlspace. I'd have to be real careful not to sit up and bang my head, but I could fit.

Petey stared at me in awe. "If you say so."

I helped him collect his toys and bring them back to the top bunk.

5

I'M NOT GOING to say it was a pleasure staying at the Slaughters, but after sleeping in jail and being locked up in a psychiatric ward, I was learning to adapt.

Sure, the house was overcrowded. There was never enough to eat at mealtimes, and every inch of the place was grimy. I worried that vinegar and diaper smell was seeping into my pores, and I'd smell like that for the rest of my life.

The worst part was the prayers at supper. Harold Slaughter would make us hold hands, bow our heads, and his voice would rise up fiery, nearly deafening my ears, pleading to Jesus to forgive us wretches of the host of sins on account of which we'd ended up without families. He was worse than them evangelical ministers on TV, crying and blustering about the price of sin. I'd always thought they weren't anything but showmen and hypocrites. But Harold Slaughter scared the heck out of me. He had nothing but disgust for all us kids, and that fervor spouting from his mouth made me feel like he was on the brink of breaking out in violence.

It wasn't even the hot words he said. You could just see it seething inside him on his flushed, fleshy face and sharp, bespectacled eyes. I figured he must've done something awful himself, and he'd gotten it in his head he had to take up sheltering children who'd been damned to hell as some sort of penance. Or maybe he liked having hard luck kids around because it made him feel superior. Lord knows what Harold Slaughter would've had to say if he found out I'd done unnatural acts with boys and got stiff at night pining for Preston. He always made sure to speak about sodomites, adulterers, and brazen women, right there at the dinner table.

The one good thing I could say about staying at the Slaughters was since I was the biggest and the oldest, all the other kids stood aside when I came around. Some even froze or shrank away from me.

I'm sure a lot of them had gotten beatings from their daddies and mamas, or worse. It hurt my heart to think about, but at least I never worried about my safety. I just stayed to myself and wrote letters to Duke and Dolly and Little Douglas and Preston and even Uncle Benjamin. I was so bored, I thought about writing letters to my teachers, though I didn't have their addresses.

One day, I asked Darlene if I could use the phone to call my brothers and sister at their foster home.

"Phone calls cost money. You got a dollar? Two dollars I figure for makin' a call 'cross state."

I dropped my head. Of course, I didn't have a dime to my name. Though I thought Mr. Applewhite had said the state paid the Slaughters a stipend that included me using the phone. I was too humbled to bring that up.

She glanced at the letters I was holding in my hand.

"Mail costs money, too. I ain't one of them machines spittin' out books of postage stamps."

"Suppose I cleaned up after dinner? Or mowed the lawn? You think then I could earn the money for a phone call and the stamps?"

Darlene frowned. "Chores already part of our agreement to take you in."

"What if I did something extra?"

Darlene thought on it. Then she pointed the wooden spoon she'd been using to stir her big pot of gumbo on the stove at me.

"Tell you what. You get the bathroom me and Daddy use spic and span every day after breakfast, and I'll think about it."

I skulked off. I wasn't sure I could trust her to keep her word, but at least it was a chance to reach my siblings and Preston.

I was on my third day of scouring her toilet, tub, and sink and mopping the floor, when Darlene appeared at the bathroom door with a moody expression on her big, overfed face.

"There's a man out front. Say he's your granddaddy. On your Mama Philippa's side."

My heart stopped beating. I searched her face as though she could explain how such a thing was possible. Darlene, in turn, studied me in an odd sort of way, like she was noticing something different she hadn't seen before.

"Go on. Get yourself cleaned up. You can't be keepin' the man waitin' all day."

I pulled off my rubber gloves and went to check myself in the mirror. It occurred to me she could be playing a cruel trick. Darlene seemed like the type to do that the way she talked to me and the other kids.

But if it wasn't a trick…Grandma had said my mama's family were proper people who wouldn't take in a child born out of wedlock. *Good Lord*, the sight of myself in the mirror! I looked like a hillbilly who'd been living in the woods. Unruly hair that had grown past my ears, a T-shirt soaked through with sweat and stinking wash water. I churned on the hot water in the sink.

Darlene pulled me by the arm. "Not in my bathroom you don't. You use the one for the kids."

I scampered downstairs and shut myself inside the kids' bathroom. I quickly washed my face, stripped off my shirt and washed my armpits. Then I decided I'd better wash my hair in the sink though all I had was soap and water. I dried off with a towel and ran to the bedroom. I scrounged out an unworn shirt from my shopping bag of clothes. Everything was either too big or too small, and I settled on a faded polo shirt that at least covered my tummy even though it was tight in the shoulders. I felt for the necklace box in the pocket of my shorts to confirm it was still there.

I didn't realize the stir I'd caused until I bustled down the hall to the front door. Looked like the whole house of kids had drawn up to the foyer to gape outside, and some was peeking out the front window of the living room.

I stepped out to the porch and set my eyes on a uniformed chauffeur standing by a glimmering, black Bentley limousine parked on the shoulder of the highway. I glanced around, thinking someone must be putting me on. The only time I'd seen such a vehicle was when a really posh family was caravanning from Kramer and Sons funeral home in Le Moyne.

The chauffeur tapped on the window in the back, and he opened the door. A gentleman stepped out, and I think all my organs stopped working. Well, except for my knees, which were nearly knocking together. I'd never seen a more beautiful and elegant man in my life. It was like he stepped right out of a movie screen showing one of them high society dramas Grandma Tilly couldn't get enough of.

He had a full head of silvery black hair, a trim moustache and beard, and kind, long lashed eyes. He wore a pinstripe navy blue suit, which he seemed perfectly at ease in.

"Arizona Fanning?"

I shyly nodded my head.

The man smiled and waved me over. *My granddaddy?* It was like he was Daddy Warbucks and I was Little Orphan Annie from that movie with Albert Finney and Carol Burnett. I put one foot in front of the other and made my way across the lawn. It hurt to look him in the face knowing how low-born and country I must've appeared, but from the corner of my vision, his eyes were wide, enlivened, like he didn't mind.

"I can see your mama in you. Why, just look at that face. I'm your grandaddy Bondurant, and I sure am pleased to meet you, Arizona."

His kind words gave me the courage to look him in the eye

while I shook his outstretched hand. His grasp surprised me. Not that it was too hard. It was just so warm and full of affection, like he'd been dying to meet me for years, which didn't make a lick of sense.

"I should say, technically I'm your *step* granddaddy. Your grandmother divorced your mama's father not long after your mama was born."

He took a half step back behind the open car door where we'd have some privacy. The houseful of kids was still gawking at us, though Darlene came out to try to shoo them away so she could do all the gawking herself.

"I married your grandmother in 1966. Your mama was fifteen. The same age as you."

He smiled at me. I smiled back. I remembered the necklace. I brought it out of my pocket and showed it to him.

A tender phase passed over his face. "Yes. I remember. I was with her when she picked that out at Adler's on Canal Street in New Orleans. She hadn't had a daddy for her first communion." His face flushed a bit. "Well, of all the things in the store's fourteen glass counters, that's what she wanted."

The initials caught my attention. *P.B.* Philippa Bondurant. I guess that meant he'd adopted her and given her his name unless by some coincidence, her father's name also started with a B. I felt shy asking him about that.

Meanwhile, he retrieved an old photograph from the inside pocket of his suit. He held it out for me. His fingernails were perfectly manicured while mine needed trimming and had dirt underneath. I tried to hide my fingers a little while I held the photo. It was black and white and looked like two Southern belles dressed up for an occasion in their curled bangs and fancy lace trim dresses.

He stood closer to point things out. I could smell his pleasant Stetson cologne. "That's your mama. That's your grandmother."

The two women looked more like sisters. *My mama.* She was real pretty and regal looking. I know I said I didn't want another mama before, but I needed so badly to believe I came from something good. Even though she'd passed, though she might as well have been a stranger, that photo of Philippa Bondurant made me feel I had a connection in the world. I had the same heart-shaped face, the same dark hair, the same big eyes, the same snub nose. Truth be told, her mother, my grandmother was even prettier. She could've been a movie star.

"That's a photo from Philippa's cotillion. She was sixteen."

I went to hand it back to him before I smudged it with my fingers.

"That's for you, Arizona. There's plenty more to show you at the house."

I shifted awkwardly. Where was I going to put the photo? I'd ruin it in the pocket of my shorts.

"I can take it for safekeeping." He carefully put the photo back in his jacket pocket. "We've lots to talk about, Arizona. I can't tell you how happy I am to see you. How'd you like me to take you to lunch? It would be nicer having conversation over a hamburger and a root beer float, wouldn't you say?"

My stomach grumbled. That sounded like heaven. I nearly jumped right into his limousine.

He chuckled and held up his hand. "How about telling Mrs. Slaughter where you're going first?"

I ran back to the house. Darlene was still standing on the porch. She had a nosy, befuddled look on her face, but thankfully she didn't put up a fuss when I said I was going to lunch with my granddaddy.

AN HOUR LATER, I was feasting on the most delicious cheeseburger I'd tasted in my life and washing it down with a chocolate malted at an old-fashioned diner off the highway. I was trying not to be a slob about it, but I'd been so hungry all the time living at the Slaughters. Back then, I could eat three deluxe burgers at the Sonic Drive-Thru and still have room for a fourth.

The man I now knew as my step granddaddy didn't seem to mind me using my hands to feed my greedy mouth and chomping away. He watched me with a quiet smile and slowly worked on his root beer float. Naturally, he was a mannerly gentleman. I tried to imitate how he sat down to eat, putting my napkin on my lap and keeping my elbows off the table.

I finished my cheeseburger and fries and noticed his eyes twinkling.

"Arizona, I'm getting the impression them Slaughters aren't feeding you so well."

I wiped my mouth with my napkin and folded it neatly back on my lap as he had. I didn't know what to say. Seeing as I was going back to Darlene and Harold's house, it didn't seem right to complain.

"You're a quiet one. That's all right. I understand you've been through a lot lately. I'm so sorry to hear about your Grandma and Grandpa Fanning. I'm sorry about everything you've been through these past few weeks."

I looked up at him. He probably thought I was slow, not saying anything the whole time. Truth was, it was like I'd forgotten how to string words together. He spoke so well with his soft, well-bred French accent, I was scared I'd sound like a dummy. I finally brought words out.

"How'd you find me?"

"Your Grandma Tilly gave me a call earlier this month. She wanted to let me know she'd told you about your mama." He bit at his lower lip with one tooth, and some strain showed on his face. He looked young to be a granddaddy. If I hadn't known, I'd have thought he was the same age as Gus. Though it occurred to me, him being my *step* granddaddy, he could be younger than my grandmother. I had so many questions to ask him.

"Your grandma, she also told me about the troubles you've been having with your daddy." His big, brown sorrowful eyes bored into me. "Arizona, if I'd known before what kind of man Augustus Fanning would turn out to be…" He glanced off to the side, picking at his beard. "I suppose it's not my place to say. But I've always believed a father should never raise a hand to his son."

"You can say whatever you want about my daddy. I'll beat you to it. He's a no-good drunk."

He stared at me for a moment, and then he broke out in a laugh. A good-natured, appealing laugh. It made me laugh, too. Then he turned real sober again. "Your grandmother and me, we should've taken you in after your mama died. It's been my greatest regret. Times were complicated back then. Your grandmother, well, she took losing Philippa hard. To this day she's not the same woman. I don't expect you to understand, Arizona. Especially seeing as we just met. But I'd like to make it up to you."

"I still don't understand how you found me." It struck me as something of a miracle considering the places I'd bounced around. My own brothers and sister had yet to hear where I was.

"Your grandmother read about the fire. She only told me two days ago. I'd been out of town for a business trip. I drove over to John's Island as soon as I could. Came to find your daddy's house empty, and then I made some inquiries." He looked at me squarely. "I'm going to tell you something Arizona, and it's not to brag. I'm a very influential person in Louisiana. I can make your troubles with your daddy go away like that." He snapped his fingers. "You're my grandson. I haven't done right by you. But you let me make it right, there's nothing I wouldn't do."

He had me mesmerized. I'd already figured he was an influential person. He had a driver and a Bentley limousine, and he wore suits that probably cost more money than my daddy ever had in his bank account.

"How do you mean?"

"This business with the court. I spoke to the judge. Your case is being dismissed on Tuesday."

I dropped the spoon in my chocolate malted.

"After that, it'll be up to you. You can stay a ward of the state and live with some foster family like the Slaughters until you turn eighteen. Or, you can come live with me and your grandmother."

My head reeled. I suppose a little part of me imagined he'd come swooping in to raise me as his own the moment Darlene told me my granddaddy was at the door. But the scale of that possibility, well I couldn't even wrap my brain around it. For sure, I'd rather live with him than a family like the Slaughters. Though I also had my siblings to think about.

"You fixed things with the court *for me?*"

"That was a little thing, Arizona. And I don't want anything in return. I'd like to be your granddaddy proper, but that's up to you. These past fifteen years, I haven't been in your life, and I'd understand if you had feelings about that."

I'm sure I did have feelings about that, but they were buried beneath a ton of more immediate concerns.

"What about my daddy?"

He frowned impartially.

"He still has parental rights over me, don't he?"

If my daddy kept getting better as my Uncle Benjamin had said, I was certain he'd do everything in his power to make my life a misery.

"I'm pretty sure I can bring Augustus around to an understanding. Your Grandma Tilly mentioned he had designs to sell your younger brother. I can't tell you how much that disgusts me, Arizona. A man like that ought to be locked up, and the key thrown away. He's scorching a path to get there. But in the meantime, I don't think it'll take much to persuade him to leave you be."

I gathered the persuasion he was talking about was money, and he was right. My daddy would swallow his pride for cash any day of the week.

Then I got to worrying again about Little Douglas, Dolly, and Duke. I wasn't sure how much I could impose on my granddaddy, a man I'd just met. I wasn't even sure what to call him so I asked.

"I hope you'll call me granddaddy. But that's yours to choose.

My full name is Gaston Polydore Bondurant." He snorted a little laugh. "Bet that sounds like a mouthful. Back when I was in school, the nickname Poly stuck, so my friends just call me that."

I looked at him in wonder. *No.* To me, Gaston Polydore Bondurant fit better. He was my fairy godfather, shown up to whisk me away in a horse-drawn gilded carriage. I tried to blink away the stars in my eyes. I still had my brothers and sister to look out for.

"Granddaddy, would you help my brothers and sister too?"

I told him about them being stuck in a foster home and how I'd promised them we'd stay together.

He grinned at me handsomely. I don't know why, but it made me blush.

"How 'bout this? I've got some business to do the next few days up in Alexandria. I'll send Buck, that's my driver, to pick you up on Sunday. Take you to visit your brothers and sister. Take you anywhere you want to go as a matter of fact. Then I'll meet you at the courthouse Tuesday. Soon as the judge gives his order, I'll take you straight to the house, and we'll get you settled in. When the time's right, we'll talk to your grandmother about the possibility of your three siblings moving in."

I was smiling so hard, my face hurt.

"Thank you. Thank you, Granddaddy."

6

I FELT HIGHER than a mountain, like I could walk on air the next few days. I'd heard the expression God works in mysterious ways, but I never paid it much heed. Well, he sure did. Out of a pitch-black pit, he'd raised me up into the light. I was someone worth saving, someone with a good lineage, come from important people.

Darlene Slaughter's attitude toward me turned around one hundred eighty degrees. She followed me around the house like a shadow, wanting to know this, that, and the third about my grand-daddy. You could see from a mile away, she was scheming to make out from my change in fortune. She said Gaston Bondurant ought to know she'd taken good care of me. She pestered me for his phone number so she could tell him herself, and she tried to sweeten me up by saying she'd mail my letters and let me use the phone as much as I wanted to.

I didn't give her the phone number he'd written down for me. I just told her I'd be leaving after my court hearing on Tuesday.

That night before dinner, Harold Slaughter sermonized about the evils of avarice and pride, all the while eyeing me with contempt. I scooped some fish sticks and hush puppies onto my plate while he was blustering, and I even stabbed food on my fork and fed it to my mouth. The other kids stared at me like I was about to get dragged off for crucifixion. I ignored them and went on eating. Harold Slaughter could preach all he wanted to, and meantime I was having dinner. And he couldn't do one damn thing to stop me.

On Sunday, Buck came by to pick me up just as granddaddy had promised. He drove me to my sibling's foster home in Iberia Parish. Duke had given me the address over the phone. It was a little white farmhouse with acres of cornfields, a barn and a silo, and a chicken pen.

Well, I gave them quite a surprise showing up at the door unannounced with a limousine parked on the roadside. Dolly and Little Douglas attacked me with tearful hugs, and then they took my hands and tugged me around back where Duke was packing husks of corn into crates. He dropped what he was doing, ran over and nearly tackled me. Seeing the three of them after so long, I was riding high emotions myself.

We sat down under a shade tree, and I explained everything as best I could. In my excitement, I hadn't thought through telling them our mama wasn't my birth mama.

It took some time for the shock of that to pass with Duke and Dolly. With Little Douglas, it went over his silver-haired head. He just wanted to climb all over me and try to wrestle.

Once I got him settled, I fixed on Duke and Dolly.

"Like Grandma said, it don't make a speck of difference. We're blood, and we always will be."

Dolly leaned against me where I was propped against the tree trunk with Little Douglas between my legs. Duke sat off a little way, chewing on a piece of straw. His face and limbs were russet brown from working outdoors.

"Daddy still saying he joining that traveling carny company," Duke said.

"You seen him?"

"They let me visit him just yesterday, over at Ochsner Acadia Hospital. He getting out today or tomorrow. They won't let him drive, and he say he want us home to help out around the house."

Dolly yanked at my arm. "Come home with us."

"You know I can't do that." I studied Duke. He was always hankering for Daddy's attention. I wanted to put things delicately, but I didn't know how.

"None of you should go home with Daddy, neither." I held Duke's eyes. "You heard what he wants to do."

"Where else we supposed to go?" Dolly said.

"That's what I was getting around to tell you. My granddaddy, he said we'd talk to my grandmother about taking youse in."

Duke scowled and looked off in the other direction.

"It's a good home," I told him. "He's a man of fine character, and he's wealthy. He'll take good care of us."

"That's fine for you, but he's not our family."

I heaved a breath and looked up at the sky. "You got a better plan? You want to take Little Douglas back to Daddy so he can sell him off for a case of bourbon? You want to watch me and Daddy fighting every night so bad one of us gets taken out on a stretcher?"

"He changed. He promise he ain't gonna spar with you no mo'."

I sucked my teeth. "And why wouldn't he say that? He needs us. Who else he got to take care of him? But listen here, you know the kind of man he is. Never once kept a promise to any of us."

"With the carny show, I can make some money," Duke said. "Soon as Daddy's good to work, he bringing me along. Say he bring you along, too."

"Gus Fanning said that?" I snorted and looked him in the eye. "After the names he called me, he's *bringing me* along? That make sense to you, Duke?"

"He tol' Duke he forgive you if you apologize," Dolly said.

I looked over my sister twice. Then I fixed on Duke. "All right. Let's just say they're figure skating in hell, and Daddy's rehabilitated. What about your younger sister and brother? What are they supposed to do while we're traveling around the country with Daddy?"

"He say Dolly and Douglas can stay with Uncle Benjamin while the three of us are working summer and fall. Then we'll all live together the other half of the year."

Daddy must've recovered all right. He was spinning stories and filling my brother's head with foolishness. Sure, we'd be one happy family, with Duke and me dropping out of school. Even if Daddy had changed—and I was sure he was incapable of that—what kind of future would we have?

I looked at Duke sharply. "Duke, he's lying. I seen Uncle Benjamin while I was in the hospital. He came to visit me. He don't want to take in any of us. Now I'm your older brother. It's up to me to tell you what's what. And I'm saying, I'm promising you Daddy don't care about nobody but himself. He was fixing to sell us off one by one. Don't you remember? That's the reason Grandma took us away from him in the first place."

I watched him take that in. I could see he was resisting what I was saying, but he still had respect for his older brother.

"I'm tired of living with strangers," Dolly said. "But if you say we gotta live with your granddaddy, I guess that's that. When we gonna meet him?"

"I don't know, exactly. But soon. Once I get settled. Meanwhile, the three of you have to stay strong and stick together."

After that, we got caught up about regular things, laying on the grass under the tree. Duke's chores around the farm. The foster family's daughter who was the same age as Dolly and let her listen to her record player in her room. I made them laugh, telling them stories about the high and mighty Slaughters and how bad their house stunk. I was glad the three of them ended up in a decent home and seemed to be doing all right.

Then their foster mother came out from the house and called them in for supper. She said I could stay and join them, but I only had Buck and the car until eight o'clock, and I had something else to do.

I TOLD BUCK to park down the street from Preston's house. Lord knew I didn't want to call attention to myself. Mrs. Montclair wasn't even letting him take phone calls from me, and here I was, showing up at their doorstep out of thin air. I suppose word had traveled about my fight with Daddy. People must've thought I was a criminal, and us Fannings hadn't been popular to start.

Sundays, Preston's family had supper early, around five o'clock, so when I arrived at six thirty, I wasn't sure where I'd find him. I couldn't just knock on the front door. So, I stole up around the side of the house to see if he might be out back tossing a ball with his younger brother, Earl. Maybe I could find a way to quietly get his attention. It was a nice, mild July evening, but the yard was deserted.

I studied the house, and my ears pricked up at a familiar sound. Why, of course. I crept around to a low window of the basement. The light was on, and I peered inside to see Preston in his boxing gloves beating that big Everlast bag his daddy had bought him.

I tapped on the glass. Sweat sprouted from my temples. He was making a racket, and what if I couldn't pry him away from his boxing bag? Worse, what if I got the attention of Mr. and Mrs. Montclair, and they chased me from the house? I pressed up to the windowpane and tapped a little harder. Finally, Preston stopped boxing and looked around. When he saw me, he shot straight over to the window.

It was one of them casement windows that don't open, so we had to try to communicate through the glass while being quiet about it. He spoke and gestured, telling me to meet him behind the shed in the backyard. I snuck over there and waited for him.

When Preston came around, slick with sweat in his sleeveless T-shirt, I sure was glad to see him. But pins sank into my heart at the same time. He wouldn't look at me directly. He must've thought I'd abandoned him. We stood together without saying nothing at first.

"I ain't got much time. Press, can you forgive me? I tried calling. Your mama never let me through. I didn't have any other way to reach you. My foster mama wouldn't give me stamps to send you letters."

"What happened? I heard you been locked up. They let you go?" While I fumbled with how to explain, Preston got a panicky look on his face. "You run away?"

I shook my head and told him this and that. I wished like mad I had more time. It was a lot to explain.

"Once I'm settled with my granddaddy, things'll be better. He's got a car and driver. You can come up and visit, and I can come and see you here."

"Your granddaddy has a car and driver?"

The way he said it made me grin.

"His name's Gaston Polydore Bondurant. I'm not sure how he made his money, but he lives like a king."

"Bondurant?" Preston shrunk up his brow like he was placing a memory. "Now I remember how I heard that name. The Bondurant family. My uncle and cousins work in one of their factories over in White Castle. They own all the sugar mills across the South. And they manufacture candy. The company name is B & B. Bondurant and Bondurant, I think."

I'd seen the name B & B on chocolate bars and lollipops. Then there was B & B sugar you could buy in any grocery store I'd ever set foot in. I didn't give that more than a thought or two at the time.

I handed Preston a slip of paper with Granddaddy's phone number. "I don't have the address where I'll be staying, but after Tuesday, you can reach me there."

Preston didn't even look at the paper. He was all out of sorts.

"I suppose your folks don't want you seeing me again."

"There's that." He kept glancing at me funny.

"Press, I ain't changed. But if you got something to say to me, I guess now would be a good time. I didn't mean to hurt my daddy so bad."

"I know what he done to you, Arizona. You don't never have to apologize for giving Gus Fanning what been coming to him a long time." He shifted his weight. "It's just...how far away you gonna be?"

My granddaddy hadn't said where he lived, and I told that to Preston.

"You ain't coming back to school next year, are you?"

I didn't know what to say, so I said nothing.

"You ain't gonna be around in two years to run off like we say."

"Look here. I ain't had a choice about anything that happened to me the past few weeks, and I can't say where I'll be next Thursday, let alone two years. But I came to tell you, I'll wait for you if you wait for me. What do you say, Press?"

He fussed around. "I thought I'd never see you again. Now you pop up out of nowheres, and you can't say when I'm gonna see you next."

"Press, you understand the reason, don't you? You're making me feel like I left you on purpose."

"It ain't that." Preston glanced at me, and I knew he was holding back tears. "I know it's not your fault. But you going off getting settled somewhere you can't even say. Somewhere you gonna forget all about me."

"Stop thinking that way. Press, I ain't never gonna forget about you." I remembered I had something for him in the pocket of my shorts. I brought it out in my closed fist. "Here's something. It ain't much. Nowhere near as special as your woodworking award. But I want you to have it."

At the diner, they had a rack of knickknacks by the cashier counter, and I'd asked my granddaddy if I could buy a little something for a keepsake. I picked out a furry rabbit's foot keychain in green, which was Preston's favorite color. I pressed it into his hand.

"Now when we're away, we'll both have something to hold on to and remember we got a piece of each other."

He turned over the rabbit's foot in his hand, and I pried a grin out of him. "It's a promise, Press. I'm coming back for you."

Preston pinched me in the side and brought me close. "Dammit, Arizona. You better stay true. I don't know what I'm gonna to do without you."

We kissed there behind the shed, and for a while, it was like time and space peeled away. Someday we'd find a place where we could be together without having to hide, without having to steal time when we were supposed to be doing something else. I swore to myself that night I'd never give my heart to anyone but Preston Montclair.

7

THE JUDGE DISMISSED my case on Tuesday like my granddaddy said he would. He'd found some fast-talking lawyer in an expensive suit to represent me, and I was remanded to my grandparents' custody while a petition for my father to relinquish his parental rights worked its way through family court. The whole proceedings didn't take no more than ten minutes.

I surely didn't want a violent criminal charge hanging over my head the rest of my life, but I felt hollow afterward. The courtroom was filled with strangers. I knew Duke and Dolly wouldn't be able to come, but neither did my granddaddy and grandmother nor my uncle and aunt.

Buck was there in the back row in his formal chauffeur outfit, and he gave me a pat on the back, which I appreciated. Though the truth was, the only reason he was there was he was getting paid to pick me up and drive me to Granddaddy's home. He insisted on carrying my shopping bag of mismatched clothes, which he stowed in the trunk of Granddaddy's Bentley before he drove me off.

A few days back, I'd imagined the day as triumphant. Instead, I was lonesome and heartsick and wondering why my life had turned out in such and such a way. I could blame Gus Fanning, but that only spread so far. I'd been losing people who were supposed to love me since the day I was born, which spoke to something deeper than the evil doings of my daddy. I told Duke, Dolly, and Little Douglas I'd find a way for us to stick together. I'd promised Preston the same. But it felt like I was fighting an enemy dead set on me losing everyone I cared about, and whatever or whoever that enemy was, it was much more powerful than me. Was I destined to be alone in the world? What kind of future did I have? I could think about it for hours and not come up with any answers for what I'd done to deserve being thrown out like the trash.

I glanced glumly out the window of the limousine. I don't know how long I'd been brooding, but along the way, Buck had driven out to the countryside. When I scooted over to the window, I saw a wide muddy river no more than a short run from the side of the road. I knew from my geography books the Mississippi cut through Baton Rouge and flowed south to New Orleans. I remembered we'd left the courthouse on the east side of the river, so based on the river being on the right side of the car, we was headed south toward the big city.

I read the signposts for the towns we passed through: Carville, Dutchtown, Geismar. I'd never heard of them, but they sure were quaint little country hamlets with ancient Greek Revival and Victorian mansions. Some of them might've been antebellum as far as I could tell.

A sense of wonder grew inside of me. Them properties had immaculate lawns, big flowering trees, royal palms, gazebos, brick-laid paths—certainly not like anything I'd seen in Le Moyne Parish, even in Franklin Acres. It was like we'd entered some fairy-tale land.

We passed by a road sign announcing the town of Darrow, and the homes grew even grander. I just about had my nose squished up against the window to stare. Some of the big houses were set far off from the street by vast wooded lawns, so you had to press up to the window to catch 'em.

The car slowed down to a halt, and I near swore out loud at the sight of the place Buck was turning into. It was fortified by a brick wall, and that wall was so high, I couldn't see the top from my seat. We waited for its giant wrought iron gates to open up. Above those gates, a name had been sculpted in gothic letters. Whittington Manor.

We drove up its gravel drive, which was a road unto itself. Great oak trees flanked each side—I couldn't count how many— and they grew high and formed a sort of tunnel through which a whale could pass through. I wanted to roll down the window and stick my head out of the car to see everything, but I restrained myself. I would've looked like a damn fool country bumpkin, and though I undeniably was, I didn't need to draw attention to the fact.

I glimpsed the manor house, but I didn't see it in its entirety until Buck rounded an ancient fountain in the front, which looked like it had fallen out of use. Buck parked the car and opened the limousine door for me. I stepped out and stretched my neck back, looking up at two columned and terraced stories of one behemoth of a main house. It gleamed pearly white.

I was certain a mistake had been made. The plantation mansion I was standing in front of was not the kind of place where anyone *lived*. It had to be as big as the White House in Washington, D.C. It was a museum, not a home. It was the gosh darn Library of Congress I'd seen in slide shows in my American History class.

Buck directed me along, carrying my dingy shopping bag full of used clothes. I might as well have been unwashed and naked walking into the place. Everything towered above me.

For such a massive house, I recall how quiet it was. That house was big enough to garrison an army, but I didn't see or hear nobody when we passed through its double doored threshold and entered a grand hall with a crystal chandelier that might've cost enough to buy up John's Island with plenty left over to rebuild the entire place. A curved, walnut bannister staircase swept down from the second floor. The space was dizzying. The ceiling went on past the second floor, forty, fifty feet? Decorative mirrors swam in my vision. I felt like I must have died to end up in the place, and contradictory emotions swelled inside me. Was this heaven or hell?

Footsteps clacked down wood floors from a distance. The house echoed like a cave. I stood with Buck for an awkward span of time, awaiting the person who was to greet us.

Eventually, an older man appeared from one wing of the house. He had slicked back gray hair and a pock-marked face, and he wore an immaculate Chesterfield suit. I stood straight and tried to push out of mind the faded slacks, oversized dress shirt, and scuffed up wingtip shoes I was wearing. The fellow had the manner of a *maitre'd* at a five-star restaurant.

"You must be Master Arizona." He had a Northern accent. His intelligent eyes appraised me, and he shored up a brief, welcoming grin. "I'm Mr. Wainwright."

"How do you do?" I reached out to shake his hand, but he just gave me a nod.

"Mr. Bondurant has charged me with acclimating you to Whittington Manor." He glanced at the plastic shopping bag Buck was holding for me, and his face ticked like we'd brought in a road-kill from the highway.

He looked to Buck, and the chauffeur handed him the bag, bowed his head, and retreated the way we had come. I was lonesome for him already.

"Shall I show you to your quarters?"

Nothing I could do but nod.

Mr. Wainwright led me swiftly upstairs.

I WAS CINDERELLA swept away to a castle. I passed by so many lavish things, I didn't know where to look. Landscape portraits along the walls that looked like they went back one hundred years or more. Rooms as big as my Daddy's house. Old fashioned gas sconces, which had been fitted with crystal light bulbs. The only thing I knew about plantation mansions was what I'd seen in that movie *Gone with the Wind*, which Dolly and I watched on Daddy's black and white TV every Thanksgiving. But I knew that house was worth a fortune. Anybody could see that.

Mr. Wainwright directed me down the carpeted main hall of the second floor, which was wide enough to drive a golf cart through. My eyes devoured as much as they could.

You could get lost in that mansion, and that's no lie. It occurred to me my brothers and sister could have some real fun playing hide-and-seek, though I doubted childish games were allowed in such a grand place. It was as quiet as a mouse, and adding to my initial impressions, it didn't seem possible anyone really lived there.

It's not that it was picture perfect, exactly. I spotted dust high up in corners of the ceiling, and the Oriental carpeting was faded, spotted, even threadbare in places. The wood moldings were chipped and grooved, and the plaster walls held stains from leaks. But it felt like that wear and tear was from some past occupants many years ago. When we passed by places where the late afternoon sun poured through giant, paned windows, I spotted grayed silhouettes behind the furniture. Nothing had been moved for ages.

Mr. Wainwright led me to a spacious, sunny bedroom. It had a high ceiling with crown moldings and a masculine decorative motif with Grecian wallpaper in blues and bronze. The four-poster bed would be the biggest thing I'd ever slept in. Twin doors opened to the second-floor terrace, which looked out to the forested back end of the grounds. Mr. Wainwright showed me an adjoining private bath and toilet done up in real marble. *Holy Moley.* I had my own apartment.

He set down my shopping bag on a dark wood cabinet and started rummaging through my clothes. That was rude. I was embarrassed to have him see my lousy stuff. But I didn't say a word. I reckoned it was his job to unpack a guest's belongings, and in any case, he'd be seeing my hand-me-down gear soon enough.

He made two piles on the counter of the cabinet. One stacked high, and the other had just a few pairs of briefs and socks. He stopped and fretted.

"I lost everything when my Grandma's house burnt to the ground," I told him.

That didn't scare up any particular reaction. He went to the closet, opened it up. Inside, some button-down shirts, a suit jacket, and a couple pairs of trousers hung neatly on padded hangers. Everything looked fresh from the store.

"Mr. Bondurant sent me ahead to purchase some furnishings for you." He looked me over, up and down. "I didn't know your preferences or your measurements. They'll require tailoring."

He didn't look happy about that. I was starting to think he wasn't too keen on me.

"I ain't picky." I tried out a grin.

"You are living in Whittington Manor, Louisiana's oldest plantation estate. We have been host to presidents and European royalty. Proper dress is required at all times." He added, "I *am not* picky. We also speak proper English in this house."

My mouth twisted up on one side and stayed there. Mr. Wainwright went back to the cabinet and tossed all my clothes back into the bag like he was handling rotten produce.

"Mr. Jackson will take these to Saint Anne's Convent, in the event there's anything of use for the sisters' charitable work with the destitute."

"Who's Mr. Jackson?"

"You were just standing with him in the front hall."

"Buck?"

"You will refer to the domestic staff by their surnames. I am Mr. Wainwright. Mr. Bondurant's chauffeur is Mr. Jackson. The housekeeper is Mrs. Laroche. And so on."

I didn't like his tone. I was well aware I had a lot to learn about etiquette, but that didn't make me dumb.

"When does my granddaddy get home?"

"Mr. Bondurant is the chief executive of the largest corporation in the southeastern United States. He is either working at the corporate office or traveling six, sometimes seven days a week. He never returns home before seven o'clock."

The Admiral clock on the mantle of the wall showed it was a little after five.

"I suppose I should meet my grandmother then."

"You should suppose nothing. Mrs. Bondurant will see you when she wishes to." He gave me another snooty look over. "Have you been baptized by the church?"

I guess all my sin must've been showing. "My mama wanted me baptized. My Mama Lou, I mean. The one who raised me. My daddy wouldn't allow it."

Mr. Wainwright pursed his lips in a manner that said he wasn't surprised. "I'll put that on a list of things to remedy. We shall see to it directly. Thereafter Father Timothy will prepare you for your first communion." He grasped the handle of the shopping bag, readying to dispose of it swiftly and privately.

I sat down on the bed and delayed him. "Did you know my mama?"

His face ticked, and he halted. "I have been steward to Whittington Manor for twenty-five years. Yes, I knew Miss Bondurant, God rest her soul."

I remembered my step granddaddy had said he'd married my grandmother when my mama was fifteen years old. I was curious if Mr. Wainwright had treated her like low down scum, the way he was treating me. I could bet money on how he felt about her getting knocked up by my daddy, though I wasn't bold enough to ask him about that.

"What was she like?"

His face flushed. "You should not ask impertinent questions. To put it more simply for your understanding, you should watch being flip with me, boy."

"I know what impertinent means. And what's impertinent about asking about my mama? You said you knew her, didn't you?"

"My relationship with the Bondurant family is and always has been entirely professional. Mr. Fanning, I can now say I *know* you. You shall be relieved to hear if someone was to inquire what *you* are like, I would be obligated to withhold my personal opinion."

I hooted and rolled my eyes. "You sure know how to express an opinion without saying it in plain English. Was that part of your steward training?"

Mr. Wainwright fixed on me with his fist clenched so tightly around the handle of my shopping bag, his knuckles turned white. "Mr. Fanning—"

"Arizona. Everybody calls me that. Mr. Fanning's what they call my daddy. Well, my teachers at least. And the bill collectors."

"Let me make something clear, Mr. Fanning. You are a ward of Mr. Bondurant, which makes me your ward*en*. During this unusual period of your residency at Whittington Manor, disrespectful behavior toward me or any member of the household staff will not be tolerated. I am fully empowered to correct it."

I was just about ready to test that, but any further exchange was squelched by the sound of footsteps gaining up on us from down the hall. I recognized that heavy-footed, confident gait. Mr. Wainwright did as well. He brought out a handkerchief from his jacket pocket to dab his brow and stood a little straighter.

Grandaddy appeared in the doorway, and his eyes brightened when he saw me. I stood, and we met halfway into the room.

"I'm sorry, Arizona. I wanted to be there at the courthouse." He grimaced in self-reproach. "I had meetings with our distributors, and I just couldn't shake myself free."

He held my arms. I gazed up at him in wonder. Any sore feelings I had melted away. He was an important man with a national company to run and never mind he had to be one of the wealthiest men in Louisiana. Being in his presence, I felt mighty important, too.

"Look at you. My grandson." He glanced around. "I see Mr. Wainwright has been helping you settle in."

The two of us averted each other's eyes. I was suddenly so full of happiness, Mr. Wainwright hardly mattered.

"This house is something else." I spun around. "This *room* is something else. I'm not sure if I'm settling in or dreaming."

Granddaddy smiled. "It's not an easy house to get used to. It took your mama some time as well. But you'll settle in just as she did. Mr. Wainwright will assist with that. Anything you need, you just ask."

I wanted to hug him. *Good god*, call me a baby, but I needed a hug. Everything seemed so formal in the house, though, I thought it was best to hold off and hope he'd hug me first.

"When do I meet my grandmother?"

He blinked. "She'll join us for dinner tonight."

Something wasn't right. He took me by the arm and sat me down on the bed, taking up a space next to me.

"Arizona, you should know your grandmother isn't well. No, it's nothing physical. I mean to say, she hasn't been right in the head for a very long time. Not since your mama passed."

I had no idea what that meant, but it made me lower my eyes and feel a bit queasy.

"There's no reason for you to be worried. But we must be gentle with her. I know she'll come around to loving you. I fell in love the moment you stepped out of that awful woman's house outside Baton Rouge. For Ginny, it doesn't come as easily."

"You saying she's not going to like me?"

"Of course not." He stood and stepped over to the closet. "She'll be right impressed by the handsome young man you've become." He sorted through the hanging clothes. "You don't have much here. Mr. Wainwright will take you over to Rubenstein's so you'll have a proper wardrobe."

I traveled over to him. "Who's Rubenstein?"

"Rubenstein's is New Orleans' finest men's clothier." He pulled out a bright powder blue button-down shirt and a checkered tie and showed them to me.

I nodded. That shirt was my favorite too.

He handed me the shirt and a pair of gray striped trousers. I held them up against me. They were both going to be a little roomy, and the sleeves and legs were too long.

"Mr. Wainwright will mark them for tailoring, and Mrs. Laroche will have them cut and sewn in time for dinner." He looked at his house steward. "I think seven thirty. In the Camellia dining room." He turned to me. "It's Mrs. Bondurant's favorite."

He clasped my shoulder and winked. "I'll leave you to get ready for dinner."

I wished he would've helped me dress instead of being stuck with Mr. Wainwright. He directed me down the hall to a tailoring room where I stripped down to my grayed briefs and tried on the shirt and trousers. Mr. Wainwright took up a measuring tape, chalk and pins, and then he shuffled me around for measurements in places I'd never known figured in to the manufacture of a man's clothes. He marked the shirt and trousers with chalk, and then he cuffed and pinned hemlines. All the while, he kept his nose up like he might catch something from me.

He took the shirt and trousers away and sent me to take a bath.

A FEW MINUTES behind schedule, Mr. Wainwright led me briskly down to the ground floor and over to the Camellia dining room. Mrs. Laroche hadn't finished with the adjustments to my shirt and trousers until quarter after seven. I'd been sweating bullets, worrying I'd have to show up for dinner in the ugly clothes I'd worn to court.

Then Mr. Wainwright came around with the tailored garments, and boy, I sure felt classy when I buttoned up, tucked in, checked myself in the mirror and had Mr. Wainwright knot and fix my tie just so. I'd always thought dressing up was a misery you had to go through for big occasions like school photos and funerals, but the shirt and slacks fit me so well, I fancied myself a gentleman. I still sorely needed a haircut, but my bathroom was stocked with a gel to groom my wavy hair, and I also found a nice-smelling cologne, and you could bet it wasn't from a drug store. Gazing at my reflection, I realized I hadn't looked so swanky the one time my Mama Lou made my Daddy drive us over for Christmas dinner at her parents' country club, and *that* was an occasion. That night, I was all dolled up for Tuesday supper.

The Camellia dining room was a sight to behold with its textured pink floral wallpaper, giant teardrop chandelier, and fresh flowers with pink spiral blossoms in vases and urns all over the place. The walnut table with its swirly mahogany veneers could seat a dozen people, but we was only three. Granddaddy sat down at one end, and I figured my grandmother would sit at the other. There was just one place setting in between the two of them, so I headed there. The table had been set with white linen, delicate blue and white china plates, cloth napkins, and fancy silverware like something out of Buckingham Palace.

A well-dressed, dark-skinned man, one of the household staff, filled the crystal goblet in front of me with ice water from a pewter pitcher. I couldn't even bring myself to take a drink from it. I was scared to touch anything. Anyway, my grandaddy stood up all of a sudden, and he looked at me like I ought to do the same.

Virginia Bondurant, or Ginny as Grandaddy had called her entered the room. My eyes bulged out of their sockets. She sure didn't look like a grandmother.

After that talk with Granddaddy, I expected a woman who was older and more fragile. I mean, I'd seen her photo at my mama's cotillion from 1967, so I knew she'd been pretty and young back then. But Virginia Bondurant was a blonde-haired beauty such as I'd never seen. She didn't look like she'd lost her marbles. In her black brocade dress and pink and yellow floral print scarf, she looked to me like the type of fashionable lady I imagined living in Paris, France.

She sat down, and Granddaddy and I followed suit. I was in such a state of shock, it didn't occur to me to say how do you do? Virginia sure kept up with her beauty treatments and her slim figure. She had to be fifty years old. I suppose she could've been shy of fifty if she'd had my mama in her teens. I watched her fit a skinny cigarette into a fancy holder. That dark-skinned attendant swept over to light it, and then he brought over a martini in a wide brimmed goblet on a silver tray and set it carefully in front of her. I watched as she raised the goblet with her black gloved hand and took a healthy gulp.

Call me a country hick, but I could've just sat there and watched her all night long. Then she turned a glance to me, and I was suddenly as jumpy as a leapfrog. I had no idea what was the proper thing to say upon meeting my grandmother for the first time. She was worldly and educated and used to formal manners. I searched my granddaddy's face, praying for some cue.

"Arizona, say hello to your Grandmother Bondurant."

I turned to her. "Good evening, ma'am."

Her lips curled in amusement. "*Ma'am*," she repeated in an imitation of my country accent. "That's charming. I can see your upbringing in Le Moyne Parish hasn't spoiled your manners and refinement." She took a sip of her martini and carefully wiped away a smudge of rose lipstick on the lip of the glass. "I detest being called 'ma'am.' I don't need to be reminded of my age. And don't even think about calling me *granny*. I'm much too young to be a grandmother. I was just a girl when I had your mama."

I wanted to scratch my head, though I didn't want to look like a fool. "What should I call you then?"

"You may call me Virginia, Aristotle."

I didn't correct her. At the time, I thought she was just being funny, and I sure wanted her to like me. I ventured to take a sip of my ice water, and then the servant drifted over to unfold my cloth napkin with a flourish and place it on my lap. For a strange stretch of time, nobody said a word. I could hear the ticking of the big dialed clock on the wall behind me.

Then the servant wheeled in a dining cart with a tray of chilled shrimp. He made up our plates one by one, Virginia first, then Granddaddy, then me. He arranged the shrimps along with lemon wedges and a mound of bright red cocktail sauce.

I wasn't sure I could eat cold shrimp. They looked like they'd be chewy, and I worried I'd gag right there at the table if they had a funky taste. But considering where I was, considering I didn't want my grandparents to think I was ungrateful, I waited for Granddaddy to cut a piece of his shrimp, pick it up with the tiny fork from his table setting, dab it in the cocktail sauce, and take a bite. I imitated what he'd done and prayed for the best. It didn't taste half bad. I had one heck of an appetite, but I made myself count to ten in my head between bites since that seemed to be the pace at which cultured people like my granddaddy ate.

"Where in heaven did Gus Fanning come up with the name Aristotle?" Virginia declared.

"His name is Arizona," Granddaddy told her.

That set her to snickering. She washed down her amusement with another draw of her martini. "Well, that makes more sense." She wagged a limp, gloved hand at me. "Have you brothers or sisters who also bear the names of our fine United States? Utah? New Hampshire?" She looked at me expectantly and drew on her cigarette.

Now I was getting the picture with her. She was brimming with mischief, and I didn't like her saying that. Though Grandaddy had said she wasn't well and needed to be treated delicately. I tried stretching my mind open and letting her have her fun.

"I have two half-brothers, Duke and Douglas, and a half-sister Dolly."

She tapped the ash of her cigarette into the glass ashtray at her side. "I see a pattern. Gus likes 'd's. I suppose it reminds him of his grade reports from school."

I chuckled. "Did you know my daddy?"

She polished off her martini, waved her hand, and the server came around to refill her glass from a silver shaker. Virginia had pushed around her shrimp a little, but she hadn't eaten a thing.

"Your daddy is not the type of man one keeps company with in polite society," she said. "We call his type a catfish. Bottom of the swamp, laying in the muck. Oh, they taste delicious battered up and fried. But you don't keep them lacquered on the mantle for the guests to see."

She laughed at her own joke. The way she said it made me blush and squirm inside. I think she was drunk, which shocked me a second time that night. Sounds stupid probably, but back then I didn't think rich people got drunk, especially ones who were as sophisticated as Virginia Bondurant.

She took another big sip of her drink and swirled the rest around in her glass, looking like she might slosh her gin right over the brim. Then, to my dismay, she fixed on me again. "So, what about you? Poly was right. You're pretty. I guess you find every now and then a dandelion that grows out of a cow pie."

"Ginny," Granddaddy muttered.

She shooed him and smiled at me in delight. "Are you going to grow up to be a catfish like your daddy, Alabama? I bet you'll find plenty of girls idling around, hoping you'll ask them back to the barn."

"Ginny, that's enough."

"Oh, for heaven's sake, Poly. He's not a child. I'm just making conversation." She turned to me. "The boy doesn't mind, does he?"

I wasn't sure whether to give her a yes or a no. I ended up just giving her a shrug.

The server cleared our plates and pushed the dining cart away. I sat in silence, keeping my hands off the table and fingering my napkin. I'd looked forward to meeting my grandmother, but now raw feelings were festering inside me. She drank too much, just like my daddy. She was unpredictable, and as pretty as she was on the outside, she was calculating and mean.

"Arizona is a straight A student," Granddaddy said. "His teachers marvel at his academic potential."

I dropped my head and blushed. It was true I was an honors student, though I had no idea how my granddaddy had found that out. Had he gone to my school? Talked to my teachers? Asked to look at my school records?

"Is that so?" Virginia swallowed down the rest of her second martini. It could've been her third or fourth if she'd gotten started before dinner. Another helper, this time a dark-skinned woman, came in to tidy up the table and put new plates in front of us. She also refilled Virginia's drink, fetched a fresh highball for my granddaddy and topped off my glass with ice water.

When she left, Virginia went on. "You're full of surprises, Arabia. Your mama didn't have a head for school. She enjoyed her dance classes, though. She was more of what you'd call a social butterfly." She twinkled with a clever grin. "*Academic potential.* Lord knows, you didn't get that from Gus Fanning. No Fanning's made anything of himself. Poor family's always been the lowest of the low. Isn't that right, Poly?" She didn't bother to wait for a response. Her eyes were on me again. "Your granddaddy always had a charitable streak. Can't pass by a mongrel on the street without stopping to give him scraps."

Granddaddy's voice rose. "Ginny, can't you be kind?"

It blew my mind that Virginia Bondurant and me were kin. We had nothing in common, which was probably the one way we could agree on. The tension in the air was getting to me, but I didn't want to be the cause of a scene. For all I knew, my grandmother could send me straight back to the Slaughters, and then I'd be back where I'd started with no hope of helping out my siblings.

"It's all right, Granddaddy," I said. "I know where I come from, and I'm just happy to be in the company of well-bred folk."

Granddaddy gave me a kind nod, and then he turned his careful attention to Virginia. She looked amused again. You could've searched me why and come up empty-handed.

She pointed her cigarette at me. "It's a tall step up for you, and don't you get used to it." She took a draw and exhaled a plume of smoke. "I gave in and agreed to let you sleep in the house. Though you'd be more comfortable in the stables, wouldn't you? Along with the swine and the chickens?"

A nervous laugh bubbled up in my chest. I looked down at the table. Granddaddy was exchanging more words with Virginia. I was so out of sorts, things weren't registering to me. Then Virginia's raised voice shook me to attention.

"Two nights I said the boy could sleep here. My generosity can only spread so far. I won't have him dirtying up the place, not to mention pocketing the silver."

"Ginny, we talked about this."

"You talked. I listened. I never gave you a yes or a no. And I'm saying right now, you can dress the boy up like putting lipstick on a pig, but you can't change his nature." Virginia set down her drink. "Look here, Poly. You're fixing to rewrite history with this boy. The only Fanning made a name for himself was his great granddaddy, Luke, and everyone knows that was for *all* the wrong reasons."

I knew I shouldn't, but I couldn't help looking her in the eyes. I'd never been told what Luke Fanning did to earn the family such a bad reputation.

"You don't know?" Virginia snickered. "The boy doesn't even know his genealogy."

"This is not the time," Granddaddy warned her.

She waved him off. "Luke Fanning and all those girls he kept locked up in his cellar? You never heard about that?"

I slowly shook my head.

"Oh, he loved his little girls. Luke used to drive his pickup by the grade school over yonder in Franklin Acres when they were letting them out. He'd lean out his window, catching the attention of a lonesome one waiting for her mama to pick her up. He'd say her mama had sent him to fetch her for one reason or another. Always had some candy to lure them into the truck."

Virginia cocked her head in a supposing manner. "How many of them did they find? Six or seven?" She turned back to me, acting all chummy again. "You see, what he'd do is lure them to his farm, then he'd knock them unconscious like stunning cattle and put them in the cellar where he'd do all kinds of filthy things to them."

Granddaddy looked like he was ready to stand and shut her up.

Meanwhile, Virginia lit up another cigarette and blew out a stream of smoke in his direction.

"It went on for quite a span. All those families scared to death about what happened to their little girls! They thought it must've been some drifter, passing through town, preying on their kids, but it turns out the monster was right under their noses, living among them. Holding open the door for them at the Five and Ten. Sitting along with them at their pew on Sundays."

She laughed. I had no idea why. The woman was deranged.

"Your grandmother won the Miss Louisiana pageant in her day," Granddaddy said. "She got high marks for her personality interview. Always could run her jaw."

I could taste the venom in those words, though it seemed to go over Virginia's head. Or she was too clever to show she was rankled. She had a quiet way of cutting people down.

"Let me finish the story. The boy's got a right to know, now doesn't he?" She turned to me again. "So, as I hear tell, somebody tipped off the law about your Granddaddy Luke."

She was giddy now, swirling her martini, having her fun at my expense. I didn't want to believe her. Though who makes up such a horrible story? I had to hear the rest.

She tipped her drink toward me. "It sent Luke into a panic. Why, he could've just run off, given it a try as a fugitive. See if he could make it across the border to Mexico. He had the time, and I'll tell you why." She leaned toward me with her elbows on the table, slouching drunkenly. "Before the police arrived that night, he went down to his cellar and slit each and every one of those little girl's throats. Then he got his shotgun and rounded up his wife and sons and lined them up in the work shed out back. He shot them all, and then he swallowed the muzzle and blew his own brains out."

She threw back her head and laughed. "Talk about a flair for the dramatic. Well, Luke was just plain stupid. Figuring he might make it look like a scene from a home invasion when the law showed up. Something out of that Truman Capote book, *In Cold*

Blood. The problem was, your Grandpa George survived. His mama fell on him or something like that. In any case, Luke's own son, Little George, spilled everything to the authorities."

She screwed another cigarette into her holder. "You know that story traveled house to house across the state without a single word about it printed in the papers? They must've figured some things were too gruesome to be written about. Worried it would give the children nightmares." She brushed an ash off her sleeve. "So, that's the story about your great-granddaddy. I don't think he'd be the source of your *academic potential* either, wouldn't you say?"

I was too horrified to speak. The servant just then wheeled in the main course. The aroma of whatever roasted meat was beneath the big domed tray made me sick. I envisioned some part of a child's corpse steaming in there.

"For the love of God, Ginny," Granddaddy burst out. "Why'd you go and do that? Scaring the boy half to death."

Virginia made a childish face at him. Then she squinted and purred to me. "Did I scare you, Abalone? Why, you look all grown up in that handsome shirt and tie. I'm sure you've seen more gruesome stories on TV."

I looked her in the eye defiantly. "You didn't scare me."

She raised her eyebrows.

Granddaddy threw his napkin down on his plate. "This is no sort of thing to be telling your grandson over dinner."

Virginia shrugged blamelessly. "A gentleman must learn the arts of dinner conversation. A story like Unlucky Luke Fanning, well, that's one you can keep. You'll get all the girls moaning and shivering, wanting your sturdy arms around them."

"That's not funny," Granddaddy scolded her.

"What do you think, Appaloosa? You find it funny?"

My upper lip trembled. I forced a big, hateful smile at her.

"You see there, Poly? The young man's got a sense of humor." She puffed on her cigarette and fixed on me. "That's something your granddaddy is sorely missing." She swayed her head this way and that. "He takes everything so seriously. And you know what else? He swore off touching me. Probably afraid he won't be able to get it up anymore."

I wanted to slide down my chair and hide under the table. What kind of woman says something like that about her husband in front of company?

"I explained to Arizona, his grandmother is working through some mental problems," Granddaddy replied stiffly.

She gave him a hardened glare. "Oh, I'm working through them all right." She gulped down the rest of her martini. "It's just so hard when one's mental problems keep yapping at you night and day like a dog."

Granddaddy stood up from his chair. "You're not well. It's time for you to go to your room."

I braced for an explosion, looking down at my plate, though I couldn't help peeking from one to the other. Virginia picked up her swizzle stick and chewed on an olive, staring at Granddaddy. The servant had stopped in his tracks, not knowing what to do about serving the main course.

"You see how he treats me?" she said to me. She glared at Granddaddy. "I'm not one of the lackeys in the office you can push around."

He stepped over to her. "Stop making a scene."

"What for?" She glanced at me. "For *his* benefit? He's used to it. Aren't you, Armageddon? Sparring at the dinner table is a tradition where he comes from. Black eyes and split lips are de rigueur in Le Moyne Parish."

"He's your grandson."

"I'm not denying it. I can see his mama's features on his face. He was probably born with her same lustful ways." She shrank up her face. "Your mama never did know how to keep her legs closed around country scum. You better not be knocking up anybody. I agreed to take you in because your daddy wouldn't have you, but I'm not taking care of any low born floozy's whelp."

At some point, Granddaddy had summoned Mr. Wainwright, and they each took one of Virginia's arms and lifted her from her chair. Virginia shook around in protest, but not so much. Once up on her feet, she nearly collapsed from a dizzy spell, and the two men had to hold her up.

"It's not fair," she whimpered." Why's everyone always telling me it's my fault?"

I'd seen some horrible things in my life, but watching that awful woman get pulled along sobbing and babbling, I wasn't sure if I'd ever be the same.

8

AFTER THAT DINNER, I figured I'd be heading back to Social Services straight away, forget about asking my granddaddy to take my brothers and sister in. I guess he'd known all along what my great-granddaddy had done and didn't care, but I felt stained ugly by that history. I was afraid of even facing my granddaddy after that, and I went to bed hoping in the morning he'd have a car ready to take me to a home for wayward boys where I belonged.

What happened next, I can't explain. I suppose I was just then learning my life was like how people spoke about the weather in bayou country—you don't like it, wait an hour or two. After that hurricane in the Camellia dining room, a strange calm fell over the house the next few days. Everybody went about their business as though nothing had happened. It gave me time for my feelings to settle. If nobody was marching me out the door, maybe that night hadn't been so bad. I started to think it wasn't my fault what my great-granddaddy had done. He'd died sixty years or more before I was born. He might've passed along his criminal inclinations to my daddy, but I'd heard about traits skipping a generation. Grandpa George had been a good man so maybe it was that kind of thing. I hadn't inherited anything from Gus Fanning, from his blond hair, blue eyes to his cruel personality.

Anyway, later that week, things came into focus, and I knew one thing for sure. I hated Virginia Bondurant. I don't think I'd ever met a woman I hated more in my entire life. I knew exactly what she'd been trying to do, making me feel like country trash. She was wicked, and I didn't care if losing her only daughter had made her sick in the head like my granddaddy wanted to explain. I swore I'd say it to her face.

I wondered if my mama had hated her, too. Virginia couldn't have been a good mother to her, and maybe that was why my mama ran off with my daddy. I couldn't fault Mama Philippa for wanting to get away from that evil woman.

However it came to pass, nobody spoke a word about the to-do. I didn't see Virginia again for many days and thought I might be lucky enough to never see her again. She and Granddaddy had their rooms far down the hall from mine, and maybe Granddaddy had given her a good talking to for her behavior, scaring her from coming out of her bedroom. Maybe she just preferred to live like a hermit or maybe she really did have some kind of sickness that kept her in her bed. I was plenty happy not to see her around the house, and she never came downstairs for breakfasts, lunches or dinners.

I barely saw Granddaddy either. I gathered I was staying on at Whittington Manor, but I might as well have been a guest in a hotel. Mr. Wainwright woke me up every morning at seven o'clock to get washed and dressed for nothing special. The cook Mrs. Gundy made my breakfast, and Mr. Wainwright gave me two books to read. One, a dumb phys ed workbook, and the other, a King James Bible. I didn't have much interest in either, but I carried them out to the wooded grounds of the estate every morning and set myself up in a shady spot for the day. I got so bored, I read that bible and started doing calisthenics.

One Saturday, Granddaddy took me to St. Anthony's Church in town where Father Timothy baptized me as a Catholic. Afterward, we went to lunch at a fancy restaurant where we had turtle soup and something called Texas quail. I finally worked up the nerve to ask him if my grandmother was going to let me live with him.

Granddaddy pinched up his brow like I'd said something funny, and then he told me I could live at Whittington Manor as long as I pleased. I was so relieved, I laughed out loud right at our table. I wanted to fit in with him and be the kind of person who belonged at Whittington Manor. It wasn't just that I didn't have anywhere else to go, or that I liked having a big, fancy room and a butler and a cook catering to me. Maybe those things figured into how I was feeling, but most of all, I needed someone to want me, and a man like Gaston Bondurant wanting me, well, that had to make me somebody real worthy.

He also told me he was headed out to Chicago for business, and after that, to Boston for a two week stretch.

That made living at Whittington Manor awfully lonely that summer. The only person I spent time with was Mr. Wainwright, and I told you already about his low opinion of me. After my baptism, he gave me a typed list of passages from the Bible I needed to memorize for my first communion with Father Timothy at the end of the summer. He added I should prepare for my first confession. I'm sure he thought I had plenty of material for that.

Well, one bright spot was the day Mr. Wainwright told me we were going to New Orleans after breakfast. I'd been dreaming about seeing the city for years, though I'd pictured going with Preston. Mr. Wainwright said it was time to pick up new clothes for me at that gentlemen's clothier Granddaddy had mentioned.

Buck drove us there, and I just about strained my eyeballs gaping from the window of the Bentley. New Orleans was more stylish and grand than I'd imagined. I'd never seen trolley cars. Heck, you could fit what I'd seen of the world on a postage stamp. There was skyscrapers and billboards and a great big football stadium in the center of town. We cruised right through that lake of concrete and steel on a raised highway like we was flying. Then we came to the old part of the city, what they called the Vieux Carré or French Quarter.

Oh, it was colorful like people said. Those two-story Creole townhouses with their long balconies came in every color of a Crayola crayon box, and the people were colorful, too. It was early afternoon on a Wednesday, and the narrow streets were teeming with gentlemen in hats and seersucker suits, ladies in flouncy dresses, families of tourists, and black street performers every quarter block. They were tap dancing and singing and playing saxophones and trumpets with crowds circled around them. I thought we must've arrived on a holiday, but Buck said the Vieux Carré was like that all the time.

I was itching to get out there and join the fun. Everyone looked friendly, and why wouldn't they be? They were having the time of their lives.

I spotted a pair of swishy fellows who looked like they had not a care in the world, strutting the streets with bright bandanas around their necks, open shirts, and tight, cutoff jean shorts. I saw other clusters of men who looked like they could be of my persuasion—neatly groomed with pretty faces, and a certain dainty manner about them. I was curious as heck to ask them questions and find out how they lived.

That wasn't possible, of course. Mr. Wainwright was my chaperone, and we debarked from the car right in front of the gold lettered marquee for Rubenstein's department store on Saint Charles Avenue.

Fool that I was, the place scared the heck out of me. Everything was posh and immaculate, and the clerks were just as well-dressed and snooty-looking as Mr. Wainwright. An older fellow in a business suit strode over to us and gave Mr. Wainwright a great big smile and a handshake. He was the highest ranking salesman, I imagined. Only the best handled Gaston Polydore Bondurant's business. I had a feeling my granddaddy spent a lot of money at that store. The fellow tipped his head to me and whisked us through the establishment's many aisles.

I'd only known clothes shopping as a yearly outing to the Family Dollar with Mama Lou and my brothers and sister. After

Mama died, Grandma Tilly took over taking us shopping for back-to-school clothes. In either case, Duke and I were lucky to walk out of the store with two new shirts and a pair of jeans apiece while Dolly got a few new dresses, blouses, and skirts.

I felt mighty important at Rubenstein's. The salesman walked me through every aisle from hats to shoes, suggesting this and that. Everything was finely made, and the salesman let me try on anything I wanted to. Calvin Klein. Ralph Lauren. They even had racks of clothes by European designers, which I liked best.

Truth be told, I turned a bit greedy that day. I needed just about everything, and I'd never had a taste of the finer things in life. Besides, I wanted to fit in now that I was living with my granddaddy. I'm not ashamed to say I wanted to be a fine gentleman like him. No Fanning had ever made anything of himself, Virginia had said. I was going to show her how wrong she was.

It didn't take good breeding to fill out a cashmere pullover or brushed cotton trousers. The salesman told me I was slim and well-proportioned, fit to wear anything the store had to offer. Mr. Wainwright had final approval, but he was less concerned with price or quantity. He just had his say on what would be stylish and appropriate for my age. We had store clerks running shirts and sweaters, trousers, shorts and jeans, socks, underwear and shoes over to the cash register counter all afternoon long. Then I tried on linen suits for summer, wool suits for fall and winter, and velvet suits for the holidays. A tailor pinned and marked them up for adjustments right there in the store.

Whatever Buck couldn't carry, Mr. Wainwright told them to deliver, and I ain't lying when I say it would fill the better half of a delivery truck. We spent a small fortune in a span of hours. It left me thinking I could get used to living that way.

That excitement faded over the next few days. It was the middle of the summer, and I was stuck in that big, empty house without much to do. Every day, I asked Mr. Wainwright if I could visit my siblings over at the Petersons, and his answer was always the same. Buck, or Mr. Jackson, as Mr. Wainwright called him, didn't have the time to drive me on such an extended trip. If I cared to, I could check back with him later in the week.

I had my suspicions Mr. Wainwright just enjoyed making my life miserable. My granddaddy was out of town for business, so what else did Buck have to do? That cruel man wouldn't even let me use the phone. He had some baloney story about there only being one phone for the family's private line. It was in Granddaddy's study, and outgoing calls needed to be authorized by him. The business line was strictly for business, he said, and the phone was kept in a secretary's office in the back end of the house by the kitchen.

One afternoon when I had the house to myself, I did some exploring, and I'll tell you the strangest thing about that mansion. I couldn't find a single phone in any of the two dozen rooms I looked through. Granddaddy's study was locked up tight and so was the door to the servant's wing.

I took care not to blow my top at Mr. Wainwright. With Granddaddy being away, he held all the keys and the purse strings in the household.

Granddaddy did give me a phone call one night around eleven while he was in Boston, but he sounded so tired, I was shy about complaining. I figured I'd work things out about phone calls and visits when he came home.

Whittington Manor had a big library, so I spent my days working through it. A thick, Russian novel, *Crime and Punishment* by Mr. Fyodor Dostoevsky, caught my interest and kept me busy. One thing you can learn by reading is the world can come up with problems a lot bigger than yours, and that *Crime and Punishment* was one good story filled with destitution and desperation and moral dilemmas I'd never thought about.

I had to force myself to put down the book at times. I was dying to get to the end to find out what was going to happen to poor Rodion Romanovich Raskolnikov. But I also needed to write letters to my siblings and Preston since I couldn't ring them up on the phone.

I filled pages and pages telling Preston every detail of my days at Whittington Manor and my trip to New Orleans. I begged him to not be sore at me for going without him. Surely Granddaddy would be all right with Preston coming over for a visit. It was on my list of things to talk to him about when he came back from Boston.

I took my suppers all alone in a wood-paneled dining room near the kitchen, just paging through my book for company. One night when I was finished, Mr. Wainwright told me my grand-daddy had arranged equestrian lessons for me. I was to meet my instructor at six o'clock the next morning.

I had no problem with that. Horse riding sounded like fun, and better to do it early in the day. It was the time of year when the summertime heat got so thick, you broke a sweat just tying your shoes, as Grandma Tilly used to say.

The next morning, Mr. Wainwright had me up at five o'clock to take my bath and shave, and when I came out of the bathroom, he'd laid out riding gear I'd only seen people wearing on television. I dressed in britches, a white button-up shirt, boots, and a cap. Downstairs, Mrs. Gundy put out a plate of eggs and toast so I could get in a quick meal before my lesson. While I was eating, conversation traveled from the hallway and steps gained up on the dining room. Mr. Wainwright walked in with a young man who was done up in the same gear as me.

I just about dropped my jaw to the floor. Mr. Wainwright introduced him to me as Mr. Jolly. He was a broad-shouldered, six-foot, sandy haired, blue-eyed fellow, handsome as a movie star and with a big, dimpled smile to boot. I was fifteen, going on sixteen, so you'd understand I thought I'd fallen in love right then and there. When I stood up to shake his hand, I felt light-headed and meek.

Mr. Jolly gave me a firm, brotherly handshake and a firm, brotherly nod. He had a warm, affectionate demeanor, and he didn't let on for one minute what a girlish mess I was. I'd been so lonesome for company, it was like he'd dropped from heaven. Meanwhile, I'd been spending my days dreaming about love affairs with dashing, complicated Russian men of the intelligentsia. Mr. Jolly wasn't the type I pictured in those private thoughts, but boy, he was a living, breathing fantasy right there in front of me.

I followed him out to the grounds behind the house and onward to the stables. Free of Mr. Wainwright's supervision, he told me he was going into his last year in college at Louisiana State University in Baton Rouge, and if I preferred, I could just call him Dan.

"I grew up with horses," he told me. "My Daddy owns a ranch in Fort Polk. That's Western Louisiana, near the Texas border. You heard of Pleasant Colony?"

I shook my head. I didn't know if he was talking about a town or some new TV show.

Dan grinned at me playfully. "He's only the Kentucky Derby winner from 1981. Same year he won the Preakness Stakes. We raised him from a foal. I broke him in when I was about your age. My daddy's had about a dozen thoroughbreds gone on to compete in Grade I races. Don't you worry, Arizona. I'll get you all caught up on your horse racing history."

I hid my face and grinned. I'd never had an interest in horse racing, but I sure liked Dan talking to me.

"I just thought you should know, you'll be in good hands. I've been training professional riders since I was in high school. Nowadays, I only take a few students over the summer, but when Gaston Bondurant calls, he goes to the top of the list. He's an accomplished rider himself."

I wished I had something to say to him about that, but I didn't. I just hoped he'd keep talking to me. I sure liked the sound of his voice.

"Next year, I'll have my degree in animal science. I'm hoping to set up my own horse ranch after that."

That sounded mighty impressive, and I had no doubt Dan Jolly could do anything he put his mind to. He was everything I wanted to be when I grew up: charming, handsome, and athletic. I was plum in awe of him and humbled to be in his company.

We reached the stables, and Dan showed me Granddaddy's two fillies. He set me up with the smaller one. I'd only seen horses from a distance grazing in the farm house fields when Mama Lou took us kids for drives up Highway 90. Those two fillies were beautiful creatures, mottled brown, thick with muscle, with majestic roan manes and big lashed eyes.

Dan said my horse was named Duchess. I thought that was fitting. She sure looked regal to me. He'd be riding the bigger girl named Bonnie. Dan told me my grandaddy had him exercise them twice a week. I couldn't believe I'd never noticed, though that damn estate was so big, I realized there were probably plenty of things going on every day that escaped my attention.

My first lesson was learning how to equip a horse with a bridle, reins and a saddle. That part wasn't so hard. Duchess took to everything real easy. She was as gentle as can be. But once we led the horses out of the stable, I had to mount her.

I was terrified of looking like a fool in front of Dan. I was hardly an athlete like Duke. I got by in sports, but gym class was never my favorite, particularly the phys ed teachers who sized me up as a lost cause from the start. Dan told me what to do, putting my boot in the stirrup, hiking myself up with my hands, and throwing my other leg over the saddle. To say I struggled was putting it nicely, but Dan was patient, saying I was doing just fine.

Then he got a grip on my hips to help me raise myself. I sure liked that for all the wrong reasons. It made me want to fall back and see how good it felt for him to catch me in his arms. I had the sense not to try that. I put all my strength into straddling the saddle, and at last I found myself atop Duchess.

Dan climbed up on Bonnie effortlessly and drew her up alongside to teach me how to center my weight, hold the reins, and use them to move Duchess along. It was simple stuff, but good golly, I was such a scatterbrain around him. I lost track of everything no sooner than the words were out of his mouth. That face of his just melted me to butter, and his thick legs wrapped around his saddle got me short of breath.

Dan had the patience of a saint. He never let slip I was an idiot, though he had to be thinking it. Eventually, I picked up walking Duchess forward, which was a fine pace for me. I felt awfully wobbly in the saddle, apt to tip off if a strong breeze came my way.

Dan explained we'd keep to the main trail through the grounds. Until that day, I hadn't realized how much wooded property my granddaddy owned. Beyond the outbuildings for the main house, there were acres of oak trees and sycamores and flowering magnolias. Some of the bigger trees were dripping with Spanish moss. The air was sweet from all the wild vegetation.

It took all of my attention to mind my balance, but when we came along a lake, I couldn't help take a gander around. The shoals were covered with flowering lily pads, and I heard the steady croak of toads. A white gazebo sat on a bluff overlooking the water. I remembered Mr. Wainwright had said Whittington Manor went back to the early nineteenth century. That set to mind people from an olden age strolling through the grounds like Scarlet O'Hara and Rhett Butler. The estate had been home to folks from high society all the way back to the time of the Confederacy.

Dan led me along and stepped up the pace, moving on to a trot. That was a lot more brutal on my bottom and my thighs, but I managed to keep up with him and hold in my complaints.

He turned to me. "You're doing great, Arizona. How you feeling?"

"Good," I lied. The inside of my thighs were being chafed raw. I tried to put that out of mind. It was worth it to spend some time with Dan.

"Your granddaddy won a blue ribbon at the Evangeline

Downs." He smiled at me. "You've got equestrian champion in your genes."

I grinned for a moment, then I remembered something. "Gaston Bondurant is my step granddaddy. He married my grandmother two years before I was born."

Dan shrank up his brow. "Is that so? You look an awful lot like him. I just assumed."

I blushed a little. "He's just about as much family as I got left." I was shy about getting into the details. "My grandparents who raised me, on my daddy's side, they passed."

Dan's face turned stricken. Good God, he was sweet. He barely knew me, but he looked like he'd lost Grandma Tilly himself.

"I'm sorry to hear that, Arizona." He gave me a grin to cheer me up. "Well, you could do worse than having Gaston Bondurant take you in. He's a good man, wouldn't you say?"

I nodded.

"And you've got me to look after you. Mondays, Wednesdays, and Fridays. Six o'clock to nine. Gonna have you riding like a blue ribbon winner youself by the end of the summer." He gave me a wink. "What do you say about that?"

My face bloomed. Three days a week of seeing him suited me just fine. It made me want to be the best rider I could, though it was hard to imagine I'd ever be competing.

"Where you going to school next term?"

I had no idea, and I told Dan so. I'd barely thought about it with everything else going on.

He fixed on me in his warm but firm way. "You best figure it out. Keep up with your grades and get yourself into a good college."

I grinned and nodded.

"I bet your granddaddy would like you to go into business. What do you wanna do?"

"Teach maybe. I love to read." I told him about Mr. Dostoyevsky's *Crime and Punishment*. I probably sounded like a lunatic raving about the story, but I couldn't stop myself. It had been so long since I'd had anyone to talk to.

"That'd be a kick. The first Bondurant ever to be a school-teacher." He smirked. "Well, schoolteacher and prize-winning equestrian on the side."

I couldn't stop grinning. He was being a bit flirtatious, unless I was misinterpreting things. I figured I must've been. Dan Jolly was a man's man. I couldn't picture him liking boys. Still, I felt right honored he'd said those nice things about me.

Later along the trail, I noticed a little cottage on the far side of the lake.

"Is that still part of Whittington Manor?" I asked Dan.

He looked that way. "Sure is. The grounds go on for another mile and then some."

"Does somebody live there?" It seemed strange so far off from the main house. I didn't see any roads leading that way.

"I'll tell you a secret, Arizona. Now, you best swear not to repeat it."

I eyed him firmly. Anything Dan told me, I'd take with me to the grave if need be.

"That's where your granddaddy's brother lives. Nicolas Bondurant. He's the other half of B & B Enterprises, but you'll probably never see him."

"How come?"

Even though we were far away from anyone, deep in the forested grounds, Dan lowered his voice a bit. "On account of him not liking being seen. He was in the Vietnam War. I never heard what happened to him, but it had to be something awful. He just keeps to himself in that house, painting and drawing pictures, and he has been for something like eight years since he came stateside. Your granddaddy has Mr. Wainwright bring him his food and gear once a week. It's a crying shame if you ask me."

I felt the same way staring at that lonely cottage. A man hiding away in the woods, never to see anybody again. Well, I remembered thinking about doing the same thing after Grandma Tilly died, but those dark feelings had passed.

We were at least one hundred yards from the house, so all I could make out was a glimmer from the sun hitting the home's bay window facing out to the lake. Then that window went dark like somebody had dropped the drapes.

9

LIFE HAD TAKEN a turn for the better at Whittington Manor. I had my mornings with Dan to look forward to three times a week. Maybe that don't sound like much, but it felt like everything to me. Even when we weren't together, I thought about Dan Jolly night and day. The way he talked. That smile of his that turned me inside out. His thick legs gripping Bonnie's sides. Well, I pictured things I wouldn't write down in my journal for fear of somebody seeing them. Suffice it to say, I'd fallen for him hard.

I prayed at night he'd think about me the same way. Dan never spoke of having a girlfriend. He never talked about girls at all, so that gave me some hope. I combed my brain for some way to talk to him about how I felt or some hint to drop. I wore myself out running through ideas in my head. Nothing seemed right, and I was scared to death he'd be disgusted by me.

With Preston, we'd just about known each other's minds from the moment we made friends in sixth grade, and all it took was him to have the guts to kiss me one night over the summer before we started junior high. Dan Jolly was entirely different. He was a college man. He probably had no interest in someone as young as me, even on the small chance he liked men the way I did. That got me feeling so sad sometimes, it hurt deep in my gut when we were together.

Now I hadn't forgotten about Preston, and it's not that my feelings for him had wore off. But I was so lonesome that summer, I needed someone to fill up the space in my heart. Looking back, maybe I needed something bigger than Preston. Dan was like the perfect older brother I'd never had and the perfect man I'd always wanted to be with rolled up in one.

I still wrote Preston letters and signed them *With All My Love.* Meanwhile, Preston hadn't sent back one letter in three weeks, nor did he call the house, and I'd given him the phone number. I guess I was beginning to doubt my own promise to never love any other man. Preston's mama had made it clear she didn't want him having anything to do with me, so how were we going to make things work anyhow?

Granddaddy finally returned from that trip to Boston late one night. It was after supper, and I was holed up in my room reading another fine book by Dostoyevsky called *The Brothers Karamazov.* I heard Granddaddy's steps down the hall, set down my book, and looked to the door, hoping he'd stop by before he went to bed.

When he appeared in the doorway, I jumped down from my bed and ran right to him, giving him a big hug like a little kid. Granddaddy laughed and gently disentangled himself from me.

"It's good to see you too, Arizona." Granddaddy was still dressed for the office, and he looked tired. He directed me through the room so we could both sit down on the bed. Only then did I realize he had a small package done up in gift wrap in his hand.

"I know I been gone a long time. But it hasn't all been business."

He handed me the package, and I went straight to work ripping off the wrapping paper. It was a journal with a beautiful calfskin cover, and a gold pen to go along with it.

"Thank you, Granddaddy."

He glanced at the spiral notebooks on my bedside table. "I

know you like writing. Figured you could use an upgrade. And you've got a birthday coming up."

Would you believe I'd forgotten about my own birthday? August 12th. That was only a few weeks away. I smiled so hard, my eyes welled up with tears.

Granddaddy patted my back. "The journal is just a pre-birthday gift. I saw it in a display window walking along Newbury Street in Boston. Made me think of you." He clasped my shoulder. "But there'll be a lot more than that at your birthday party. We'll have it right here at the house. You can invite whoever you want."

I gawped at him. A birthday party for me at Whittington Manor. That was going to be something else. I knew right away I wanted Duke, Dolly, Little Douglas, and Preston there. Then I asked if I could invite Dan Jolly.

"I don't see why not. I take it your riding lessons are going well."

I blushed and nodded.

He glanced at his hardcover copy of *The Brothers Karamazov* tossed on the bed. "You been reading, too. That's good. Never a bad idea to get a jump start on school."

I was glad he'd brought up the subject. I had no idea if I'd be doing my junior year back at my high school in Le Moyne Parish or at a new school in Darrow.

"What am I gonna do for school?"

Granddaddy reached into the inside pocket of his suit jacket. He brought out a glossy tri-fold brochure and passed it to me.

"I mentioned I was up in Boston for more than business. I paid a visit to my old prep school."

Middleton Boys Academy. The cover of the brochure had a photo of a big brick building with a white tower and a columned threshold. I'd never heard of it, but I could put two and two together. It was an elite New England boarding school. That made me light-headed and dizzy. I sure would love to go to a school like that, but I was hardly the kind of person who belonged at such an exclusive place.

"Now Arizona, they don't typically take students transferring in just for their last two years. And they most definitely don't take students who haven't submitted a full application and come for an interview by their February 1st deadline. But I pulled some strings and came up with an offer they couldn't refuse." He unfolded the brochure. "See here. They've got the best writing program in the country. And you can study abroad in Florence, Italy, Barcelona, Spain, and Geneva, Switzerland. Tell me you can beat that."

I was floored. Granddaddy had done all that for me? I'd be going to a school with the brightest, wealthiest people in the country. Part of me was hungry for it. I'd sure be making a name for myself, and I'd be starting from ten, twenty floors above ground level.

But all the way in Massachusetts? I'd be leaving my siblings behind. Who knew how often I'd get to see them?

Granddaddy must've read the worries swirling in my brain.

"It's your decision, Arizona. If it's too far for you, there's a nice Catholic school in New Orleans. St. Bartholomew's." He frowned impartially. "Nothing wrong with the place. We could have Buck drive you to class in the morning and pick you up in the afternoon. You'd get a solid education. No frills, but plenty of good families send their sons there."

He turned back to the brochure. "At a place like Middleton, though, you'd be in the pipeline for an Ivy League college. Harvard. Yale. Dartmouth. Heck, you could go anywhere you wanted. I just know you've got the head for it, son."

"Where'd you go to college?"

"I went to Harvard." His eyes glimmered from the happy memory. "First in the family. Then I went on to the Wharton School of Business for graduate school. That's Princeton University in New Jersey." He chuckled. "Put my daddy through the fits. 'No Bondurant's gone anywhere but Tulane University,' he'd tell me. Well, Tulane's a fine school, but I wanted the best. And Arizona, you can study just about anything at Harvard and get yourself a job wherever you want with that name at the top of your résumé."

Lord, I wanted to say yes to Middleton. I wanted the ivy-covered halls, the trips to Europe, and the prestige of being a Harvard man. Only one thing held me back.

"Can I have some time to think about it? I ought to talk to Duke and Dolly is all."

"Of course you can." He pulled me close and kissed me on the head.

My heart nearly burst. Being loved by my mama and Grandma Tilly was one thing. I don't mean to sound ungrateful. I'd have been nothing without their love. But growing up, I'd always felt like something was missing; and I found it right then that night. A daddy who loved me and thought I was worthy. Well, Gaston Bondurant was my step granddaddy, but it sure felt like he was more than that.

I TOLD YOU I was learning my life was like the bayou country weather. That went both ways. Wait around a little and it might get better. Wait around a little, and it might get worse.

That night when Granddaddy told me about Middleton Academy and my birthday party, I felt ten feet tall. But then he gone and left me again, this time saying he had a week-long business trip in Baltimore. I traipsed after him to the car, and he gave me a hug and a kiss before Buck opened the door for him to climb inside. I watched his black Bentley roll down the tree-lined driveway out to River Road and onward to the airport from there.

Stupid me, I forgot to ask him about letting me see my brothers and sister and inviting Preston over. I thought about it just after he left, and I went to Mr. Wainwright straight away. He still had excuses for Buck not being able to drive me anywhere. But when I brought up making a phone call, he finally gave in. He opened up my granddaddy's study and showed me the phone on the big executive desk. The old busybody made a point of leaving the door wide open, and I was sure he was sticking around within earshot.

I called the Peterson family. The mother put my sister on the phone, and I talked with her and Douglas for a while. Duke was out on a tractor with Mr. Peterson doing his chores.

Dolly didn't sound like herself. She was quiet and moody, and then Little Douglas kept asking when I was coming home no matter how I tried to explain that wasn't possible. I told them I loved them, and we were sure to see each other on my birthday. The conversation left me with a heavy heart.

Meanwhile, I still did not receive a single letter from Preston Montclair. My birthday party invitations had gone out, and Mr. Wainwright assured me he'd sent one to Preston. Preston couldn't even respond to that?

Glum as I was, I still had my lessons with Dan Jolly. I was getting better at riding Duchess, and my troubles washed away in Dan's company. He always seemed genuinely happy to see me, and I sure was happy to see him. He was handsome and kind and always brought a smile to my face. When I told him I had the opportunity to enroll at Middleton Academy, he said I'd be a damn fool to turn that down. They only let in one in ten students. Besides, they had an equestrian program.

I felt bolder around him, not dropping my eyes when he looked me in the face. I stole longer glances at his body while we trotted down the trail side by side. One sticky morning, he threw off his jacket and said it'd be fine if I left mine back at the stables. While we rode, he popped open the top two buttons of his shirt and rolled up his sleeves. His poplin shirt clung to him while he worked up a sweat, and his sturdy, golden haired forearms glistened. I admired the little curly hairs sprouting from his chest.

I'd been waiting for something to happen for so long, I couldn't hold back that day. Preston had forgotten all about me. Anyway, it started when Dan and I slowed down to guide the fillies along a minor trail off the route along the lake.

I told Dan, "I sure like spending time with you."

He grinned. "I like spending time with you too."

I don't know what I expected, but I was left with nothing to say. Dan sounded like he hadn't caught my meaning. Then he moved along, and I had to follow him single file down the narrow trail.

When we got back to the stables, dismounted, and stripped the gear off Duchess and Bonnie, I hiked up more courage. Maybe you'd call it recklessness or the crazy ideas them Brothers Karamazov put in my head or just plain desperation. Typically, we'd scrape off our boots, put away the gear where it was supposed to go, and he'd send me to strip down and wash up in the old shower stall in the stable. That morning I tarried around once the girls were back in their pens.

Dan looked at me. "Everything okay, Champ?"

Butterflies swarmed in my stomach. I looked at him grimly and eased up in front of him. "I sure like spending time with you."

It was the same damn thing that come out of my mouth before. I felt like an idiot and wished he'd catch the hint.

He smiled again and rustled my hair. "How 'bout I take my shower first? Give you more time to spend with Duchess and Bonnie?"

That wasn't what I'd been fishing for, but I gave him a nod. I watched Dan grab his barrel duffle bag and stride down to the shower stall.

I was steaming hot and feeling like grains of sand were slipping through my fingers. I couldn't wait another day to tell Dan how I felt about him. The feelings were tearing up my insides, and I just had to do something about it. So I got even bolder that day. I crept up on that shower stall, listened to the water churn on, took a long glance in every direction to make sure no one could see. Then, Almighty Jesus, strike me with a lightning bolt, I called out to Dan and didn't wait for a reply before parting the curtain and stepping into the door frame.

Naturally, I gave him a scare. He swung around to hide

himself, but he was still a scorching sight, wearing nothing but some soap suds sliding down his calves.

Dan looked over his shoulder with a nervous grin. "Something you need, Arizona?"

I bit my lip. "I just wanted to tell you I like you, Dan. I mean, I *really* like you. You think you could like me too?"

I stole a glance at his face. Nearly knocked my feet from under me. He'd gone ashy, and he took a peek this way and that like somebody must be coming along to wrestle him into the backseat of a police car.

Eventually, he turned back my way with a sympathetic gleam. "It's natural what you're feeling, Arizona. But I can't feel the same about you. I'm not that way. Even if I was, I'm your teacher. Don't you know your granddaddy would skin me alive?"

He might as well have punched his fist into my heart. I dropped my head, wishing I could die.

I must've looked a wreck. Dan faced me fully, stepped out from the shower head, and placed his hand on my shoulder. "You're a real special person. Don't you ever forget that."

I shook my head. I didn't feel special at all.

Dan shifted around and looked into my burning, watery eyes. "Tell you what, Champ. If there's something you want, I don't suppose there'd be a problem letting you have it every now and then." He pointed his finger at me. "So long as you swear you can keep a secret."

I followed his gaze down his beautiful body. I looked up at him, and he gave me a wink. Dan drew the shower curtain tightly closed. I knelt down between his legs and shut my eyes, dreaming this was love.

IT BECAME A regular thing after my riding lessons, and I don't care what nobody says. Those special moments with Dan Jolly were my heaven and earth. It didn't matter he never said he loved me or he never gave me anything but a pat on the back in return.

I knew in my head it didn't mean the same thing to him, but a man's more than sense and reason. I felt like Dmitri Karamazov from that Dostoyevsky novel I was reading. He had a lousy father, too. A lousy father who went on to try to steal Dmitri's inheritance from his mother and then he tried to get between Dmitri and Grushenka, the woman he loved. It didn't matter to Dmitri that Grushenka didn't love him back. He kept pursuing her his entire life.

I guess that's how it was with me and Dan Jolly. Sometimes the person you love doesn't love you back, but that doesn't mean you give up. We're all put on this earth for a purpose, and mine was to love Dan even if it meant I'd be miserable all my life like Dmitri Karamazov. Dostoyevsky taught me not everyone in the world gets happiness, but you still fight on.

That made a lot more sense to me than my religion lessons with Father Timothy. He had me read parts of the Bible and answer questions about them every Saturday to parse out the morals that would make me a good Catholic man. I never mentioned it to Father Timothy for my grandaddy's sake, but whoever wrote that book sure didn't know how to tell a story. They were all too short and never told you who the characters really were.

Like the story of Jacob's ladder. It had potential, but it felt like it was written by a third grader. Jacob runs away because his brother Esau wants to kill him on account of being jealous that their father likes Jacob better. Then Jacob has a vision about a ladder to heaven, and God appears to tell him he won't ever have to worry about anything. Jacob can go back home because God will watch over him.

There's nothing in the story about Jacob's hopes and dreams, nor why his father favored him over Esau. There was no *pathos*, as my ninth-grade English teacher, Mr. McDougal, used to say. That's when the drama of a story creates an emotional reaction. I teared up every other page reading *Crime and Punishment* and *The Brothers Karamazov*, but all I did reading the Bible was roll my eyes.

Those Bible stories just seemed incomplete to me, and every ending was the same. God either swoops in to make everything right, or he punishes people who don't have faith in him. No one really learns anything about themselves or the world except they best stay on God's good side since all he cares about is people worshipping him. I told Father Timothy what he wanted to hear about the importance of faith and keeping to God's command-ments, but to me God just seemed selfish, and the stories seemed made up like fairy tales, and none too good ones at that.

I guess you could say that summer taught me I wanted to learn all I could about the world. And not just through books. I wanted to get out and have experiences of my own and meet people from all different walks of life. At times, I was conflicted, remembering my siblings, thinking about Preston and the promises I'd made. My heart hadn't turned cold to them, but deep in my soul I wanted something more. Like now that my eyes had been opened to the world outside Le Moyne Parish, to possibilities like being with a man like Dan Jolly, I couldn't just shut my eyes again and go back to living like a Louisiana country boy.

About a week before my birthday party, Mr. Wainwright told me that directly after my lesson with Dan, I needed to get washed up and dressed to come with him and Buck to get fitted for a new suit at Rubenstein's. I didn't mind, even though it meant I had to cut my time short with Dan. I hustled through taking a bath, put on new clothes, and I ran out front to meet Mr. Wainwright at the car.

We made it halfway down the drive when I realized I'd forgotten the journal Granddaddy had given me. I liked to keep that with me at all times in case some new idea occurred to me and especially since we were going to New Orleans where I was liable to have some observations.

So, I made a great big fuss, begging Mr. Wainwright to tell

Buck to turn around so I could fetch my journal from the house. Maybe I'd gotten better at getting my way, or maybe I'd just caught the old prison warden in a softer mood. He huffed and told Buck to turn around, and I jumped out of the car and scurried up the stairs to get the journal in my bedroom.

Halfway down the second floor hall, I sensed something different. It could've been as subtle as a slight displacement of the air or some familiar lingering scent. As I neared my room, I spotted a muddy heel print on the carpet in the hall. That hadn't been there before. I'd been sure to take off my riding boots and slip into my tennis shoes before coming back into the house. I looked down the hall in the direction of that footprint. The house was still, but I was overcome with curiosity.

I passed my room and kept following the heel print. I'd never gone down that corridor out of respect for Granddaddy. That's where his private quarters were, and I suppose more to the point, that's where Virginia Bondurant slept. But like I said, I was growing bolder by the day living in Whittington Manor. Something strange was going on, and now that I was a resident of the place, I had rights to know about it. I saw a door half open up ahead, and then I heard a gasp and a whimper like a woman in distress.

My first instinct was to rush in there and see if everything was all right. I caught myself. My grandmother hated me, and if I was wrong about her needing help, she'd be none too pleased I'd barged into her room. So before doing anything, I stepped real light-footed to the open doorway to have a look.

I could tell it was my grandmother's room all right. Though the curtains were drawn over the windows, I could smell her perfume, and I spotted a lady's fancy vanity desk and mirror. The deeper part of the room was shadowy, but I heard that odd sound of a struggle. I angled around so I wasn't blocking the light from the hallway, and I strained my eyes to see.

I was like Lot's wife struck to a pillar of salt from the sight of sin. At the foot of the bed, a bare-skinned fellow with his riding britches pooled at his ankles was pressed up against a woman who was mostly turned away from me. But I could make out her long blonde hair and see her nightgown thrown open in the front and hiked up her back. It was lurid and disgusting. Dan was clasping her bare breasts needfully, nuzzling his lips against her face and forcing himself inside her in desperate thrusts.

I could tell he wasn't really taking her against her will, brutal as it looked at first. Virginia threw her head back and grasped the back of his hair like a whore in the throes of ecstasy. I felt sawed in half. I forced myself to look away, and I staggered to my bedroom, rushed to the bathroom, and threw up in the toilet.

10

THE NEXT DAY, I told Mr. Wainwright I wasn't taking riding lessons no more. He argued with me about it, complaining that my granddaddy had paid Dan Jolly for a full month. I answered that wasn't my problem, and he could lecture me until the pigs flew, but I wasn't taking lessons from that man. Then I blurted out if my granddaddy wanted to know the reason, he could ask me himself.

I stared at the busybody defiantly and watched a blink of knowledge pass over his face. Nothing happened at Whittington Manor Mr. Wainwright didn't know about. He played it off in his grumpy way, but he didn't dare take me up on that offer. Mr. Wainwright stormed off, and I could bet he was going to call Dan Jolly and cancel his services. He'd make an excuse like I'd come down with something or other and wasn't up to it.

That week was my birthday party. You can imagine I wasn't in the mood. Not only was I stinging from Dan's betrayal, but I was also reeling over what it meant for Granddaddy. We'd both been cut down to size in one fell swoop. I hadn't counted for much, so that wasn't such a big deal for me. But with regard to Granddaddy, well, it roused up complicated feelings.

I know now it ain't fair, but I was ashamed of him. He was my role model, the epitome of strength and respectability. But all along, he allowed his mean wife to make a fool of him, carrying on with a man he'd welcomed into his home and paid to take care of his horses. It wasn't just a one time thing, either. After I'd thrown up, I staked out a spot just inside my bedroom door, and I over-heard Dan telling Virginia he'd see her Friday next. Sounded like their arrangement had been going on for months, maybe longer. How could Granddaddy be that blind?

Like I said, it wasn't right for me to feel that way. I ought to have been spitting mad at Virginia and Dan for disrespecting Granddaddy so brazenly, so unforgivably, so hurtfully. And I did detest them both, but every time I came around to pitying Grand-daddy, it twisted into cruel disgust. What kind of man lets his wife make a mockery of him?

I wished I'd never seen it, and that tortured me, too. Suppose I'd just minded my own business and kept on being none the wiser? I wouldn't have to shy away from looking my granddaddy in the eye, feeling ashamed of him then feeling ashamed of myself for feeling that way. I'd been thinking I wanted to learn everything about the world, but I'd discovered there are things you're better off being ignorant about. Things so stinking ugly, they're like a conta-gion, and they get you feeling stinking ugly yourself.

With all that on my mind, it was awfully hard to walk into my birthday party raring for a celebration. It should've been spectacu-lar. I was dressed to the nines in a heather blue and white striped suit and a white fedora. They'd put up a big white tent on the south lawn with a stage for a five-man jazz band and a dozen tables with white tablecloths and ocean breeze orchid centerpieces with balloons. The tent had a dance floor and a great big banner that said *Happy Sixteenth Arizona*. Waiters circulated with punch and fancy canapés. Chefs worked on grills cooking chicken, sausages, and shrimp.

That tent was a good thing. The sky was gray and rumbling. The weather forecast called for thunderstorms.

Granddaddy had invited a couple dozen of his executives and clients from work, and some of them brought their families. In my lousy mood, it felt like a farce. None of the guests knew me. They'd just come because Gaston Bondurant had told them to.

He ushered me along to say how do you do to all those well-dressed strangers bearing friendly smiles and wrapped gifts. I put on being gracious as best as I could. Meanwhile, it was forty-five minutes into the party, and I didn't see Duke, Dolly, or Little Douglas anywhere. Preston neither, not that I had high hopes of him showing up.

I found myself idling on my own because Granddaddy had run off to greet someone or other. I'd never imagined feeling so lonely at my own birthday party, but there I was. Then things got worse.

I spotted Dan Jolly strolling over from across the tent, pointing a big grin at me. He had a gift-wrapped box in his hands.

My eyes scoured the place for Mr. Wainwright. Hadn't he had the sense to cancel Dan's invitation? When I found him in the crowd, well, he was staring at Dan, and he looked as fit to be tied as I was.

Dan headed toward me. Was it just plum bad luck some wires got crossed, and Dan didn't get the message he was no longer welcome? I didn't want no gift from him. I nearly ran, but why make myself look more stupid than I already felt?

"Happy Birthday, Arizona."

Naturally, Dan looked as handsome as a bridegroom in his madras suit, pink shirt and tie, and clean-shaven face. I still managed to yawn at him.

"You clean up real well. Bet you'll have the girls fussing with each other over who you're going to ask to dance. I'm glad you're feeling better. Just in time for your big day."

I gave him an ugly squint. "If you're looking for Virginia, you best slip into the house and find her upstairs. That's why you came, isn't it?"

His face paled as he started to get the picture.

He pushed his present toward me, trying to shrug things off like I was joking around. "I didn't come for anybody but you.

Here, take it. I won't spoil the surprise entirely, but I can tell you it's something you might use out on the trails at Middleton."

I crossed my arms. Dan shifted around with a nervous smile.

"Well, c'mon Arizona. It's your birthday."

He nudged the box toward me again. I didn't budge. Dan looked at me flummoxed and slid his gaze this way and that. I don't know if anyone was watching, and I didn't care.

Dan forced a chuckle. "I'm starting to get the impression we're not friends no more."

"Why don't you leave before I tell my granddaddy what's been going on?"

Dan's eyes popped. I could see the panic gripping him. Dan glanced around again and tried to lean in and direct me to the periphery of the tent.

"I don't know what's in your head, but it's nothing we can't fix by talking things out."

I shirked away from him. "I don't want to ever see you again. I sure as hell ain't in the mood for *talking things out.*"

Dan shook his head, left my gift at a nearby table, and marched away in a hurry.

That turned out to feel awfully good in the end, and then I spotted Duke, Dolly, and Little Douglas wandering into the tent. I hustled over to them, feeling so much love I might've bowled over some of the guests.

Well, they looked all kinds of out of place and moody. Truth was, they did stick out like sore thumbs. Duke in a pair of hand-me-down dress pants that rode up his ankles, a baseball cap and his faded school bag thrown over his shoulder. Dolly in a dowdy poofy-sleeved dress with a big lace bib. Little Douglas chewing on the cuff of his oversized Western button-down. But they'd never be out of place to me. I gave them each big hugs and kisses. Only Little Douglas gave me back much of a hug.

"I was starting to worry you weren't going to make it."

Duke shrugged his shoulders. Dolly stared at me like I'd transformed into a million-dollar diamond behind a display case.

I scooped up Little Douglas and led everyone over to a table. A waiter came along and brought us glasses of punch. I sat down with Douglas on my lap. Dolly sat down next to me, turned away, twirling a strand of her hair. Duke took a seat next to her. He brought out a wrapped package from his backpack and set it down in front of me. "We all pitched in from our weekly allowances. It ain't much."

"I already know it's the best gift I'll get all day."

I ripped through the wrapping. It was a jumbo box of Lemonheads, which were my favorite candies. I smirked at Duke, leaned over to give Dolly a kiss on the head, and I hugged and tickled Little Douglas. "You all want something to eat?"

Duke perked up some. I caught a waiter's attention and told him to bring over four big plates with everything. Duke and Dolly kept looking at me funny.

Once the food got brought over, the three of them chowed down and the tension lifted a bit. I cut up a piece of chicken for Little Douglas and carved kernels off a corn cob to help him eat. I missed taking care of my little brother, and I was proud to see he could nearly handle a fork on his own. For a while, us four having a meal together felt like home—Duke and I making faces at each other for laughs, Dolly being picky, all of us yapping at Douglas to not play with his food. Duke emptied his backpack on the table to show me a beat-up baseball mitt and ball the Petersons had given him. Unfortunately, rain drops had started pelting down, otherwise I would've tossed the ball around with him out on the lawn. Instead, I let him take his swipes at me about my uppity outfit, looking like some city slicker, he said with a big snort laugh.

"How's living with the Petersons?" I asked Duke and Dolly.

"It ain't like this." Duke rolled his eyes and finished sucking the meat from his drumstick.

I caught Dolly staring at a pair of young ladies drifting by our table. They wore summery gowns, wide-brimmed silk hats, sparkling earrings, and lots of jewelry. I'd never met them, and I

guess I'd gotten used to being around wealthy folks. I suppose I'd
have been as wide-eyed as my sister a few weeks back.

When the girls passed by, she turned to me. "You never said
your mama's family was millionaires."

I'd written to them about Whittington Manor. At least three
letters apiece since we'd last seen each other, and I told them so.
They said they never got any of the letters.

"My step-granddaddy owns B & B Sugar. He's one of the
wealthiest men in Louisiana." *And he wants me as his own.* That's
what I was wanting to say to them, not to brag, just hoping they'd
see I was someone special after all, and they'd be happy for me.
Duke looked at me uncertainly, and Dolly had a real sour expression on her face.

"Don't matter that he's wealthy, does it? We still all Fannings."

Dolly clucked. "It don't matter to you. You living easy. We still
ain't got no home. I guess your granddaddy ain't gonna take us in
like you say?"

Part of me wanted to tell her to watch her tone. But I glanced
away. My granddaddy had a big company to run, and I hadn't
found the right time to talk to him about taking them in. That
didn't mean I hadn't been thinking about them and missing them
real bad. I didn't know how to put the words together to make
them understand.

Dolly gloated at my shame. "What it mean to you saying you
looking out for us?" She shrugged. "Don't make a difference
anyway. End of the month, Duke's going on the road with Daddy."

My temperature spiked. Duke hid his face. He knew how I felt
about that idea. I stared my brother down. Eventually, he looked
at me.

"He family."

"And what's your sister and your little brother?"

Duke looked down at his lap again.

"I'm talking to you, Duke Fanning. If you gonna run off on
Dolly and Little Douglas, you better answer for it like a man."

"Why you picking on him?" Dolly said. "You run off on us, too." She pulled Douglas over to sit on her lap.

In a span of months, she was all grown up, sass and all. I gave her a firm look.

Dolly crossed her arms over my little brother. "Why you even invite us? To show off?"

"Dolly, you gonna tell me I had any options other than living here? It ain't been easy all the time, you can believe me that."

She put on a wide-eyed gape. "Oh, it must be so hard snapping your fingers to get a servant to bring you anything you want. Must be hard sleeping in silk sheets every night."

"I'm still responsible for you three," I reminded her. "And we were talking about Duke going on the road with Daddy. I won't have it. I've still got the phone number for Social Services. None of you are going back to living with him."

Duke threw up his hands. "What am I supposed to do? The Petersons want the two of them out by the start of school. They only want to keep me so I can work on the farm."

My stomach burned. I'd thought the Petersons had agreed to take them in for the long term.

Dolly sneered. "Social Services already found me a home with a pastor and his wife up in Jonesville. And remember that couple Daddy had over to the house? They taking Little Douglas. All the way to Texas." Her face scrunched up ugly, and she cried. Little Douglas started sobbing, too.

That sliced through my heart. I pushed up from the table. "I'm going to talk to Granddaddy right now."

I lifted Little Douglas into my arms to comfort him, and I waited for Dolly to look me in the eye. When she did, I nodded to her. Then I gave Little Douglas back to her and went to find my granddaddy.

THE PARTY TENT was crowded now that rain was teeming down. The jazz band had hit its stride, and the dance floor was filled with couples doing the swing. I felt like a prairie dog while I cased the tent, perching on my toes and stretching my neck to look over and around people. The stringed lamps were lit up since the early evening sky had gone charcoal gray, but it was still pretty dim. I worried I might never find Granddaddy.

Finally, I caught sight of him at the far side of the tent. He was holding court with a group of gentlemen, recounting some story that had everyone smiling. They all had highballs in hand. I wove around people to get to him.

When I did, he seized on me to introduce me to this fellow and the other. I felt like I was going to burst standing there while he and his friends went on and on.

"Arizona, son, how you enjoying your sixteenth birthday party?" Granddaddy asked me.

"It's fine."

They all chuckled in an uneasy sort of way. I didn't have time for meeting people Granddaddy worked with and making pleasant conversation.

"Wait till you see your birthday cake." Granddaddy winked to his friends. "This one I had made special at Swiss Confectionery."

"Granddaddy, I need to talk to you."

He raised his eyebrows. Then he smoothly told his friends, "Excuse us, fellas. But don't you go nowhere. The party's just getting started."

He took my shoulder and led me along to a more secluded area aside the bandstand. Granddaddy looked at me expectantly.

"Can my brothers and my sister stay with us?"

His eyes sparked, and then he eased into a grin. "I don't see why not. We'll just have to check with their foster parents. Make sure it's okay with them to have the kids stay the night." He glanced around. "We can ask Mr. Wainwright to ring them up."

I fixed on him. "I don't mean just the night. I mean, can they stay *on* here? Like we talked about before I moved in."

"Stay on? How you mean?"

"I mean, can they live here?"

He shifted his gaze. "You saying as in a permanent arrangement?"

"I am. You told me you were going to work on it once I got settled in. Grandaddy, I'm settled in."

I didn't like his amused expression. "Arizona, it's not as simple as that. You're my son. My grandson, I mean. You and your grandmother are blood, so having the courts grant me guardianship was easy. But I can't take in your half brothers and sister just for the asking."

"Please, Granddaddy. They got nowhere to go. Nowhere *right* to go. My brother Duke's talking about going with my daddy to be a traveling carny. Dolly and Little Douglas are going to be split off to live with strangers."

I felt like I was crumbling saying it.

Granddaddy bulged his lip. "I'm sorry to hear that. It's a terrible situation Gus Fanning put those kids in. But the law's the law. If I took those kids in, I'd be harboring minors. A man can go to jail for that. You wouldn't like that, would you?"

I didn't understand what he was saying. I just knew my heart was breaking because I couldn't take care of my brothers and sister.

"You can't just split us up."

"I'm not the one splitting you up, son. Gus Fanning gone and done that. Now, look here. This is your birthday party. It's not the time or place for you to be getting upset about this."

Maybe the matter with Virginia and Dan Jolly was still on my mind. I looked him boldly in the eyes.

"You said you're a powerful man. You can't help three kids who ain't got nothing?"

He stared at me crookedly. "What's gotten into you? I understand you care about your half-brothers and sister, but you best show me some respect."

"Show *me* some respect." I waved my hand. "Look at all you got, and you're telling me you can't make room for three kids who got nothing?" I wiped hot tears from my face with my jacket sleeve. "I don't need this big party. I just need you to help."

Words caught in my throat. I turned from him while my eyes bled tears.

Granddaddy gripped my arm, trying to make me look at him. "Listen here. There's wanting to help, and there's having the ability to help. You need to understand the difference. You're a Bondurant now. Them kids you grown up with, they'll get along fine with their own kind. Better for them to be raised in the environment they're used to."

I bit down on my shaking fist. I felt like I'd been socked in the gut.

"You're special, Arizona. Remember that. You belong here because you're mine. Them siblings of yours, they're your past. You're on your way to becoming someone important, and you need to understand that."

He'd never spoken to me so sharply. I was a steaming pile of mush. I tried to sniff back my tears, stand straight, be the kind of man he wanted me to be.

Granddaddy rustled his hand into the pocket of his slacks. The world was throbbing in and out of my vision so I wasn't so clear about what was going on until I looked down and saw he'd pressed a wad of cash into my hand. It could've been five hundred dollars or more.

"You go on and give them that. There's help. Right there. And I don't want to hear another word about this the rest of the night."

He nudged me along. I was dizzy with defeat. I nearly tripped over my own two legs stumbling away from him.

Approaching the table where I'd left Duke, Dolly, and Little Douglas, I awakened a little and brought out the handkerchief from my suit jacket to clean up the sweat and tears from my face. Though there was no disguising how things had gone with my granddaddy.

I went to Duke, gestured for him to stand up, and I tucked the money into his pants pocket. I sucked in a breath to steady myself.

"He says you can't stay, but that's from him."

Duke's eyes widened. Dolly stood up and put her hands on her hips.

"So, that's that. We splitting up. All because of you."

I was broken, but those words raised what was left of my self-respect. "All because of *me*?"

"If you hadn't hit Daddy with that bottle, none of this would've happened."

Blurrily, I faced her. "Dolly, you take that back."

"He was right about you," she snapped. "You're a no-good faggot. Gone dragged us all to hell."

I lunged wildly for my sister, but Duke got in the way. "That what I am to you? A no-good faggot? Who fed your ungrateful mouth how many years?"

Duke wrangled Dolly away from me. She looked scared, but I wasn't done.

"You come to my party and call me filthy names? Act like it's me who broke up the family? You listen here, country swine, I ain't never going back to that sad drunk what made you. I'd bash his head in again if given a second chance, and don't think I won't do the same thing to you if you ever call me that again. You want to hear me say it? I *am* better than you. Just take a look around. I'm *somebody*, and what're you?"

I'm ashamed to say I didn't mind the sight of my sister trembling and weeping. But when I noticed Little Douglas cowering behind her and Duke's eyes beseeching me to cool down, well, I hadn't felt that miserable since the night Grandma Tilly's house burned. Meanwhile, guests had drawn up around us like they were watching a street brawl.

"Duke," I sputtered.

Dolly shouted at me. "I hate you." She yanked at Duke to pull him along toward the car lot.

I tried with my brother again. "Where you gonna go? How you gonna get home? You don't got to leave."

Duke looked split down the middle. In the end, he gave me a tight-lipped frown and patted his pocket with the cash.

"We got bus fare now."

Tears seared my face as I watched him turn his back and usher Dolly and Little Douglas along.

I staggered out of the tent and into the rain. Then I broke into a run, heaving tears, no destination in mind, just wanting to disappear from the world.

11

I DON'T KNOW how long I ran that night, but it was enough to be deep in the woods beyond the outbuildings of Whittington Manor while lightning flashed overhead and thunder boomed. I was soaking wet and my lungs were burning, but I kept pushing on. Fool that I was, I'm not sure what I hoped to accomplish. Just getting as far away from my birthday party as I could.

I found the horse trail and followed it for a while, and then I stumbled off the shoulder into the shelter of trees. Rain beat down, and the wind kicked up. At some point, I ended up in a little clearing, and sheet lightning lit up the sky and shocked me to a halt.

That lightning was so bright, it shone on a dark, glassy body of water. I realized I must've come as far as the lake. For a moment, the fanfare of lightning overhead stole my breath away. The air tasted charged, like putting your tongue to a battery. Then a big gust of wind flooded through the woods, and jagged lightning struck so close to me, the snap of it sent my ears ringing.

I heard a violent crack above me, and then my legs gave out. Darkness ate up my vision, and all my strength was sapped away. I thought I might have died, and part of me welcomed it. Sometimes being alive hurt too much.

I DIDN'T DIE. When I woke up, as best as I could figure, something had fallen on my head. A tree limb most likely. But I wasn't in the woods no more. Somebody had carried me into a house.

My brain was all worn out, so it took me a minute just to stitch that much together. I was propped up on somebody's couch, covered in a knit blanket. My rescuer had taken off my jacket, loosened my shirt and tie, and pulled off my shoes. I was groggy, and the back of my head ached some. I touched that spot delicately and felt a swollen lump. Somebody's bath towel was draped around my neck.

I didn't have the foggiest idea where I was, but I wasn't sore about it. I was grateful it was dry. I could hear rain drumming on the tin roof overhead, and through the big bay window across from me, I saw the dark and stormy night. Someone had brought me to his cabin in the forest.

The walls, ceiling, and floors were exposed wood. The place where I was laid out looked like a living room, though the furnishings were strange. Unframed canvases were helter-skelter, some on easels, most just propped up against the walls along with mismatched chairs. A long worktable dominated the room.

It was kind of creepy. I was surrounded by portraits, all of the same young woman. They were done in wild brushstrokes, kind of abstract, if that's the word, or could be the artist hadn't gotten around to finishing them. That big worktable was covered with oil paints and brushes and other kinds of supplies I didn't recognize. The artist had some metal work projects laid out there as well. I couldn't tell if those were finished either. They were all surreal and kind of menacing in my mental state. Then I noticed some pencil sketches tacked up on one wall. *B&B Enterprises*. A collection of hand-drawn logos?

Like waking up in the middle of a dream you can't quite remember, these things were familiar in a way I couldn't place at first. A cabin by the lake. I'd seen it before, but I couldn't call up when, where, or even if it had spun out of my imagination.

Footsteps shuffled toward me, and a stranger came around the couch. He was tall. I had to stretch my neck to see his face. He had overgrown, sandy hair, damp from the rain, a week's worth of a beard, big sorrowful eyes, a kind face. I guessed he'd slipped into dry clothes since rescuing me. He wore a 1970s graphic T-shirt, loose drawstring trousers and nothing on his feet. He was a lean fellow with broad shoulders and long, ropey arms. Arms that had carried me who knew how far?

"Glad you're up and awake. I was worried about you. How you feel?"

He said it so routinely. Like he knew who I was? I was sure about him then. He had Granddaddy's strong jaw and fine blond hair, though he wore it longer. He was more of a Bohemian type, but he had to be my granddaddy's younger brother. The wonder of meeting him made me forget my bodily complaints.

"Yes, I heard about you," he said. "I got a feeling you heard about me as well." He stooped down and offered his big hand. "Nicolas Bondurant. Pleased to meet you, Arizona."

I remembered then the dread and pity I'd felt when Dan Jolly told me about my granddaddy's brother. But Nicolas wasn't a weathered, hard luck Vietnam veteran like I'd pictured. I couldn't tell his age exactly, but he looked too young to be what I thought a veteran was like. He had me bound in a spell, a gentle, strong-bodied recluse who'd fought through a storm to come to my aid, probably saved my life.

He leaned over to take a look at the back of my head. He smelled nice from whatever deodorant soap he used to bathe and his laundered T-shirt. Meanwhile, I must've stunk like a wet dog.

"Well, it doesn't look too bad." He gazed at me from an eye level crouch. "Should get it checked out, but the problem is the phone lines are down along with the electricity. So, if you want to get cleaned up, it'll be a cold shower, not a warm bath. I got the generator running on gas, but that's just enough to keep the lights on along with the fridge."

"Thank you," I finally managed to say.

He held up his big hand and tucked his thumb and pinkie together. "How many fingers?"

"Three."

He moved his pointer finger back and forth to see if I could follow it with my eyes, which I could. Then he brought out a pen flashlight to take a closer look at my eyes.

Nicolas clicked it off. "Your pupils look all right. You got a headache?"

"A little bit. Mostly I'm just sore around the bump."

"You got lucky. There was a tree limb down as thick as your two legs just a foot or so from where you fell. You got beaned by one of its branches. Still can do some damage."

He took my wrist in his hand to feel my pulse. "Feel sick, like you might throw up?"

"No, sir."

"You know what day it is?"

"August 12th." *My birthday.* What a day it turned out to be.

"I was a Medical Specialist, Fourth Class in the Army, in case you're wondering why I'm harassing you with all the questions. That's not a doctor, but I had my training." He released my wrist, gave me a frown. "I'd feel better if we could get you to the hospital over in Donaldsonville. Get an X-ray just to be sure. But that won't be happening until the morning." Nicolas stood. "I've got some aspirin, and I'll get you set up with an ice pack for that bump. You want coffee? Kettle's working just fine on a gas burner."

I nodded. Something warm to drink sounded wonderful. Now that I was coming to, I was freezing cold in my waterlogged clothes.

I pushed myself up a bit. "I'm getting your couch all wet. You suppose I could dry off?"

Nicolas held out his arm for me to grasp, and I stripped off the blanket and carefully raised myself to my feet. I really didn't feel so bad. I wasn't dizzy, but just to be safe, Nicolas helped me along to his little bathroom and sat me down on the toilet. He left me to fetch something and came back with a pair of pajama bottoms and a long-sleeved thermal T-shirt.

"There's towels in the cabinet. You'll be swimming in these, but they'll have to do." He handed me the clothes and eyed me somberly. "You sure you're okay handling things yourself?"

"Yes, sir. Thanks."

He gave me a wink and shut the door to give me some privacy to change clothes.

I couldn't have ended up in better hands. Nicolas was like an angel, swooping me up in the middle of a lightning storm and bringing me to safety. I was thinking he must be the kindest soul I'd ever met. There was something fascinating about a fully-grown man who'd gone to war yet had such tender ways.

I stripped down and dried off with a towel. Nicolas was right about me swimming in his clothes. The pajama bottoms had a drawstring so I could tighten them at the waist, but the cuffs bunched up at my feet. I rolled them up and threw on the thermal shirt. It smelled like the soap Nicolas used and made me feel warm and comfy even though it was at least one size too big.

I hung my wet clothes neatly over the shower rod and stepped out to the house. Nicolas was heating up a kettle on his gas burner in the kitchen. I went back to the couch. As far as I could tell, it was the only place to sit, and I figured I'd be sleeping on it overnight. I only saw one other room, which must've been where he slept.

Nicolas came over with two mugs of coffee and a blue ice bag tucked under his arm. I took one of the mugs from him, and he pulled over a stepstool for his. He gave me the ice bag to place on my bump, fished out an aspirin bottle from his pocket, and shook out two pills for me to take. I swallowed them down with some coffee. It was the bitter instant kind, but I'd never been choosy. It warmed me up just fine.

He pulled over an old chair with a vinyl seat cushion so he

could sit across from me, and we sipped our coffee together. He snuck a few curious glances at me. I knew I owed him some explaining, but I was shy talking about it.

"You gonna tell me what you were doing out in the woods in the middle of the worst storm of the summer?"

I tucked my legs beneath me on the couch. "Do I have to?"

Nicolas half-smiled. "I suppose you don't. But if your search party shows up here in the middle of the night, it might be nice for me to get ahead of the news."

I hadn't thought of that. My granddaddy was probably worried sick. And pissed as hell I'd disappeared from my birthday party with all his friends at the house.

"How'd you find me?"

He scratched his stubbly square jaw. "I like watching storms." He pointed his eyes over to the bay window. "I was out there on the deck, just gazing at them fireworks in the sky. Lots of folks, they get scared of thunderstorms. Especially those who've been in the service. It gets their brain remembering missile fire and machine guns." He tucked a strand of copper hair behind his ear. "Well, there's plenty of things you're better off not remembering. But living out here, you've got nothing but nature. And she can get loud sometimes, but it's only because she can't help herself. And when she wails and rages with her pyrotechnics, I just think it's beautiful. The world provides so many things for free, it's a wonder to me why man needed to invent television and radio and movie theaters. All you need is to pay attention to what's around you. You'll see more wonders than any man could come up with in his head."

I liked watching thunderstorms, too, and I liked the way he talked, like a poet. I liked looking at his big, strong hands as well as other parts of him, though I was trying to tame my wandering eye and not be rude. I kept my gaze on his face, which wasn't so hard to do.

"Anyway, I saw a lightning strike just down the bank of the lake and thought I saw somebody struggling. So, I hiked over and found you." He fixed his soulful eyes on me. "What's your side of the story? We ought to get them matched up right."

"It's dumb." I chewed my bottom lip.

"How old are you?"

"Sixteen. Just today."

I peeked at him. I hoped he didn't think I was young and immature. Nicolas had that kind, half-smile on his face again.

"Happy birthday. If I knew you were comin', I'd've baked a cake."

I bowed my head. It was stupid, but it made me grin.

"Well, Arizona, when I was your age, I did some dumb things too." I watched him look toward the window. "Went swimming in this here lake in the dead of winter. I caught it good from your granddaddy a few times for sneaking friends over to the house to drink his whiskey."

I wished my story had been as simple as that. I didn't know where to begin explaining how I'd ended up in the woods. Meanwhile, I had a lot of questions for him. I hadn't thought before about my granddaddy's brother growing up at Whittington Manor.

"Did you know my mama?"

Nicolas nodded slowly. "She was just two years older than me." He sipped his coffee. "I was away at school most of the time while she lived here. But we were friends." His eyes brightened. "You look like her."

I glanced around at his portraits. The shape of the faces was similar enough to say they were the same woman, and the coloring and hair looked a little like the photo of my mama.

"No, that's not her. It wasn't like that," he said with a tiny smirk. "Philippa was just a good friend."

He knit his hands around his mug. "I knew a girl before I went off to Vietnam. Sara. Well, Arizona, funny thing. I made it through a war, came back, and found out she died. Hit by a drunk driver. I guess you can see she stayed on my mind."

"My mama, my mama who raised me, she died in a car accident too."

"My brother told me you haven't had an easy life. I'm sorry about your grandparents."

His eyes were so pained and earnest, it brought out my pain too. I teared up and dabbed my eye with my sleeve. Then I looked up at him, real serious. "You ever feel like you don't belong anywhere in the world?"

That probably sounds like too much to ask someone I just met, but I guess I felt he might understand. Nicolas came over, sat down at my side and stretched his big warm arm around me, just gingerly at first. That made me drop my head and cry again. Nicolas held me a little tighter, not saying anything, just letting me sob against him. I gripped his shirt with my outside hand, and we sat tucked up while I cried from all the pain in my heart.

I hurt something awful, but I also hadn't felt so comforted since Mama Lou was alive. That probably don't make any sense. We barely knew each other, but Nicolas made me feel like I finally found a man who understood me and thought I was all right the way I was.

The tears stopped coming out of me, and I felt peaceful. I let go of Nicolas' shirt, sat up a bit, and dried my face with my sleeve. Nicolas brought his arm down between us.

"Arizona, I reckon I do know something about not belonging anywhere in the world. The secret is, you don't know where you belong till you find it." He gazed deep into my eyes. "You'll find that place."

I wasn't as sure as he was, but it made me feel better. I was tired of thinking about my troubles and now wearing Nicolas out after I'd already made him rush out in the rain to drag my dumb self from the woods. I looked around at his artwork. I recognized the big lettered crown I'd seen on sugar bags at the grocery store and another design from candy wrappers.

"You draw the designs for B&B?"

He nodded. "I'm the wizard behind the curtain. But that ain't much. It's your granddaddy who runs the business."

I still thought that was impressive. Looking over at the paintings, I said, "That girl Sara, were you in love?"

He twitched his nose. "She was my one and only. I guess you'd call me a late bloomer. Not like Poly, your granddaddy. He had a girl from the first day of his co-ed religion classes. Sara and I met our junior year of college. Tulane University. We went steady for three years." He glanced off thoughtfully. "I'm not going to lie and say things were perfect between us. But sure, we loved each other. I asked her to marry me the night before they shipped me off to Nam."

"I'm sorry. Sorry she died, I mean."

Nicolas stood and collected our empty mugs. "You don't have to be. It was a long time ago." He brought the mugs over to the kitchen.

"How long?" I wanted to know everything about him.

"Sara died in 1975. Nine years." He tinkered around at the kitchen counter. "Hey, you want something to eat or drink?"

I wasn't hungry. I was still a little thirsty and told him so.

"You've got your choice of water or Lipton's iced tea. From the mix."

"Water's fine."

Nicolas came back with two glasses of water with ice cubes. I hoped he'd sit down on the couch with me again, but he went back to his chair.

"You ever sell any of this here art?"

"Nope. It's what the doctors call therapeutic."

I thought it was more than that. I mean, I didn't know anything about art, but his paintings looked as good as modern ones I'd seen on TV. I especially liked his metal sculptures. I recognized one was shaped from copper piping and looked like an owl. I'd never have the imagination to create anything like that.

What I wanted to ask him the most was why he lived in the

cabin so far from everyone else at Whittington Manor. But I shied away from it. I didn't want him to think I found him strange.

"Were you close with my granddaddy when you were growing up? I mean my *step* granddaddy."

Nicolas sipped his water. "Well, you've got to understand, there's eleven years between us. He's always been something between a father and an older brother. But we always did get along." He picked at his stubbly chin. "Our daddy died when I was twelve. Poly was twenty-three. Left him the man of the house. Our mama, she'd been sick as far back as I can remember. She died just short of a year after our daddy passed. In a way, Poly took up being both father and mother to me."

I was a little sad Granddaddy had never mentioned his brother to me before. "How old were you when he married Virginia and brought my mama to Whittington Manor?"

"I'd have been fourteen. It was only the second wedding I'd been to in my life, and I was his best man."

I pieced things together and realized my granddaddy had to be a lot younger than Virginia as I suspected. Nicolas was two years younger than my mama would've been, which made him thirty-one. That meant my granddaddy was forty-two, and he'd only been twenty-seven when my mama died in 1968. Virginia had to be at least six years older than him, probably more.

I gave Nicolas a crooked grin. "How'd you get along with my grandmother Virginia?"

Nicolas drew up a tight smile on his face. "Now, I'll tell you something about your grandmother Virginia Stewart. She was quite the starlet in her day. Miss Louisiana 1950. Third runner up for Miss America. She had a modeling contract with Neiman Marcus department stores. But that ended when she got pregnant with your mama, and she married Wilson Packard. He was the son of a big shot oil company mogul, and he had a reputation as a ladies man, if you know what I mean. If memory serves, their marriage only lasted four years. Ginny returned to New Orleans a humbled woman, back living with her parents, past her prime to take up modeling again. All the same, she had her sights on a second husband who could bring her back to respectability. And she found herself a second and a third and then there was your step granddaddy."

He drank down some more of his ice water. I watched him, transfixed.

"Ginny was well into her thirties, but she still had the looks and charm to hook a man of society. Poly had tinkered around with some serious relationships with women, but nothing that stuck. And he'd just taken over our daddy's company, which made the idea of settling down appealing." He half-smiled. "I mean no disrespect, but I think he figured he'd done good marrying a beauty queen."

I snorted. "She's a witch."

He frowned impartially. "I won't make excuses for Virginia. She was high-strung even before she lost your mama. There's some pain she's harboring. With some folks, it makes them kinder. Others, they lash out, hoping to find someone to take the misery off their hands."

"She don't want anything to do with me. She made that clear the night we met."

I almost told him about her affair with Dan Jolly, but I stopped myself. As easy as it was talking to Nicolas, that didn't seem right to mention.

Nicolas looked at me sympathetically. "I don't know what to tell you about that, but I'll say you're in good company. Ginny told off half the population from Lafayette to Slidell. The two of us, we had some real good spars."

He grinned, which made me grin too.

"What was my mama like?"

"Now, Philippa, she was a good woman for all the reasons Virginia isn't. She had a big heart, your mama did. Friendly to just about anyone she met. Never stuck up, always down to earth. Why we used to have a lot of late night talks just like the two of us are having." His eyes twinkled, the way my granddaddy's did.

"Philippa always did make me laugh. I remember once she told me maybe I was better off not having a mother or a father, considering the pair she'd ended up with."

I smiled. I felt the same way with respect to my daddy. That made me wonder about something else.

"Did your parents love each other?"

Nicolas pointed his finger at me. "You're lucky you're talking to me. Some people would say a question like that's too nosy."

"Like Mr. Wainwright."

He tipped his glass to me. "Yep. Like Mr. Wainwright."

I looked at him expectantly.

"Sure, my daddy and mama loved each other. I never seen it, but Poly used to tell me stories from when they were younger. They were high school sweethearts. Used to tear up the town courting, and my mama had a fine career ahead of her as an illustrator. She made children's books and had a weekly strip in the funnies of the *Times-Picayune*. That's the biggest newspaper in New Orleans. But she had what you call a nervous condition. It cropped up in her mid-twenties. She got scared of leaving the house and had all kinds of worries about catching sicknesses. Back then, it was something people didn't understand. I sure didn't understand when I was young, and it made things hard on all of us. She and daddy drifted apart. But after they died, we found letters our daddy had written her, and he sure loved her, back when they were courting."

That made me sad and wonder if his mama had passed on her condition to him. He didn't seem like he had nervous problems, but then again, he kept himself secluded from the world. I wasn't about to pry into that.

"You think my mama loved Gus Fanning?"

Nicolas raised his eyebrows then eased back in his seat. "I can't say, Arizona. Would it make a difference one way or the other?"

The way he said it made me think maybe I'd been wrong worrying about that. I mean, I'd grown up thinking a mother and father ought to love each other if they were going to have a child.

And if they didn't love each other, that meant the child wasn't meant to be and maybe something was wrong with him.

But I'd since learned a lot about families. My daddy, well, I doubted he was capable of love, but he'd made me, Duke, Dolly, and Little Douglas. I wouldn't say that meant any of my half-siblings were lesser than anyone else, so it shouldn't mean I was any lesser if my mama hadn't loved my daddy.

While I pondered those things, Nicolas stood up to collect our glasses. "What do you say about turning in for the night? I'm early to bed, early to rise. And soon as them telephone wires are up again, you can bet your granddaddy's going to be burning up the phone lines looking for you."

I didn't want to think about that. I gave him my glass and got up from the couch, wanting to help in some way.

"You make do on the couch for the night?" he said. "I've got an extra pillow, sheets and a blanket. You'll probably do just fine with a sheet this time of year."

I told him I was plenty happy with that. Nicolas brought me the pillow and the sheets, and we said goodnight. I listened to him brushing his teeth in the bathroom, stepping over to his bedroom, and not long after his night light clicked off, I was lights out, too.

12

I SLEPT LIKE a baby that night. I don't think I slept so well in months, which was funny considering I was laying on a beat-up couch and for weeks I'd been sleeping on a queen-sized poster bed in my own suite. I guess I needed the rest after an eventful day, and I felt warm and safe in Nicolas's cabin. I would've slept through the morning, but goings-on in the kitchen woke me up. I smelled fried eggs and bacon.

Nicolas was over there, washed and dressed for a new day in a T-shirt and a ripped and faded pair of denim jeans. The wall clock read seven thirty. I remembered he said he was an early riser. I said good morning, hurried to the bathroom, washed my face, and joined him in the kitchen.

In the daylight, I noticed things I hadn't the night before. Besides the bedroom and bath, Nicolas's cabin was just one room. The kitchen area was in the front, and his big stained and grooved wooden worktable took up what could've been a dining area, and it pushed into the living room space. Seeing as I was awake, Nicolas went to raise the shades over the big bay windows, which looked out on a deck and beyond, the lake.

The storm had passed, and it was bright and sunny. I strung along with Nicolas as he went out to the deck and dried his picnic table with a towel. That made for the only place we could sit down and eat in his whole house, but it sure was a great view of Whittington Manor's wooded lake. Ducks and geese were gliding down on the water, and I could see clear across to the gazebo by the riding trail.

I followed Nicolas inside and asked what I could do to help. He pointed to the kitchen shelves and told me to bring down plates, mugs, and utensils. Together we carried everything out to the deck, and then Nicolas served the eggs and bacon right from his cast-iron frying pans.

"That gas burner comes in handy," he said. "The lines are still down so I'm afraid that means no hot water."

One thing hadn't changed in the daylight. He was handsome. Maybe more so now that I could see the fair hairs on his forearms, and the kiss of the sun on his nose and upper cheeks. I dug in to my eggs and thought it was the best breakfast I ever ate, probably because it had been made by his hands.

I watched him staring out to the lake. He was quieter than last night. I was dying to know what was going through his head.

"What you got planned today?"

"I was just thinking it looks like a good day to fish."

I took a sip of my coffee and hiked up some nerve. "Sounds like fun. Suppose I might go with you?"

He didn't turn his head, and every atom of his face stayed in place. "You fished before?"

I nodded. Truth was, I'd only been twice with my daddy and Duke, and that was years ago. We went to Bayou Teche, and one time Duke caught a big bass, but I never caught anything. I chose not to mention that.

"Gonna be a lot branches down on the trail, but they say right after a storm is the best time to catch crappie." He frowned. "But you ought to show yourself at the house. There's folks right worried about you."

That sent a pang through my belly. "I don't want to go back there. Not today."

Nicolas fixed on me sternly.

"Please can't I stay? I won't be no bother. I swear."

He kept watching me. So, I told him about my fight with Granddaddy and everything that happened with Dolly and Duke. Well, to be honest, I left out some of the words Dolly and I threw back and forth, and I bet you can guess which ones. But I gave him the gist of how bad it was, and that was plenty enough to get my heart breaking again and sore at Granddaddy for not lifting a finger to help my siblings.

"I just know I'm not ready to face him. If he gets hot-tempered with me, I'm liable to say something I'll regret. Can't I stay here for a while? Just until things cool down?"

The outdoor lightbulb above the deck fizzed on. A few breaths later, the phone rang inside the house.

Nicolas smirked. "Lookie there. Right on cue."

I near got down on my knees and begged him not to, but Nicolas strolled into the house to answer the phone.

Breathlessly, I listened to him pick up the receiver. I strained to hear every word he spoke.

"Good morning to you too....Mm-hmm...No, everything's fine. Just lost the electricity is all, but it's back up...You don't say?...Why, yes I did...He's eating eggs on the deck...That's right…"

I crept over to the door frame. Nicolas was leaning against the kitchen wall with the phone receiver on his ear. He glanced at me just once. That man ought to have been a poker player. I couldn't read a thing on his face.

"So, he told me...He's fine, Poly. Caught a branch on his head in the woods, but he just needed some rest...Yes, I'm sure about that...He's saying that's not such a good idea...Yeah, just a little cooling off period is all...Uh-huh...No, it's no bother...Yep...I will...Au re'oir to you too."

Nicolas hung up his phone. He went to the sink, turned on the faucet, and started scouring a frying pan.

He left me with my heart in my throat for a good thirty seconds, and then he called over his shoulder. "Best time to fish is the morning. How 'bout getting the table cleared while we still got a chance to bring some crappie home for supper?"

I was so thankful, I ran over and embraced him from behind.

Nicolas chuckled. "I'm not your daddy, fool."

"Thank you."

"It's only for one night, y'hear?"

"Yes, sir."

I rushed back to the deck to help him clean up after breakfast.

WE HIKED OVER to a spot by the lake where there was a shelf of rock above the water, which made for a better place to fish than the rain-flooded bank. Nicolas had dug out an old pair of running shorts I could tie up at the waist so they didn't slip down my legs. He also gave me an old polo shirt, which hung loose around my skinny frame, and a pair of his own briefs. I had to wear my dress socks and shoes from last night since he wore elevens and I wore nines. I looked like a clown and dirtied up my nice wingtips from Rubenstein's, but the hell if I cared. I was spending the day with Nicolas.

He had an extra fishing rod for me, and he showed me how to tie on a hook, fix the line with weights and a floater, and—the part I liked least—how to skewer a worm on the hook. He cast out to the green-brown water, and I followed with a pitiful cast that barely made it beyond the bank.

I reeled the line back for another try, and Nicolas gave me pointers on where I should be holding the rod, how much line to leave out, laying the line on my index finger, and using both hands to give the rod a flick. I did better my second time.

It turned out the fish weren't biting that day. That was fine by me. The only thing I liked less than getting a worm on a hook was pulling a barb through a fish's mouth. After standing for about an hour, hoping to reel in a crappie, Nicolas sat down with his legs hanging off the ledge. I sat down too and eased up close. I liked being near him. I liked his clean, manly smell.

"They must've heard you were coming, and you scared them off."

I scowled. "How you even know there's any crappies in this here lake?"

"I know. I've been fishing this lake since before you were born."

I was feeling a little cheeky that day, wanting to see what Nicolas looked like when he got flustered.

"Maybe you fished out every last crappie."

He curled up his mouth on one side. "Hmm. I never had trouble before. Only thing I can figure is the fish don't like a boy from Le Moyne Parish disturbing their natural habitat."

I bumped my shoulder against his. "Now, that's plain cruel. You know I got roots right here in Darrow."

"You got roots in Metairie. That's where your grandmother's family's from."

"You saying them crappies are prejudiced? They only like people who been raised right here in Darrow?"

"Could be."

The sun was serving up some heat. I'd sweated through my polo shirt, and Nicolas's neck was glistening and his sweat pooled on his shirt collar. That gave me ideas.

"Maybe I need to make a proper introduction." I reeled in my line, set the rod aside, and I stood up and pulled off my shirt.

Nicolas's eyes smiled for a moment, but then he went back to sassing me.

"You jump in there, you can forget about catching fish the rest of the day."

I kicked off my shoes, peeled off my socks, and threw them at him. "In Le Moyne Parish, we catch fish with our bare hands. I suppose that's too much work for you snooty Darrow folk."

Nicolas reeled in his line. He looked like he was fixing to give me a clip on the head. It made me laugh seeing his feathers ruffled.

I took a quick glance around. We was a long way from the

main house, and mossy oaks hedged in the banks of the lake on either side. I don't know what got into me that day, but the idea of skinny dipping was exciting. So, that's what I did. Dropped my shorts and briefs and cannonballed right off the rocky ledge before Nicolas could catch me. I even hollered like a country boy doing it.

That lake water was pungent, but it was heavenly refreshing. It was only about four feet deep where I'd jumped down, and the bottom was slimy with long blades of weeds. I swam out a little and treaded water, looking up at Nicolas fretting on the ledge.

"I should've sent you back to your granddaddy, you damn fool."

"Hold on." I pretended to study a spot in the water. "I think I see a crappie."

I dove beneath the water and dug out a big fistful of mud from the floor of the lake. I shot back up and shook my head.

"Nearly caught one." Then I flung the mud at Nicolas. It splattered a few inches from his foot.

He looked steaming mad. He shrugged off his shirt, peeled his boots from his feet, stripped off his jeans and briefs, and came barreling into the lake with a gigantic splash. I laughed and clapped water at him. Nicolas stretched out his arms and lunged to catch me.

I ducked away from him, but I'd be lying if I said I put much of an effort into it. Nicolas got a wrestling hold around my neck. I batted him and squealed, but he was plenty strong enough to dunk me for being a brat.

When I resurfaced, hollering for him to let me go, he ground his fist into my scalp.

"How you like that?"

"Lemme go."

Nicolas loosened his hold on me. I seized the opportunity to jam my fingers into his sides.

He thrashed and giggled. Then we rounded each other in the water, smiling and sizing each other up.

"Now you gone and frightened the crappies away," I teased him.

He put on a scowl. In a blink, he leapt for me again, catching my arms while I tried to kick away. He pinched at my ribs, sending me twisting and shrieking. Good Lord, I loved wrestling with him. It got me stiff between the legs.

Nicolas trapped me around the shoulders. "Look here, son. What do I gotta do to teach you to behave?"

I stopped resisting. He could hold me all day long, and I wouldn't mind. I searched his face and brushed my knee between his legs. He'd gotten hard too.

That was one horrible idea. Nicolas shirked from that contact, released me, and backed away. His poor face looked tortured, and I was scared to death he was disgusted by me. Why'd I gone and pushed things like that? I wanted to hide, but I couldn't steer my eyes away from him.

Something in Nicolas reset. "Just got a little too worked up is all." I wasn't sure if he was referring to him or me. He looked off to the side and waved his hand. "C'mon. Best get you out the water before you make more of a mess of yourself."

He trudged toward the bank. The muddy water clung to me, and I realized I'd have to clean up real well before setting foot in his house again. I gave Nicolas a lead, and then I made my way over to climb up the shelf.

We looked away from each other while we dressed. Nicolas threw me a towel he'd brought along, and I wiped the mud from my limbs and feet. I felt like I should say I was sorry, but then my brain twisted up. Maybe it was best to not bring attention to what happened. Nicolas was acting like he didn't want to talk about it. I felt like I would break to pieces if he called me a faggot and said he never wanted to see me again. We'd been getting along so well, and now it was like a forcefield was between us. I was sick to my stomach.

Nicolas started chuckling. I turned to him, wondering what he found so amusing.

"You're a lousy fisherman, Arizona."

My mouth screwed up in a lopsided grin.

"And you've got no business picking fights with men who're bigger and stronger than you."

I peeked at him, and our eyes met. Nicolas didn't look mad. I didn't know what to make of that glance, but it made me feel all good again.

"So, you can't fish, and you don't know how to fight. What *are* you good at?"

"I can fight. My daddy's twice my size, and I laid him out cold with a bottle of bourbon."

Nicolas chuckled again. "Gus Fanning?"

"Mm-hmm."

"Well, I'll say two things about that. He had it coming, and you got lucky."

I suppose he had a point.

"So, what're you good at, Arizona?"

"Reading. Writing." I shrugged. "I read two novels by Fyodor Dostoyevsky this summer. Someday, I want to be a writer like him."

Nicolas grinned. "Fyodor Dostoyevsky. Now that's something. I read all his books in college. You must be more of an intellectual type."

The way he said it was kind. Nicolas Bondurant was one special person. I told him all about *Crime and Punishment* and *The Brothers Karamazov*. I didn't even feel stupid about it. Nicolas seemed genuinely interested, and he told me some things about those books I didn't know. Like the fact that Mr. Dostoyevsky spent four years in a Siberian prison camp for treason and blasphemy. The Russian tsarist government didn't like his books bringing attention to the plight of poor folk and said his egalitarian ideas were corruptive to minors.

Nicolas started packing up our gear. "I think we're done here. And remind me to never invite you fishing again."

"You didn't invite me. I invited myself."

"I suppose that's right. You Le Moyne Bolshevik types always got to get the last word in, don't you?"

"Only when we got a point to make to the landed gentry."

Nicolas scowled. "I'm not landed gentry."

"You own half of B&B Enterprises, don't you?"

He pushed the tackle box on me to carry. "Technically. Now Arizona, I can't help where I come from any more than you can."

"So, why you ashamed of it? Living out here away from everybody else?"

I done ran off my mouth again. Nicolas's face was cross. I wanted to take the words back, but I couldn't.

The tension lifted in the strangest way. Nicolas fixed a look on me like I'd schooled him in something he'd been long overdue thinking about. I wanted to say I didn't intend for it to come out so mean. I wanted to let him know I didn't judge him for how he lived. I liked him a whole lot, and I just wanted to understand.

"Well, smarty pants, I got some work to do back at the house. But I can set you up with one of my books from college in the meantime. What do you say to that?"

I nodded and helped him gather our equipment, and I followed him through the trail back to his cabin.

I HADN'T NOTICED before, but Nicolas had two big bookshelves full of paperbacks and hardcover novels. He said I could pick whatever I wanted and read out on the deck while he was tinkering with one of his metal sculptures. I found a book called *Saul's Book* by a Mr. Paul T. Rogers. It had a modern, grainy cover, like a photo out of focus, which piqued my interest.

"This one any good?"

He gave me a beleaguered frown and shook his head. "You've got Hemingway, Fitzgerald, and Thomas Pynchon to choose from, and that's what you pick out?"

Then I was sure that was the book I wanted to read.

"I asked if it was any good."

"It's good. But don't let me hear you say you ain't been warned. It's not the kind of book you'll find in Poly's library."

Then I was *really* sure it was the book I wanted to read. I got a glass of iced tea from the kitchen, went out to the deck, and sat down with the book in some shade.

Well, from page one, my mind was blown away. That Paul Rogers wrote like a poet, and poor Stephen, the main character, was a teenage boy like me, but he was Puerto Rican and living on the dangerous streets of New York City all by his lonesome. Then I got to the part where he was selling himself to men in bathroom stalls at Port Authority bus terminal. I couldn't believe a story like that was in print. My head grew two sizes that day. I guess I'd always figured there were other people like me and Preston, but to see that kind of thing written about by a famous author, I felt a whole lot less alone in the world.

It wasn't a happy story, though. My heart bled reading what Stephen had to go through just to live, and the one man he loved was a drug addict who sold boys for sex. I couldn't tear my eyes away. I was right desperate to see what would become of Stephen and Saul. I don't know how many hours passed while I was sitting on the deck reading that book.

Late in the day, Nicolas came out. I didn't even look up at him at first. When I did, I saw he was staring at me with a crooked smile.

"Are you having dinner? Or am I eating by myself? It's crawfish stew and rice."

My stomach grumbled. I noticed then the aromas coming from the kitchen, and it smelled real good. I dog-eared my page in the book. "You need me to set the table?"

"That'd be nice."

I stood up and headed to the kitchen. Grabbed plates, napkins, and utensils out of drawers and carried them back to the picnic table. Nicolas brought out pots and served us rice and stew.

I had two helpings without saying anything. Truth be told, I was dying to get back to my book. Nicolas watched me with some interest, though he didn't say a word neither for a while.

Then he looked at me with a quiet smile. "How you liking that book?"

I took a sip of water to clear my throat. "I ain't never read anything like that. I'm liking it a lot."

"You understanding what you're reading?"

I scowled. "I ain't illiterate."

"I'm not saying you are. That book's just a whole lot of story for a sixteen-year-old. I only read it myself last year."

There were a lot of things I wanted to ask him, some things I wanted to tell him about me, but I was shy about it. I guess since he'd read the book, kept it right out in the open on his bookshelf, I shouldn't have been worried he'd be sickened by me. But I was.

"You think Stephen and Saul were in love and could've made something out of their relationship?"

Nicolas plucked at his chin. "I don't know. I don't think it's that kind of story."

I gathered my thoughts. "You think men could have that kind of relationship? Where they love each other?"

He leaned back in his chair and folded his hands behind his head. "There's all kinds of people in the world. I knew some fellows like that before I went off to the war. They were good people. Good friends."

I wanted to know more about that, but the way he said it, I worried I'd be straying back to the topic of why he lived all by himself. We were both quiet again.

"I'll tell you this, Arizona. If I met a boy who was thinking he might be that way, I wouldn't think any less of him. I'd be right honored to be his friend."

My heart started racing. I hid my face. As much as I'd been dying to tell someone that secret about me, I wanted to burrow underground like a mole.

"Guess you figured me out."

"The lake was a pretty good clue."

I shot a glance at him. The funny guy was having a good snicker at my expense. I shoved his leg with my foot under the table.

"You can't hold that against me. I got hormones running helter-skelter."

"I bet you do."

"Stop picking on me."

"All right. Does your granddaddy know about you?"

I crossed my arms. "No. And I'd prefer to keep it that way."

"He's not a bad man, Arizona. Sooner or later, you're going to have to talk to him."

I didn't want to, and I sure didn't want to go back to that lonely house.

"You may recall, I said this escape act of yours was limited to one night."

"You gonna throw me out?"

I could see him fussing in his seat in my peripheral vision, and I wasn't going to wait for him to say it.

"You don't have to bother." I pushed up from the table. "I'm leaving."

I grabbed my plate, utensils, and glass and shuffled into the house. I put it all in the kitchen sink and went searching for my clothes. I thought I'd seen them hanging on the front porch, but they weren't there. I went to look in the bathroom, and Nicolas gained up on me.

"I was trying to have a conversation with you."

"That what it was? Sounded like you had come to the point." I tried pushing past him, but he hung his hands on the top of the doorframe, blocking my way out.

"Look here. You're not going anywhere wound up like this."

"Why? You don't want me here. I can make my own way."

"How you going to do that?"

"Hike over to the county highway. See where I can hitch from there. What do you care anyway?"

Nicolas gestured with his arms to bring me in for a hug. I

wasn't having that at first, being treated like a child having a temper tantrum.

"You're nothing but a phony."

He held my gaze. "I suppose I might be."

"What'd I do?" The corners of my eyes burned, and my vision was blurry.

He took a half step toward me, still angling to calm me down. "You didn't do anything. I never said you had to leave. I just wanted to talk to you about it. You can't avoid your granddaddy forever."

"He don't want me. I don't belong in his big, fancy house. How many times I got to tell you, I don't belong anywhere."

Nicolas touched my shoulder lightly. "That's not true. You got plenty of people who care about you. Including one right before your eyes."

I looked him in the eye, fiercely. "You couldn't even be bothered to come to the house to meet me. I been here almost two months. So, why all of the sudden do you care if I stay or go?"

He didn't have an answer for that, and I went on staring him down. I had a powder keg of emotions inside me. Maybe it wasn't fair to throw them all at Nicolas, but it felt like we'd known each other our entire lives, and I could talk to him that way. I know it don't make sense. We'd only known each other forty-eight hours, but I needed his love so bad. At the same time, he infuriated me like nobody I'd ever met. Nobody that I liked, that is.

"You look me in the eye and tell me I belong here. There it is. You can't do it. That's all right. I'll make like Stephen in that book. Go on up to New York City. Find a place to belong up there."

Nicolas looked at me, cross. "Boy, you got more sense than that."

"You've got no idea how much sense I got."

"I'm telling you, you're not running off tonight."

I snorted. "What for? So, you can tell me in the morning I've got to go back to my granddaddy's?"

"The time'll come for that. He's the one who took you in. Because he loves you. Like his own son."

"Took him long enough to let me know. That ain't love. That's charity. Same reason you let me stick around for a while. I had my fill. I'll take my chances on my own. Now why don't you get out of my way?"

"Goddamn it, Arizona, I'm trying to tell you you've got a place to belong right here."

"Why? Because you feel sorry for me?"

"No. Because, believe it or not, knucklehead, I could get used to the idea of having you around."

I wanted to believe him. Truth was, there wasn't any other place in the world where I felt I might fit in. But he was getting a piece of my mind first.

"You say that, you best not take it back. I can't…"

My chin quivered. Nicolas pulled me into his arms. I fought with him a little, then soon enough, I was crying against his chest. "There. Let it out, you damn fool." He gripped me tighter, and I felt his lips graze my hair. "See? You don't have to go nowhere. You just stay with me, all right?"

13

ONE MORE DAY living with Nicolas turned into two, and then three, and he never did bring up me going back to living with my granddaddy. I finished *Saul's Book* and dug into a paperback from Nicolas's collection. It was called *The Lord Won't Mind* and written by a man named Gordon Merrick. It was another love story about two men but a whole different kind of romance, more like one of them Harlequin stories. I couldn't read that book fast enough.

Every day, Nicolas woke me up for breakfast, and after that, he got busy with his sculptures and sketches while playing his records real loud. He liked classic rock bands like the Allman Brothers and Creedence Clearwater Revival. That suited me all right, and I was plenty happy to set myself up on the deck with my book, sometimes in the sun to get some color and sometimes in the shade when it got too hot. At night, we had dinner and sat out on his deck talking about this or that until it got late. One night, he brought out his old guitar and played a couple songs by the Beatles, and after, he taught me how to string together a couple of chords myself. On a Sunday night, we brought out his transistor radio and found Dr. Demento on a New Orleans radio station. Duke and I used to love listening to that stupid show. Nicolas did, too. I had him singing along when there was a catchy tune, and we cracked up like fools.

It was the best part of my summer. I liked so much being around Nicolas. We bickered now and then, but the truth was, he meant everything to me.

One night after dinner, he let me have one of his beers, and we got a little cheeky sitting out on his deck. I loosened the top buttons of the shirt he'd leant me and swayed around the table to plop down on his lap.

"You ever think what a shame it is a good looking fellow like you hides himself in the woods all the time?" I placed his big hand on my side.

"Good looking, you say?"

I brushed the side of his beard. "You ain't bad looking. Could use a little polish. And someone to remind you to turn on your side when you're sleeping. You snore like a grizzly bear."

He closed his hand high up on my chest by my armpit. Made me breathless. It felt so good to snuggle up with him.

"I ought to call you Goldilocks, stumbling into my bear den."

I could've come up with a smart answer to that, but the way my body was feeling, I dug my fingers into the back of his thick hair. "You gimme a kiss, and you can call me anything you want."

Nicolas laughed lightly. "Arizona, I don't think that's such a good idea."

"You won't know till you try."

He leaned in and grabbed my mouth with his. *My lord*, I died and went to heaven. That was one deep, steamy kiss, and he snuck his hand inside my shirt, his rough fingers grazing my chest and tummy.

Nicolas broke things off. I opened my eyes. He avoided my gaze, looking out of sorts. "I shouldn't have done that."

I reached to kiss him again, but he turned his face.

"We can't. You're old enough to know it's not right."

"What's not right? Give it another try, and you might do better the second time around."

Nicolas half-smiled. He swiped his face. "I'm supposed to be taking care of you for your granddaddy."

My body was so heated up, nobody could tell me no. I ran my hand across his broad shoulder, admiring him. "I ain't been so well taken care of my entire life. That's all my granddaddy needs to know."

Nicolas frowned.

"What? We ain't blood." I could feel him against my thigh, which made me grin. He'd woken up down there. "You got me falling in love with you, and I think you like me, too."

"Arizona, I'm twice your age."

"How you figure? In four years, I'll be twenty, and you'll be thirty-five. I'll be catching up to you."

He shook his head. "What do you want with a grown man who lives like this? I'm not changing, Arizona. This is who I am."

"I'd say there's an upside to that. Makes it easy to find you when I need you."

He looked at me with some humor. "You never give up, do you?" He gently held my back with his hand. "You get me angry as a badger sometimes, but I like you, Arizona. You're right about that. I just don't know what I'm supposed to do with you."

I looked him in the face, smiled and blushed. "I underlined some passages in that Gordon Merrick novel. How 'bout I fetch it to give you some ideas."

Nicolas hooted. "What *are* you? I'm starting to think you got lost in the woods on your birthday looking to be rescued on purpose."

I brought his other arm around me and touched the sun-whitened hairs on his forearm.

"You been with boys before?" he asked.

I licked my lips. I didn't want to get into all that while my motor was running like a Kawasaki motorcycle. I gave him a nod. With my throat dry and cracking, I asked him, "What about you?"

He nodded, and then he crushed my lips with his, sending me soaring again. I didn't want that to end, but he got one arm under

my legs and lifted me up from the chair. Then he carried me into
the house to his bedroom.

THAT NIGHT, WE did things in Nicolas's bed that would make
a Baptist preacher keel over and spit blood. We did the things we
really liked a second time, and one we did a third. I was *his*, body
and soul. Some things were new to me, but I tell you, I'd been
born to make love to that man. He showed me the most intimate
thing two men could do together, taking it slow and gentle. I'd
never known anything could feel so good. I shut my eyes and wept.
Well, that was the thing we did three times that night. I was
burning sore, but I couldn't stop grinning.

Afterward, we lay face-to-face tangled up together. I stared at
him in wonder. I'd never felt such happiness, never thought a man
like him would want me like that.

Nicolas stroked my face. "What am I gonna do with you?"

"You say you got a college degree and medic's training, and you
still ain't figured that out? Now I been in this bed a good three
hours, and unless I just went through an exorcism, you been here,
too. I think you found a few good uses for me, Nicolas
Bondurant." I crept my hand up the inside of his thigh. "Want me
to show you again? Jog your memory?"

He smiled, really fully smiled, which Nicolas didn't do too
much, and then he stilled my hand. "That's not what I mean.
Where'd you come from, Arizona? You gone stole my heart."

I placed my hand over his heart. "I'm not giving it back
neither. Finders keepers."

He chuckled, squeezed my thigh between his and rolled toward
me. "You sure you're only sixteen?" He sighed. "Hell, I never had
sex with a sixteen-year-old even when I was sixteen."

"My mama was only sixteen when she had me."

He brushed my hair with his hand. "You saying it runs in the
family?"

"Could be. Must come from my grandmother Virginia's side."

He laughed. "Just how many boys you been with?"

I poked him in the nose. "One or two. Boys, that is. I only been with one man. That's you." I tickled his ribs. "You're the one who knows his way around the *Kama Sutra*." I'd seen that book on his bookshelf. "So, how many fellows you been with?"

He trapped my arm to stop me from misbehaving. "I sure wasn't having sex with men when I was sixteen. I had the feelings, but even if I had known someone to do it with, I'd have been too scared."

"So, how old were you when you first did?"

"Twenty-two. Oh, it was very romantic. There was this men's room in the basement of the arts hall at Tulane. Come to find out, it was place where, you know, men got together. Some of them even wrote what day and time they'd like to meet right on the stall." Nicolas sighed. "I walked by that bathroom probably fifty, sixty times after I heard about it as a freshman. But I didn't have the guts to go in there until my last semester, senior year."

He lay back and stretched one arm behind his head. "I was nervous. I nearly gave up and ran on home, but I told myself, 'Nicolas, you've been running from this all your life, and you don't have anything to show for it besides a lonesome heart.' So I hung out in that stinking bathroom. Two full hours. Finally a boy showed up who gave me a look and took me into a stall. I didn't know his name. Probably couldn't even pick him out of a lineup, and it was over in a blink. But after that, I was back in that basement men's room two, three times a week."

His face was red and glowing, which made me smile. Then I remembered something curious. "What about that girl, Sara? Were you just with her to hide? I thought you said you loved her?"

Nicolas took my hand and held it against his fine-haired chest. "Well, that's complicated. I wouldn't say that was the only reason we started dating. We got along like two halves of a whole. We had everything you could ask for in a relationship except the physical attraction. For me, it was like cuddling up with a good friend. We both knew that early on, and she didn't mind. Sara was the first person I told who I am."

I cocked an eyebrow.

"It might sound strange, but when she accepted me, it made me love her even more. I knew I couldn't give her what a husband's supposed to give a wife, but somehow it made sense for us. Maybe Sara didn't need what some women needed. Maybe the emotional part was enough for her. Could be we would've come to our senses after we'd gotten married like we'd said we'd do. But at the time, well, people were experimenting with all kinds of relationships. Free love and all that."

I didn't know what Nicolas meant exactly, but I could see it felt true to him.

"Is that why you keep painting her? To keep her memory alive?"

Nicolas combed his hand through his hair. "I guess that's the obvious explanation. Sara showed me more kindness than anyone in the world. I know now that wasn't a good enough reason to get married. I suppose I didn't want to lose her even though I couldn't be a real husband to her. I thought about that a lot after she died. Whether I was selfish. If I had let her go, maybe she would've run off and gotten married to someone else instead of waiting for me back with her folks in Georgia. Maybe she never would've crossed that road at night and gotten killed by that drunk driver. Or what about if I hadn't enlisted in that stupid war? I might've been with her that night and stopped it from happening." He stared up to the ceiling. "Just makes you think, you know?"

I took one of his hands and massaged his palm. It didn't seem fair for him to blame himself, though I'd felt the same way after Grandma Tilly and Grandpa George died. I was going to tell him that, but then I noticed a jagged scar from his wrist up his forearm. I hadn't looked at that real close before.

He turned on his side and fixed his big soulful eyes on me. "Well, anyway, I messed around with a few fellows when I was on leave in Saigon. But I've been keeping to myself until you dropped out of the sky in the middle of a lightning storm."

"Does my granddaddy, your brother know about you?"

"He sure does. I think he always did since I was little. Poly's perceptive that way."

"What did he say?"

"He said if that's the way I want to live my life, it wasn't up to him to tell me I was wrong or right. I told you he's always been more like a father to me. He said my business is my business, and he don't want to hear anyone say otherwise."

That got me thinking about my granddaddy differently. Like maybe he knew about me too and didn't care.

"My daddy was perceptive too," I told him. "And he made sure I knew how he felt about me being gay." I let him know the full story about the fight I had with Dolly. It still stung how she'd turned on me.

Nicolas looked at me. "There's two things that's plentiful in this world. Oxygen and ignorance. That's something my daddy used to say." He cuddled up tighter. "I'm sorry about your daddy and your sister. But listen here. Some people are ugly on the inside and beautiful on the outside. Some are beautiful inside and ugly the other way around. You, Arizona, you're beautiful on the inside *and* the outside. Anybody can't see that, you just let them jog on ahead. That's another one of my daddy's expressions."

He took my hand and kissed each one of my fingertips. That was the sweetest and sexiest thing I'd ever seen. I was ready to go off to the races again, but I halted when I glimpsed that scar on the underside of his arm.

"Is that from the war?"

"No." He switched up his hands and rested that arm at his side. "I was one of the lucky ones. Came home without a scratch." His eyes shifted. "I guess you ought to know what you're getting into, Arizona. That scar... I did that to myself. Just three days after I came home and found out Sara was gone. Got me sent to the loony bin at the VA Hospital upstate. Three months. Well, I was in and out of there for years. *Combat fatigue* they called it back then."

That hurt my heart. Made me wish I could take all his pain away. Something occurred to me that might make him smile.

"Guess what? I been in the loony bin too."

It didn't make him smile. It made him study me like there was reason for concern. So I told him what had happened and how I'd thought about ending it all but that was just back when. I glanced at him sidelong. "You still get those thoughts sometimes?"

"Every now and then. But my medication and my artwork keep me steady." He looked at me squarely. "I got a real good reason to live now."

That deep, green-eyed gaze of his had a throbbing, achy feeling working through me again. I placed his hand on my bottom. I wanted him to know I was his and always would be.

Nicolas put on a beleaguered face. "God help me. Talking about suicide makes you horny?"

I giggled and burned up in the face.

"All right. Let's see if this old man can keep up with you."

He circled me with his arms and made love to me again.

14

YOU COULD SAY my summer turned out dandy in the end. Nicolas Bondurant was everything I'd ever wanted, and by golly, he made me feel sexy and beautiful and most of all, he made me feel loved. We holed up four more days just making love and devouring everything in his kitchen to feed our bodies so we could make love some more. We didn't bother dressing up in anything besides boxer shorts since sooner or later, one of us would be pulling them off the other.

Sometimes we'd listen to music on his record player. Nicolas had a big collection of albums he kept in alphabetical order in wooden crates. He belonged to a mail order club, and he bought all the latest rock albums along with some British New Wave, country, and R&B. Plus he had dozens of old albums from his high school and college years: the Beatles, The Doors, Led Zeppelin, and The Grateful Dead to name a few. Some nights, we thrashed around his bedroom listening to the harder stuff like we was at a concert. I loved the garage band sound of the Sex Pistols and The Clash, the crazy wail of them British singers. Then Nicolas would put on something softer like Crosby, Stills & Nash or the Eagles, and he cradled me and led me around in slow, swaying circles. Listening to the lyrics, it was as though they were singing about our own heartaches and all the things we felt about each other.

I never stopped being in awe of him. He treated me so kind and loving, and he had such an easy masculinity, strutting around in his bare, rangy body without a care in the world. And he knew something about everything from music to cooking to medicine to carpentry to fixing the leaky faucet in his bathroom and welding scraps of metal to make art.

He knew a lot about literature, too, and he introduced me to authors like James Baldwin, Williams S. Burroughs, and Thomas Mann, all of whom were gay though they sometimes wrote about it in coded language. I wanted to read everything he'd read and become an educated man like him. They say a good book's like taking a trip around the world, reading about people and places from faraway, and you don't even need to have the money for plane fare. Well, I'd be lying if I said I got a *lot* reading done while I was living with Nicolas. We couldn't keep our hands off each other, and in our quieter times, we had lots to talk about. It was like we was on vacation and forgot what life was before.

That changed when Granddaddy called one day and told Nicolas he was coming over. Nicolas said I couldn't put it off no more. I'd been gone over a week, and it was time for me to mend fences with my granddaddy. I got cleaned up and waited on the deck, not looking forward to the conversation one bit.

I heard a golf cart motoring to the cabin and listened to my granddaddy talking to Nicolas inside the house. It sounded like a friendly conversation, and then Granddaddy, slick as always in a business suit, came out to the deck. Nicolas stepped away into the house to give us some privacy.

Granddaddy took a seat across from me at the picnic table. He had an easy manner, which took me by surprise considering I'd run off in the middle of my own party.

"It's good to see you, Arizona."

"How do you do?"

"You're looking well."

My cheeks burned up. I sure felt like I was glowing from all the screwing Nicolas and I'd been doing. Granddaddy's brother.

"I'm not going to say I haven't been sore about you running away." He waited for me to look him in the eyes. "In the middle of a thunderstorm with all the guests over at the house."

I forced a swallow down my dry throat.

"But I'm not here to fight, son. And I'm glad you found your way here. Looks like the two of you are getting along like corn-bread and chili. You happy?"

"Yes, sir."

He held out his hands the way I imagined he addressed a board room full of his executives. "I think I've got a good idea about why you left. But before I say anything, it's best I hear it from you."

I squirmed. "I'm sorry, Granddaddy." I told him about the fight with Dolly and her storming off with Duke and Little Douglas. "I didn't know what to do. But I knew I couldn't stay at the party, pretending I was happy to be there."

I could see him nodding along in the corner of my eye. "Well, that I understand. Though I wish you'd come to me. It left me with the impression you don't want to talk to me anymore."

I drew a breath, grasping for a way to explain. "It's not that I don't appreciate everything you done for me. I do. That was the biggest, swankiest birthday party I ever seen. I wanted to enjoy it, but every time I started feeling high, I got low real fast, not knowing what was going to happen to my siblings. Not being able to do nothing about it." I chewed my lip. "That don't matter anymore. Duke and Dolly made it clear they don't want anything to do with me."

"I'm sorry, son."

I peeked at him. "You say you want me to come talk to you about my troubles. But I did, Granddaddy. I tried telling you about my family, and you said you didn't want hear another word about it."

He sat back a little. "I reckon I could've been kinder when you asked about them staying over at the house. Your daddy put you in an impossible situation. You're too young to look after three kids, and I know you fear for them going back to that man. But I'll have you know, I paid Gus Fanning another visit."

My gaze froze on him.

Granddaddy gestured with his hands again. "He signed the papers relinquishing his parental rights to you. Now the decision's still yours, Arizona. You can say you want me to adopt you, or you can go back to Social Services. But I wanted you to know, I also talked to him about your siblings. I told him he best treat them right, whether he decides to be a man and take them in himself or make sure they have a good home together."

"What did he say?"

"He said he'd let a family court judge decide where they'll go." Granddaddy sniffed. "He knows he's not in a position to take care of three kids. He gave me his word he won't interfere."

He paused to catch my eye again.

"So, you've got a decision, Arizona. You can say you want to live here or say you'll live with a foster family until you turn eighteen. It's up to you. I'll just say I'd sure like it if you'd let me be your daddy. Well, granddaddy, I should say."

It stung for a moment how easily Gus Fanning had signed me over, just thrown away the idea I was his son. But seeing my granddaddy again, I remembered all the things I liked about him. He was a powerful man, and he wanted me as his own. He saw something special in me.

"If I say yes, does that mean I'm a Bondurant?"

Granddaddy smiled. "It sure does." He chuckled. "In a few years, we just might have to change the name of the company. B, B *and* B."

I didn't care about that. I just knew I'd be happy living with him and Nicolas. I stood, came around the table and gave Granddaddy a big hug. "Thank you, Granddaddy."

He sat me down next to him on the bench. "The other matter is, school's right around the corner. You give any thought to that?"

I hadn't. It felt like a lifetime ago since we'd talked about school. At the time, I'd been thinking about giving that Middleton Academy a try though I'd been worried about being so far away from my siblings. Now, I'd be far away from Nicolas. I was just about one hundred percent sure I didn't want to do that.

"I don't know what to do. Feels like I just got settled in here, and I'd be starting over someplace new all over again."

Granddaddy didn't say anything right away, though I could tell he was warming up to it. He wanted me to go to that elite boarding school he'd gone to himself.

"Think of it this way, it's only for the school year. That's September through May. Whittington Manor will always be your home. And there's breaks in the semester. I've been doing a lot of business at the Boston office, so I'll be up to show you the town, if you like. Never mind you'd be home a week for Thanksgiving and two weeks for Christmas."

"When would I have to leave?"

"Well, we'd have to get you up there over Labor Day weekend. Classes start the Tuesday after."

I'd lost track of the days of the week. But I knew Labor Day was always about three weeks after my birthday. Over a week had passed since then.

"That's one week from this Saturday," Granddaddy helped out. "Which is why you're going to have to think quick." He glanced at his wristwatch. "I need to get back to the office. How about this? You and Nicolas come up to the house for dinner on Saturday, and you can give me your answer then."

He got up from the table and gave my hair a tussle. I walked with him through the cabin on his way out.

"I sure am glad you made friends with Nicolas," he told me along the way. "I know it can get lonely up at the house. Must be nice having someone a little closer to your age to spend time with."

I wasn't sure if he was picking up more than that. Then he glanced into Nicolas's bedroom and quickly looked away. He had to have noticed there wasn't anyplace else for me to sleep.

His cheerfulness seemed a little forced all of a sudden. "I'll ask

Mr. Wainwright to bring over some of your clothes. That is, if you plan on staying here. You must be getting sick of wearing shirts and trousers two sizes too big."

"Thank you, Granddaddy. That'd be great."

He gave me a hug and a peck on the head. "Supper Saturday night. Don't you forget."

I watched him climb into his golf cart and drive off down the trail. Well, if he had put two and two together, I supposed I couldn't have expected him to not feel a little bit shell-shocked. I hoped that's all it was.

I WAITED UNTIL that night to talk to Nicolas about school. The more I thought about it, the more I didn't want go to that Middleton Academy all the way in Massachusetts. I wanted to be with Nicolas day and night. Even going to that Catholic school in New Orleans worried me. I wasn't interested in meeting new people and making friends. Besides, how were Nicolas and me supposed to have a relationship when I was off at school all day?

So, I brought it up after dinner, sitting out on the deck. Nicolas had a big Adirondack chair that fit the two of us with me sitting between his legs. We'd stripped down to boxers and brought a bed sheet out to cover up in. It was heaven like that, all warm and snug, gazing out at the shadowy lake, listening to the bullfrogs and watching lightning bugs sparking in the woods.

After I told him what I'd been thinking, I wove my fingers through his, which had been brushing the little hairs under my belly button. "What do you think I should do?"

Nicolas was quiet for a while. I wished I could see his face. I was about to turn around when he answered. "What do you want to do?"

"I want to stay with you."

I could feel him grinning behind me. Then he softly picked at my hair. "You're sixteen. You've got to go to school."

I couldn't argue with that. And it's not that I didn't want to continue my education. It was just I didn't want to be without Nicolas, not even for a day. I was getting lonesome thinking about it.

"I went to Middleton myself. That's where you go when you're a Bondurant."

I brought my feet up to the chair, tucking into myself. "I just got used to living here at Whittington Manor, and now I'm supposed to move clear 'cross the country?"

Nicolas leaned over me and rested his chin on my shoulder while he slipped his hands around my waist. "It's a three-and-a-half-hour flight. That's not so bad, is it? And they give you breakfast and lunch. Or lunch and supper if you leave out in the afternoon."

I'd never been on an airplane. That alone sounded like a big deal. I didn't have any answers. I just wished the whole problem would go away.

"Arizona, I'm not going anywhere. You know that by now. I'm not going to be the reason you sit out this opportunity your granddaddy gave you."

"You want me to go away?"

"Yes, I do. Not because I'm looking forward to sleeping alone at night, and not having you be the first thing I see when I wake up in the morning. It's because it's the right thing for you. Look here, you'll get the best education in the country. You'll learn how to take care of yourself real quick. You ought to see the world beyond Louisiana. Meet all kinds of people. This is a tiny atom of the world down here, and I don't have to tell you, it's mostly backward-thinking folks." He slid his hand around my forearm. "You're smart. Independent. Handsome as sin. You're gonna take Middleton Academy by storm."

I couldn't help grinning when he was praising me like that. My mind set to thinking maybe he was right. Part of me was just plain scared about being on my own. But I'd gone through losing my mama, taking care of my brothers and sister when we barely had money to spread through the month, and surviving on my own after losing Grandma Tilly. All that took a lot more courage than going off to boarding school.

"Will you come with me Labor Day weekend?"

A silence passed. I turned my head and grinned at Nicolas. "You gone hard of hearing?"

"You've got your granddaddy to help get you settled in."

I hadn't been expecting that. I pulled his arms around me. "I want you there, too. And Granddaddy said there's breaks. You can come up and visit and take me to all the places you used to go in Boston. Or maybe it could be the three of us." I looked at him, real cheeky. "As long as you and me get our own hotel room."

Something changed with Nicolas. I felt it first with his body stiffening up, and his hand gone cold. Then he drew back his arms and pushed up behind me in the chair. I stood and got out of his way. Nicolas wandered inside the cabin. I followed him without a clue what was going on.

He went to the kitchen and shakily brought down a glass from the cabinet and filled it with water from the faucet. I didn't know what came over him. He set down his glass of water on the counter and turned his back to me. I hovered around him, and then he swung toward me with a pained look on his face.

"Maybe you leaving for school is the best thing all around."

"What do you mean?"

Nicolas leaned against the counter, slump-shouldered. "I can't take you to school. I can't visit you on breaks." He heaved a breath, trying to steady himself. "I can't leave Whittington Manor. I haven't left since I got out of the hospital six years ago."

I stared at him, trying to understand.

He swiped his brow, avoiding my gaze. "I tried, Arizona. But it don't work. Outside the walls of this property, everything starts pressing in on me. I can't catch a breath. My heart starts racing. I get these flashes in my head." He shifted around. He was pale and sprouting sweat on his forehead and his chest. I didn't know what to do. I'd never seen anyone have a panic attack before.

"What can I do?"

Nicolas said nothing. I was dying to hold him and say everything would be all right. But he was so jumpy, and I knew when I felt nervous, the last thing I wanted was someone swooping in and touching me.

"How 'bout some air?"

Nicolas nodded, and I followed him back out to the deck. I stood off a little and watched him take some full breaths.

"So, now you know," he said after a while. "My mind's made me a prisoner to this cabin. I can't take you to school and visit you. I can't be the kind of man you deserve."

"You can get help. Go back to that veteran's hospital and see what they say."

"I tried. For nearly eight years, I tried."

"Then you keep on trying. Isn't that what you'd tell me?"

"We're not the same, Arizona. I'm a fully grown man. It gets to a point your brain stops adapting. It just gets stuck. You can't change it." He shrugged. "Well, the doctors can give me tranquilizers. Get me so hopped up on medicine I'm just a zombie stumbling around in the dark. What's the point in doing that? I'm happier being myself right here."

Now I was getting hot in the neck. "You just going to stay in this cabin the rest of your life?"

"That's right."

"Then that settles it. I'm staying here, too."

Nicolas started saying something, but I cut him off.

"Someone's gotta look after you. Especially when you get old and can't take care of yourself."

Fire sparked in his eyes. "I'm not going to let you waste your life fussing over me." He pointed his finger. "And I don't need anyone hanging around to treat me like a mental case."

I'd dug my heels in so deep, that didn't faze me. "I can explain things to you, but I can't understand things for you, Nicolas Bondurant. Now how 'bout you take a warm shower to relax you some?"

"You gonna act like you're my nurse now? You can go piss off. Thinking you know everything about me."

"I ain't read the whole book, but I done plenty of highlighting. Besides, you tell me who else you got?"

We squared off, staring at each other and not saying anything. Then his voice trembled. "I'm a grown man."

"There's a start. You gonna act like one now?"

I won't lie. I was scared inside. I couldn't make him do this or that even though I was posturing like I could.

"I never met anyone so goddamn stubborn," he said.

"You got a mirror in your bathroom. You ever take a look? But you're right. I'm stubborn. And I told you once, if you tell me to leave again, you'll get a whole lot more than my mouth."

His eyes flared. Then Nicolas turned his head, and I thought I saw a little humor on his face. I drew up in front of him and hooked my fingers in the waistband of his shorts. He was going to love me. No squirming out of it. Eventually, he snorted in resignation, and he held my shoulder blades. I wrapped my arms around his waist.

"I love you," I told him. "Now you say it back."

He squeezed me tight. "I love you, too." He leaned back a little and cocked a glance at me. "But I won't have you giving up school on account of me."

"Who said I was?"

He looked at me funny. Somehow through all that fuss, a moment of clarity had come over me.

"A man can change his mind, can't he? I'm going to Middleton Academy. You can come up to see me or you can stay down here. But you best believe we're spending Thanksgiving together. And talking on the phone and writing letters. So, you better get it out of your head I'm ever giving up on you."

Nicolas crushed me against him. His lips grazed my cheek, and his hot breath fanned my face. I melted into him. I had so many feelings, I hiccupped with tears. Nicolas held me tight, and we cried softly in each other's arms.

WE HAD A week together before I went off to Boston. That Saturday night, we had supper with my granddaddy at the house, and I told Granddaddy what I'd decided to do. The next day, Nicolas and I went to the stables and took a long ride with Duchess and Bonnie. But mostly, we stayed in the cabin, just loving each other for the little bit of time we had left. It was real emotional. Making love to him got me thinking how much I was going miss being with him that way. I hurt so bad, I wasn't sure if I'd survive.

Then the Friday before I had to leave, we were both a mess, trying to get through the day without spending our last hours weeping. That afternoon, he had me sit to sketch me on a canvas. I'd never imagined I'd be the subject of an artist, let alone being naked as a jaybird to do it, but I had no shame being naked around him. When Nicolas was done and he showed me the sketch, I felt like a celebrity. We made love right there against his worktable. It was the last time before I went off to school. That night, we were both too torn up to mess around. We just held each other in bed, and neither of us got much sleep.

15

I DIDN'T LIKE Middleton Academy for Boys at first. Sure, it was pretty with its big stone-walled halls covered with ivy, and its landscaped grounds scooped out of the forested, rolling New England countryside. Everything about that school was elegant and formal. Students dressed in navy blue blazers, white shirts, khaki slacks, and navy- and sky-blue striped neck ties. The teachers wore suits and ties, too, and frankly they scared the heck out of me. Even for athletic activities, we had to wear trousers and button-up shirts. I studied the school handbook to keep up with the routines, but I was sick to my stomach worrying about all the ways I could make a fool of myself, whether talking out of turn or wearing the wrong outfit to dinner.

Nicolas said it right. I'd only seen a wee corner of the world. I was living with boys who came from places like New York City, Philadelphia, Connecticut, and Maryland. They got dropped off by family limousines on moving-in day, and they'd grown up with maids and nannies to take care of them. Maybe, in the shower, they didn't look any different from the boys I'd known, but on the inside, I thought all that wealth and privilege made them an entirely different species.

I might as well have been invisible when the school started

filling up. Students sorted out their friends and swaggered around in big groups, happy to be back together. Some of them talked so fast and strange, I couldn't even tell you half of what they said. When I could understand their conversations, just overhearing now and then, they mentioned spending their summers at places I'd never heard of like Martha's Vineyard and Hilton Head. I could bet those were exclusive places to be. Some even talked about traveling around Europe and sailing in the Caribbean. I had a lot to learn about how rich boys lived.

Since everyone had been bunking up with their friends for years, I got my own bedroom in the upper division dormitory. That was nice for privacy, and the room was plenty big with one heck of a view of the campus. But living alone made it hard to make friends. The other students already knew who they were going to sit with at the dining hall and who they'd meet up with after class to toss around the football or study or shoot pool in the dormitory lounge. I'd heard it said before: Northerners are cold, and it was true. I said how do you do to anyone I happened to run into, but they either looked at me like I had three heads or scampered away like they was worried about catching fleas.

I was alone, and the worst was the first weekend when all the boys ran off for day trips or crew practice on the river outside of campus. At night, I could hear the commotion from get-togethers in their rooms that no one invited me to. I had nothing to do but study on my own. I told myself I was only going that school for an education. I didn't need to make friends and be popular. I had Nicolas waiting for me back home, and I'd write him letters whenever I was feeling lonesome. I wrote him every day that first week. Still, walking around campus and seeing everyone else palling around, looking like they were having the time of their lives, I felt real low sometimes.

I thought things might change for the better when a group of boys came over to my table one morning in the high ceilinged, wood paneled dining hall. I judged them to be part of the popular crowd. They were tall, good looking, athletic types, and I'd noticed younger boys making way for them in the halls. That bit wasn't so different from what I was used to. Though at Le Moyne Senior High School even the popular kids looked like they weren't fit to do more than fill the gas tank and clean the wind-shield of the kind of young men who went to Middleton Academy.

I had no idea why the five boys decided to sit down with their breakfast trays at my lonely table. I said how do you do, and they darted glances at one another and smirked. Then one of them, the leader of the pack, introduced himself as Christopher Watts-Jennings. I'd never known a man to have a double-barreled name, and his wasn't the first I'd heard that week. Christopher was a charmer with curly brown hair and a grin that said he knew a whole lot better than anyone else. He pointed out his buddies and laid into questions.

"What did you say your last name was, Arizona?"

I could tell he found my name amusing. "I was born Fanning," I told him. "But it's Bondurant now. My granddaddy adopted me."

Christopher imitated my country drawl. "You from the *Sowwth*?"

"Yes, sir. I'm from Louisiana."

One of his friends, a freckled red-haired boy, piped up. "What did I tell you? His father's Gaston Bondurant. CEO of B&B. The sugar manufacturer."

"Is that true, Arizona?" Christopher asked me. "Did your *granddaddy* buy you into Middleton?"

His friends laughed. I wasn't enjoying the line of conversation. "He's paying the tuition, if that's what you mean. What does your daddy do?"

Christopher sat back in his chair. "My father is a U.S. senator from Connecticut. You know what a senator is?"

"I do."

"Where'd you go to school?"

"Le Moyne High School."

"Never heard of it. Is that a private school? You have to take a motorboat to get there? Out on the *bye-you*." His friends chuckled again.

"No. It's a public school. In Le Moyne Parish."

Christopher mugged a woeful frown to his friends. "This is what I've been saying. They've been relaxing the academic standards. Pretty soon, they'll be letting anyone in whose parents can afford it."

I'd been trying to play nice, letting him sass me because that's just the way boys are when a group of them gets together. But that Christopher Watts-Jennings rubbed me the wrong way.

"My granddaddy might've pushed them to let me transfer past the deadline, but I met every one of the admission criteria. I'm a straight-A student. I took my placement exams last week. Made upper division fair and square."

Christopher twinkled with amusement. "Oh, I didn't realize you were a *straight-A* student. Are they still teaching creationism and reading Uncle Remus stories in Louisiana public schools?"

I could've belted him across the face. The only thing that stopped me was thinking that would only make his point about me being backward and uncivilized. Then that red-haired boy, his name was Graeme, which was strange so it stuck, he cut in looking like he was going to steer things in a friendlier direction.

"Middleton has students from thirty-two states. Our pal Gregory Carmichael here is from Virginia. He's one of the best rowers on our eight-man team."

He was looking at a fair-haired fellow next to him. I glanced at Gregory hopefully, but he didn't seem too interested in being friends.

"So, what activities are you planning on signing up for?" Christopher asked me. "Possum shooting?"

They all laughed, and Graeme joined in.

"You play the banjo, Arizona?"

I could feel myself getting red in the face. I fixed my eyes on Christopher. "I hear there's a club for fucking your daddy. I would've signed up for it, but I already had him, and he was too loose to be any fun."

That didn't just shock silent Christopher and his sneering friends. I shocked silent the entire dining hall that morning. It was suddenly so quiet, I might've had the staff in the kitchen frozen in place while the eggs and sausages burned on the griddle.

Christopher's face flushed, and he shoved up from the table. He peeked around the silent room. There must've been three dozen students staring at our table and a couple of proctors gazing our way. Christopher raised his voice to put on a show.

"What did you say to me?"

"I didn't realize you were hard of hearing." I glanced at his friends. "Any of you boys wanna fill Christopher in?"

"You watch yourself, Louisiana. We'll see how brave you are when we cross paths without any proctors around."

He looked to his friends, and they all got up giving me parting glances while they trekked off. I heard them muttering *inbred hick* and *Southern trash*. I'd been called worse. As the dining hall went back to chattering, I popped open my pre-Calculus textbook to get a head start on the day's lesson.

AFTER THAT INCIDENT, I went from being invisible to being famous for all the wrong reasons, as Virginia would've put it. People gave me a big, dramatic berth when I walked down the halls, like I stunk. Boys with Varsity Football pins on their jackets stared me down and laughed at me in class, and I got clipped and tripped jogging around the track during physical education.

I swear it wasn't just the students who were against me. My Latin teacher, Mr. Georgiou, gave me dirty looks and never called on me. With his highfalutin attitude, he'd have been good friends with Mr. Wainwright. The phys ed teacher, Mr. Phelps, turned a blind eye when the other boys called me names and tried to bait me into a fight in the locker room. I was two-thirds sure

Middleton Academy wasn't for me and just about ready to beg my granddaddy to let me come home. But two things kept me there.

The first was English class. I'd always loved English, and Miss Antonelli's English Literature course was like my refuge. There weren't many female teachers at Middleton, and Miss Antonelli had this sweet and graceful way of making everybody feel welcome. She had a short, blond bob of hair and a motherly smile. She didn't care I talked different from everyone else. In fact, I think that made her like me more. I sat at a front row desk in her classroom, and she called on me a lot and smiled when I answered her questions. I devoured the books she wanted us to read like James Joyce's *Ulysses* and J.D. Salinger's *The Catcher in the Rye*. I went to her office hour every week to talk about what I was reading. When I told her I wanted to be a writer, she told me about all the great American writers who came from the South, like William Faulkner, Tennessee Williams, and Truman Capote.

The second thing was meeting Jonathan Gutierrez. Well, I didn't so much as meet him as be in the right place at the right time. One day after classes, I saw a group of boys from the hockey team knocking around a short, Hispanic kid and calling him shameful names. I recognized Jonathan from math and history class. We'd given each other friendly looks but never said hi.

I marched right over to the boys who were harassing him and told them in no uncertain terms to leave Jonathan be. I wasn't big and muscular, but you might've noticed I have a mouth. Most times, that's all it took to handle bullies. They're not the smartest people. Besides, no one liked me in that school, so I had nothing to lose by taking on them hockey dipshits.

I stared across the three of them, daring them to call my bluff. The big dopes moved along. I guess I'd earned a reputation being Gaston Bondurant's grandson and having put Christopher Watts-Jennings in his place.

I helped Jonathan gather his books, which the boys had tossed up and down the hall. He didn't say anything to me at first. I'm sure he was embarrassed, and I knew what that felt like.

"I'd say them three are compensating for what they lack in their drawers, but that might be giving them too much credit. I don't think they've got the brains to work out that calculation."

I gave Jonathan a wink. He still looked awfully nervous. I wondered if he got bullied a lot. He was a scrawny fellow with acne rashes on his cheeks. I also sensed we might have something in common, the way he was timid around other boys.

I reached out my hand. "How do you do? I'm Arizona Bondurant."

Jonathan took my hand lightly in his. "Jonathan Gutierrez."

"Pleased to meet you, Jonathan. Where you from?"

"Los Angeles."

Well, I thought that was right impressive. "Get out. Los Angeles, California? That's high up on my list of places I'd like to see. You been to Hollywood?"

"Yeah. But I grew up in East L.A.. I'm a scholarship student. I guess someone thought recruiting Mexicans helps the school's image, but you can see how well that's going."

I didn't know what to say to that. Truth was, I'd never met a Mexican. At the time I was surprised he spoke English so well. I was ignorant about a lot of things back then.

"You're from Louisiana?"

I nodded. I'm sure I sounded funny to him and apparently, he'd heard a few things about me.

"Yes, sir. And I intend to wear it like a badge. Folks 'round here could use some help broadening their minds, wouldn't you say?"

Jonathan snorted.

"I'll tell you something else, Jonathan Gutierrez. I grew up on John's Island, which is one of the poorest places to live in all of Louisiana. I went to public school up until this year. I didn't even know places like Middleton existed."

That got him to squinting and passing his eyes over my black leather Oxfords and my silk necktie. Students had to wear a standard Middleton blazer, button down, and khaki slacks, but I'd noticed the wealthier boys had the fancier gear while others had scuffed up shoes and polyester ties like Jonathan. My granddaddy made sure I had all the best in my wardrobe.

"You're here on scholarship, too?"

"No. Well, it's a long story. To cut to the chase, my situation changed significantly when my step-granddaddy adopted me. I never knew I even had step-granddaddy until this past summer. Turns out he's a businessman who's done well for himself."

Jonathan grinned. "Your life sounds like a Charles Dickens novel. Are you a modern Pip Pirrip?"

I thought that was pretty funny, and I liked Charles Dickens. "I suppose I am."

He glanced at me, and then he hiked his book bag onto his shoulder, fixing to move along. "Thanks for standing up for me."

I looked him in the eye. "I'd do it again. Anybody tries to mess with you, you just let me know."

He nodded and ambled on his way.

I called after him, "You got anyone to study with for Mr. McKendry's history quiz tomorrow?"

Jonathan halted. He looked over his shoulder. "Not really."

"How'd you like to meet up in the library after supper?"

His face brightened. "Okay. What time?"

I shrugged. "I haven't had much luck filling up my social calendar. How 'bout you just say?"

"Seven?"

"Seven it is."

16

FROM THAT DAY on, Jonathan and I became fast friends. And what a miracle. I hadn't thought there was a single boy in all of Middleton I had anything in common with, and there were eight hundred of us living on campus. Jonathan loved English literature. He'd done so well, he was taking an advanced comparative literature course and a creative writing elective. We'd read some of the same authors, and we could talk about books for hours. I showed him the paperbacks by William Burroughs, James Baldwin, and Thomas Mann that Nicolas had loaned me, and Jonathan showed me his books by Gabriel Garcia Marquez, Rudolfo Anaya, and Reynaldo Arenas. We swapped books and had discussions about them. Jonathan also wrote short stories and poetry, and though he was shy about it, I needled him to let me read some of the things he wrote. I was mighty impressed. He was going to be a famous author one day.

We met up at the library every night, and all day on weekends. Sometimes when the weather was nice, we'd bring our books outside and find a quiet spot on the grounds and spend an afternoon reading together and talking about everything under the sun.

Jonathan had two older sisters and an older brother. His father worked at a General Mills factory, and his mother worked in custodial services at a hospital. He'd be the first person in his family to go to college, and he had his sights set on Brown University or Columbia. He told me he'd always felt like a misfit in his family and at his former school. Boys in East L.A. could best hope to take up trades like his daddy did, he said. We didn't look anything alike, but I tell you, we were mirror images in a lot of ways. Jonathan knew what it was like growing up in a crowded house and having parents who came up short at the end of the month and getting by on whatever they had at the food pantry. His older brother worked in a movie theater, and his sisters both had kids young and struggled to make ends meet working at a supermarket and a beauty salon, respectively. Jonathan aspired to bigger things. He wanted to make his parents proud.

I told him about my own family, trying not to scare him off too much. Like Jonathan, I felt like I had something to prove, but without a mama or a daddy, my situation was a little different. I shared with him how I'd tried to keep my brothers and sister together and hoped to be able to take care of them one day. I'd been nervous talking about those things with anyone at school, but Jonathan didn't think it was strange.

On Friday and Saturday nights, while most of the students whooped it up after football games, the two of us would hang out in the library until it closed at eleven, and then we'd go up to my room to listen to music or watch TV. Granddaddy had shipped me a brand new 27- inch Sony color television. It was one of my birthday gifts I'd never opened. I was living flush with a stereo, turntable, cassette player and speakers, and Nicolas sent me mixtapes every week with all the songs I loved. It sure was nice having someone to share those things with, but I did get teased. Jonathan went from calling me Pip to calling me Richard Bluedhorn-Stratton who was a character from the TV show *Silver Spoons*, played by Ricky Schroeder. Not that Jonathan minded hanging out in my room. He had three roommates, none of whom he liked. They were all stuck-up preppy types who treated him like dirt.

Anyway, we loved watching Friday night music videos, *Saturday Night Live*, and our favorite, the *CBS Late Night Movie*, which came on every Saturday at one o'clock in the morning. Granddaddy had even sent me a popcorn popper and a mini fridge, so we'd make popcorn and drink Coca-Cola like we were at a movie theater. Those old movies were corny as heck, and we cracked each other up making fun of the actors. Or we'd ham it up when there was a romantic scene, or turn off the lights and try to creep each other out if they were showing a horror movie. I'll say it now. Jonathan was the best friend I ever had. Well, besides Preston Montclair who I still thought about sometimes. Ten letters I'd sent that boy over the summer, and he never once wrote back, even when I invited him to my birthday party.

I did real well in my classes that term. They were tougher than the ones I had at Le Moyne Senior High School even though I'd been an honor's student. But on the other hand, I had more time to study, and I liked being a bookworm and doing homework. Jonathan was nerdy like that, too. I'm pretty sure he was a genius. Whenever I got stumped in chemistry or pre-calculus, he could always show me how to figure things out. The fall term went from being a nightmare to being a dream. I realized I belonged at Middleton Academy after all, and let the phonies like Christopher Watts-Jennings try to tell me different when I was getting better grades than anyone.

One Saturday night, Jonathan and I were watching one of them Late Night Movies, tucked up at the head of my bed and having a great time. The film was called *Diary of a Teenage Hitchhiker*. It was one of those slasher stories and had a cast of TV actors that got the two of us smirking at each other right away. Dominique Dunne, Dick Van Patten, and Christopher Knight, who played Bobby on *The Brady Bunch*. When we weren't laughing about the cheesy acting, I noticed Jonathan paying close attention whenever Christopher Knight came on the screen.

He asked me, trying to sound casual, "Do you think Christopher Knight's handsome?"

We'd never said boo about being gay. I suspected Jonathan was, and I suspected he gathered I was, too. He'd seen those books Nicolas gave me, and I can tell you William Burroughs wrote some things so dirty, it'd make your jaw drop straight out of your mouth and go back to reading the page a second time.

"I suppose he's good looking," I told Jonathan. "But if I was in the market for someone to butter my biscuit, I'd rather it be Greg Brady."

Jonathan's red cheeks got even redder, which made me crack up. Then a big grin split across his face. "You like boys, too?"

"Only Sundays through Saturdays."

Well, that threw open a whole new world of conversation. Jonathan wanted to know if I'd ever messed around with boys, so I told him just about everything from Preston Montclair to Dan Jolly to Nicolas Bondurant. As much fun as I was having away at school, I sure was looking forward to being back in Nicolas's arms at Thanksgiving break. I didn't tell Jonathan every detail about Nicolas just yet. He was bowled over enough without knowing Nicolas was a little mixed up from the war and technically my great uncle now that my step granddaddy had adopted me.

"I've never been with anyone." Jonathan looked lonesome about that.

"I bet you had a crush." I elbowed him. "Or maybe two or three."

He got shy and antsy on the bed. "You swear not to tell anyone?"

I gawped at him. "Now why I got to promise not to tell anyone when you know there's not a soul in this here school who cares what I've got to say one way or the other?"

Jonathan giggled. I nudged him with my elbow again to make him spill.

"It's hopeless anyway. I've got one that probably makes me masochistic and another that could get me expelled."

I rubbed my hands together in anticipation.

"You know Christopher Watts-Jennings?"

My heart dropped. "Oh, we been acquainted."

"He's beautiful, right?"

I glanced away from him and sucked my teeth. "I'll give you that. But he's also in the *Guinness Book of Records* for World's Biggest Snob."

Jonathan got long in the face. "I know. That's why I call him my masochistic crush. He'd punch me in the face if I looked at him too long." His eyes lit up. "But I can't help it. We knocked into each other filing out of bio lab last year during a fire drill. I nearly tripped over myself. Christopher told me to watch it, and then he smiled at me. I wrote about it in my journal. April 30th, 1983."

I knew something about pining after boys I couldn't have. Dan Jolly came to mind.

"Moving on. So, who's number two?"

He got all goofy again. "You'll make fun of me."

"Look here, if I can swallow down you writing love poetry about Christopher Watts-Jennings without hurling my dinner, you can bet I'm open-minded."

"Mr. McKendry." He covered his face in his hands, afraid of looking at me.

Mr. McKendry was our American history teacher. He looked like he'd only just graduated college. He had the face of an angel and thick, glossy auburn hair. He never wore his suit jacket in class, and he rolled up the sleeves of his white Oxford shirt over his beautiful, hair-dusted forearms. If you looked real close, which I was liable to do from time to time, you could see his chest hair and his nipples through the fabric of his shirt.

I sat up. "Jonathan Gutierrez, I'll bet you there's not a warm-blooded boy in Middleton who hasn't had a wet dream about Mr. McKendry. And I ain't just talking about the ones like you and me."

Jonathan gaped at me. Then he burst out laughing.

"That's a fine bottle you put on the top shelf," I went on, giving him a sharp nod.

"He's got the cutest face and the cutest butt."

"Easy now. You go popping an erection and movie night is over. I told you I got a man back home. He won't be too pleased to find out I've been having boys in my bed pointing their pistols at the ceiling."

We both cracked up like fools. Jonathan caught his breath and looked at me dreamily. "You've got a *man* back home," he repeated. "You keep a picture of him?"

I hesitated for a moment. I did have a photo of Nicolas in my wallet, but it was an old one where he was wearing his Army uniform, from right before he got sent to Vietnam.

I reached over Jonathan and pulled my wallet out of the bedside drawer. I opened it up and pried out that two and a half by three and a half photo from the inside sleeve. Jonathan took it from me greedily.

He grinned wide, and then his brow shrank up. "He's in the Army?"

"Not anymore." I leaned over Jonathan's shoulder to admire the photo myself. I never got sick of that. Nicolas looked so handsome with his crew cut and neat, Army fatigues. "That was from 1975. He was a medical officer."

Jonathan's eyes bulged. "How old is he?"

"He'll be thirty-two in December."

Jonathan's voice squeaked. "Isn't that illegal?"

"Mm-hmm. Well, strictly speaking I don't know if Louisiana's age of consent laws apply to homosexual relations. But we committed enough unnatural acts to spend the rest of our lives in jail." I carefully took the photo from between Jonathan's frozen fingers and tucked it safely back in my wallet.

"El coño, Arizona. What else have you been hiding?"

"Now why you looking at me like that? Go on and speak your mind. But you can save your breath if you're wondering if we're first cousins running moonshine out of a trailer."

"I wasn't thinking that. I just never met anyone who had a boyfriend. Let alone a thirty-two-year-old boyfriend." Jonathan burned up in the face again. He peeked at me. "How'd you meet him?"

As close as we'd become, I decided that was a story for another day. "He works for my granddaddy. We met at my sixteenth birthday party."

"Are you in love?"

"Mm-hmm."

"You miss him a lot?"

I nodded. I could see more questions stirring in Jonathan's head. I let him take his time.

"So you...you and Nicolas, you went *all the way*?"

I grinned to myself, fixing to give him some grief. "What do you mean? All the way to Disneyland? All the way to Tijuana, Mexico?"

"I mean, did you have intercourse?"

"Oh. Well." I pounced on him, thrusting my hips obscenely to make him laugh. "If you mean like this, we sure did. But he was the one doing most of the work. Scratch that. First time, I developed muscles in places I didn't even know I had."

Jonathan laughed and batted me off him.

"Stop it."

I rolled over myself laughing.

Jonathan glanced at me. "Arizona, I'm dying for the same thing. With the right guy. What's it like?"

I leaned back and folded my hands behind my neck. "It ain't bad. You ever rode a roller coaster?"

"Yeah."

"Well, it's like when the train is cranking up the first great big hill. And you're having second thoughts about why you got on in the first place. The train is slowly climbing up that mountain higher and higher to the top. Your chest freezes over, and your palms start sweating."

I glanced at Jonathan. He was rapt at attention.

"Your stomach's hovering in your throat," I went on. "And whether you close your eyes or not, your body knows things ain't right. That train's lifted you so high in the air, and you're going to drop straight down, and man, it's going to be terrifying, but it's too late now. That steep plunge is coming, and you just might have a heart attack right then and there.

"Then, just to make things more excruciating, the train stops climbing just short of the pinnacle. Makes you damp all over and festering inside with dread and anticipation. And that roller coaster lurches forward, and here it comes. You want to scream because you can't believe death could feel so good. You're plummeting straight down, forgetting any sense of yourself, just surrendering mind and body to something bigger, something primal, like you've entered another plane of existence. And every slam of the train on the tracks shudders through your body, and your mouth hangs open disbelieving any of it is possible. Like how could something so brutal make you want to cry out for more? You're shook up like you've taken the beating of your life, and when the ride finally ends, you're sweating and your legs are feeble, but you just want to do it all over again."

That got me warm in the face just saying it. I chewed my lip. The two of us were quiet for a while.

"Arizona, you should write that down. That's pure poetry."

I scoffed. "You're the one who's good with words. I was just trying to explain."

Jonathan flopped down next to me. "I envy you. You've got someone to love. I don't think anyone is ever going to love me back. I'm a short, ugly, Mexican weakling with bad skin."

I turned on my side so we were facing each other, and I could give him a good talking to about spouting such foolishness. Maybe Jonathan didn't catch a lot of glances. But we were both still growing, and once his acne cleared up and he filled out a little, well, he might come back to school next year a hot stud. I told him that, and then most importantly, I said he was beautiful on the inside. Anyone who took the time to get to know him couldn't help seeing that. Well, you know now, I got that line from Nicolas.

"You'll find somebody. I just know you will."

He sighed. "Not at Middleton. Maybe at college. Brown University has a club called the Gay Student Alliance. When we went for a day trip last year during spring break, they had a table right there in the Student Union."

"Get out."

The thought of gay people being so open excited me too.

Jonathan grinned real big. "The student who was handing out flyers at the table was really cute. I was too scared to go over and talk to him. But I wish I had."

That gave me a dandy of an idea. "I betcha they have gay college clubs in Boston." That city was crammed with colleges and universities. "I heard you can catch a train in town Saturday mornings. Gets you there in forty minutes. Gets you home before curfew."

Jonathan's eyes nearly popped out of their sockets. Then we both stood up on the bed and started jumping around like little kids. Next weekend, we were going to Boston to find Jonathan a boyfriend.

I TOLD NICOLAS about it during our Sunday evening phone call. I was excited for Jonathan, and truth be told, I was excited for me. Things really were different up North. It wasn't that gay people lived totally free, out in the open, but the *Boston Globe* had news stories and editorials I never would've seen in Louisiana.

A congressman from Massachusetts named Gerry Studds had become the first openly gay member of Congress that year. He came out because of a scandal, sleeping with a seventeen-year-old Congressional page. But the people in his district rallied around him. Folks said they didn't care he was gay as long as he was doing good by his constituents. That blew the top off my head, and then I saw an article one day about the Boston Gay Men's Chorus. Just a regular human interest story in the local section of the paper. It mentioned a neighborhood called South End where a lot of gay folks were known to live. They even had a community center for gay teenagers.

I rambled on about all that for who knows how long until it hit me Nicolas hadn't been saying a thing.

"You still there, or did I put you to sleep?"

"I'm here."

"Everything okay? You sound kind of blue."

"I'm fine. I'm glad you made a friend. And that you're having such a good time at school."

He sounded honest, but I still worried he was feeling low. I wanted to tell him I wished he could come up and see me. I stopped myself. That wasn't the right thing to say to cheer him up. "I miss you."

"I miss you, too."

"You're not getting sick of me?"

"Baby, the only thing I think about day and night is the next time I'm going to hear your voice."

That got me feeling warm all over. I tucked my knees into my chest sitting in the little booth for the communal phone in the hall.

"Granddaddy's coming up here for Columbus Day weekend, but I wish I was flying down to see you."

"You're sweet. But you should spend some time with your granddaddy. He misses you too."

It wasn't that I wasn't looking forward to seeing Granddaddy, but a lot had changed in just a month's time. Since Jonathan couldn't afford to go home for the long weekend, I could be spending it with him, maybe running off on a daytrip somewhere. I didn't mention that to Nicolas.

"You heard of Harvey Milk?" I asked him.

"Who's that?"

"He was the first openly gay member of the San Francisco City Council. He ran for mayor and probably would've won. But he was assassinated by another councilman just because he didn't like gays." I scratched the back of my head. "I'm thinking about writing about him for my American history paper."

"That so? You becoming one of them militant activists up there?"

"Could be."

"Well, I'm proud of you. But you be careful. You may be in liberal New England, but there's still plenty of hateful people up there. You promise me you take good care?"

"I promise."

"How's that boy Christopher Watts-Jennings?"

"Minding his 'p's and 'q's."

I glanced at my watch. We'd been talking for a half hour, and I was running up his bill, calling collect. So we said goodnight, but first I told him, "Don't forget you owe me a letter. I wrote last."

17

I'D NEVER SEEN autumn like I did that term. Leaves changing in Louisiana was nothing special, but the Massachusetts countryside looked like something straight out of a storybook, the trees all vibrant red, orange, and yellow. In town, they decorated the store windows with autumn wreaths, pumpkins, and colorful little gourds. People drank apple cider and ate doughnuts. That was something I could get used to. And there was a nip in the air, so cold you could see your breath at night, and everyone dressed in wool sweaters and corduroys to hike around campus, which I didn't mind either. The brisk air was refreshing, and layered clothes made me feel snug.

Jonathan and me took that trip to Boston. It was such a big, crowded city, if it wasn't for Jonathan, I'd probably have gotten lost just stepping out of the train station. I couldn't stop staring at everything and getting myself dizzy. Coming from Los Angeles, Jonathan knew about urban living. He taught me to pay attention to my surroundings and not keep all my money in my wallet. He'd done some research on the T line, which was Boston's subway system, and he tugged me along to the underground station to buy our tickets and take the train to that South End neighborhood I'd read about.

Truth be told, it was a bit more drab and gritty than I'd imagined, at least along the main drag where the wide boulevards intersected and everything was asphalt and concrete. But some of the side streets were pretty with their rows of brownstone houses and little plots with flowers and trees. On Tremont Street, we came along a block with stores and restaurants festooned with Gay Pride rainbow flags. I wore Jonathan out insisting we stop by each and every one of them to take a look.

We found a bookstore entirely devoted to gay and lesbian literature. The two of us pored through every bookshelf. I'd never known so many books existed about people like me. There were biographies, history books, romance novels, and even mystery stories and comics. I bought *The Mayor of Castro Street* by Randy Shilts, which was about my new personal hero Harvey Milk. Jonathan bought a poetry collection, and we both scooped up some dirty magazines. I could've stayed in that bookstore all day, but we had other things to do.

Jonathan helped us find our way to the gay youth center, and we made it in time for the afternoon rap group. We met a mixed group of local kids and college students. None of them had ever met a gay boy from Louisiana, so I'm not being stuck up when I say I got a lot of attention.

I tried steering boys to Jonathan, but he was so nervous, he clammed up and wouldn't say much. Anyway, we all told stories about ourselves. I realized I'd made a lot of assumptions about gay men and lesbians. Well, I'd never had anyone to teach me different. I'd thought all gay men were girly, but there were fellows in the group I'd never have guessed were gay. Same thing with the lesbians. Some of them were manly, but there were girls with long hair and makeup too.

I had all kinds of epiphanies that day. I mean, besides realizing gay people came in all shapes and sizes, I realized I'd been just as ignorant as everyone else thinking swishy boys were weak and unnatural. Some of those effeminate kids who wore makeup and nail polish, made up like Robert Smith from that British band The

Cure, they talked about having gone through hell at home just for being the way they was born. They were braver than I'd ever be, and so were the girls who kept their hair short and wore boys' clothes. I'd never talked to black kids or Asians, but I did that day. We were a big melting pot in that basement room at the community center, and the one thing we had in common was being gay. I liked that a lot.

After the meeting, a group of us went to a diner down the street for burgers, fries, and milkshakes. It was a mix of boys and girls. Two of the girls held hands right there in public. Some of the guys were punk with spiked hair, earrings, and denim jackets with patches and safety pins. One young kid had been kicked out of his house by his parents and was living in a homeless shelter. My heart bled for him, and I felt guilty for having so much when he had so little.

In the end, we didn't find a boyfriend for Jonathan, but we sure had fun. Jonathan and I stopped at a doughnut shop on the way back to the train station, and we chowed down on a half dozen doughnuts and talked about our adventure all the way back to Middleton.

We'd pretty much become inseparable outside of times we had different classes. Looking back, I can say it was inevitable what happened later that week just before Columbus Day break.

Jonathan and I were on our way to the library after dinner just joking around about something stupid. I didn't notice until we nearly ran right into Christopher Watts-Jennings and his pals. They'd been swaggering down the hall from the other direction. Jonathan and I had to stop in our tracks because the dumb jocks blocked our way. They glanced at each other in amusement and got in front of us each time we tried to step by.

Christopher eyed me with his false smile. "Where you faggots off to in such a hurry?"

"The library. You might never heard of it. It's the place people go to increase their intelligence."

His friends chortled and jeered. Christopher laughed it off, and then he sized me up to make a point.

"I see you're still wanting to spar with me, Louisiana. I told you your day would come." He threw off his blazer and cracked his neck. "How 'bout it, country boy? You want to try taking a swing at me?"

Jonathan glanced at me in a panic. I'm sure he would've preferred we take our chances running off in the other direction.

Meanwhile, Christopher caught that exchange. He stared at me, deadpan. "Are you two boyfriends?"

I looked at him squarely. "What if we are?"

That got his buddies hooting and making faces.

Christopher got right up in my face. "You should've stayed back in your faggoty, inbred town back in Louisiana."

A cold curtain fell over me. Before I could think things out, I threw out my hands and shoved him. In a blink, Christopher launched his fist and pounded me hard in the gut. I bowled over myself, but I was so hopped up on adrenalin, the pain didn't hold me back from lunging for him.

I remember getting one good jab to his chin, and then he wrestled me down to the floor. It felt like he was three times more powerful than me. All I could do was protect my head with my arms while he threw his fist into my shoulders and my ribs, over and over again. I thought, this is it. Say your last prayers, Arizona. I could feel Christopher's hatred and all the hatred of his friends lashing at me as they goaded him on.

Then a proctor whistled and ran over to break things up.

Christopher righted himself. He was still breathing fire, and he was red-faced and ugly. Humbled as I was, I was glad to see I'd managed to bloody his mouth. The proctor took him by the arm to lead him down to the residential hall director's office. Christopher slowed him down to get in one last threat.

"Who's the big man now, Louisiana? Next time I'll beat the faggot out of you for good."

I fought through the pain to wobble up to my feet and point a finger at him. "You ain't gonna live to see that day. Next time you see me it'll be the middle of the night, holding a knife to your throat."

A second later, I knew I shouldn't have said that. I could've let things pass, and Christopher would've taken the heat for the fight since he'd thrown most of the punches and made the threats. Another proctor hustled over and directed me away to cool down.

18

THAT FIGHT LED to a great big mess. Straight away, I got a lecture from the residential director, Mr. Pawlowski. Fighting was strictly prohibited at Middleton. He didn't care to hear what Christopher had said to me the first week of school or how things started that night. I think Mr. Pawlowski had already made up his mind I was a dumb, Southern troublemaker before I even opened my mouth. He said the two of us bore equal responsibility in his eyes, but it would be up to the dean of students to decide how I got punished. I could be suspended from school. I could even be dismissed.

He sent me off to the infirmary where a nurse cleaned up my split lip, bandaged the side of my ribs where the skin had been scored by Christopher's fist, and gave me an ice pack for my throbbing bruises.

Every part of my body was screaming to high heaven the next morning. It was the Friday before the three-day weekend, and I was supposed to have my morning classes and then run off to meet my granddaddy in Boston. He had said he was sending a car to pick me up at one o'clock. Instead, I had to report to the dean of students along with Christopher, and they were calling our parents in for a meeting.

I sat outside the dean's office with Christopher. We both hung our heads and didn't say a word. I'd never gotten in trouble at school, and you'd think I might've eased into it, skipping class or getting caught smoking. Here I'd dove in headfirst, risking my entire education. That dean's suite with all its oiled wood veneers and towering ceiling felt like the kind of place where sentences were handed out that would determine the rest of your life.

Around eleven o'clock, my granddaddy finally came along. I dreaded looking him in the eye, but I had to out of respect. His expression saddened when he saw my face, and then he drew a breath and took a stern account of me.

I stood up. "How do you do?"

Granddaddy came over, gave me a delicate hug, and patted my back. "I'd be a lot better under different circumstances."

He glanced at Christopher, adding things up. We sat down together in silence. Then the dean, Mr. McGovern, called us in.

Mr. McGovern had a posh office with a dark wood executive desk and four arm chairs set up in front of it. Christopher and I staked out seats the farthest away from each other. Granddaddy sat down next to me.

"Senator Jennings is joining us on the speaker phone," Mr. McGovern explained. His secretary, Mrs. Woolsey, came in to get the senator on the line, tapping away at the dean's big phone console. Once the senator's gruff voice came over the speaker, Mr. McGovern sat down behind his desk and got the meeting started.

He thanked Christopher's father and my granddaddy for joining us on short notice, and he emphasized this was a serious matter. Mr. McGovern looked like a fair-minded, decent man. Maybe it was his friendly demeanor and him being a bit chubby. It might be unfair to say, but I'd always thought of people who were round in the middle to be likely to be warm-hearted and generous. Well, he didn't look at me like I was a juvenile delinquent, so that counted for something.

He summarized the incident as it had been reported to him, which left out Christopher's comments about Jonathan and me being gay. I don't know if that was to spare me some shame, but it didn't sit right with me. I held my tongue, and it was the senator who was the first to speak.

"You're right, Mr. McGovern. This is a very serious matter. And let's get to the point. Christopher's behavior is an embarrassment with implications that go well beyond the code of conduct at Middleton. This is not the first time his impulsive nature has threatened to blemish my reputation as a public servant. I appreciate the school's efforts to keep those matters away from tabloid journalists. But I'm afraid we've reached a juncture where my son requires a more supervised environment."

I was stunned. I didn't know Christopher had gotten in hot water before. If you had told me I'd be feeling sorry for him at that meeting, I'd have busted my ribs laughing. But I was feeling sorry. A little. Christopher was an ignorant, snobby bully for sure, but did he deserve being taken out of school, away from all of his friends over our fight?

Mr. McGovern addressed the speaker phone. "Senator Jennings, I understand your concern. I was, however, going to suggest a week's suspension for the boys and a plan to mediate whatever grievance they have with one another so they can get along during their time at Middleton. We pride ourselves on being a community where every student is treated with respect."

My granddaddy spoke up. "Harlowe, this is Poly Bondurant here. How do you do?"

"I'm doing well, Poly. Good to hear your voice. It was a pleasure seeing you in Baltimore at the manufacturer's convention. I'm still dreaming about those crab cakes at the executive's luncheon."

I had no idea they knew each other. Granddaddy was always surprising me how well connected he was.

"Only crab cakes in the world are Maryland crab cakes," Grandaddy went on. "It was a pleasure for me as well. Allow me to apologize for my grandson, Arizona's behavior. This is also a matter of public reputation for me, and I can assure you this'll be the first and last time he pulls this kind of stunt. Your son Christopher here looks like a fine young man. It seems to me the boys lost their way last night as young fellows are known to do. What do you say we take their word they're going to keep on the straight and narrow from now on? Mr. McGovern here is going to make sure of that. I trust him. The way time flies, these boys will be graduating quicker than you can look over your shoulder."

We all stared at the speaker phone in anticipation. Granddaddy sure had a way of putting things smooth. I glanced at Christopher. He looked to be the most anxious of all of us, which stood to reason. He'd turned as pale as a saucer of milk.

"That's kind of you to say, Poly. And I don't doubt your grandson will turn things around just fine. But my Christopher is a different matter, and one we choose to handle with greater prudence and severity. I've already made an inquiry to a military academy in Connecticut. And until we can make those arrangements, he'll be returning to Fairfield for the rest of the fall semester."

"But Dad," Christopher burst out. "I can't leave school in the middle of the term. I'm supposed to graduate this May. It's my last season on the crew team."

"Good of you to think of those things now. But you should have thought about them before you decided to tee off like a common thug on a boy from a good family. Do you realize what a disgrace this is to me? With an election year coming up? No, Christopher, you've disappointed me for the last time. Mr. Bondurant is being extraordinarily equitable under the circumstances. I will not gamble on you conducting yourself like a civilized human being."

Christopher balled his fists while he stared at the phone. "It was just a little scrap." He swung toward me. "Tell them, Arizona. We made up. Why, we're friends now. Isn't that right?"

I didn't know what to say. I suppose I could've lied to help him out. It might have saved Christopher's skin if I'd said it hadn't been all his fault, maybe even going further to say I'd baited him into the tussle. That would've earned Christopher's gratitude and maybe made him lay off of me and Jonathan. Mr. McGovern was looking at me like I ought to say something like that. My granddaddy, too. But I couldn't push the words out, and the more they silently urged me to do so, the less I felt like doing it.

I fixed on Mr. McGovern. "You said Middleton is a school where every student is treated with respect. What do you plan on doing to make sure gay students get respected around here?"

I hadn't planned on saying it. I guess the fact the power in the meeting had shifted to me gave me the courage. It pretty well turned everyone in the room mute and peeking at the phone like the line might've gone dead.

Mr. McGovern sat forward in his chair. "I'm not sure I follow, Arizona."

"I don't know what was reported to you, but this whole thing between Christopher and me started when he called me and another student faggots. And not just last night. All the time, he harasses boys for being different." I looked Christopher in his frightened eyes. "Christopher introduced himself to me at the beginning of the term. What was it you called me? I'll help you out. Southern trash. But it didn't stop there. He got all his friends calling me names and shoving me around."

I ran my hand through my hair, trying not to look at Granddaddy who was staring at me. I addressed the speaker phone. "And Senator Jennings, with all due respect, I'm not saying that's a reason your son ought to be sent off to military school. If it hadn't been him last night, you can bet there'd have been another group of boys looking to beat up gay students. There's kids scared to death. Kids who think they've got no other option than to commit suicide on account of everyone hating them. We just come here to get an education like everyone else. What I'm saying is this here problem is bigger than Christopher trying to shame me for being gay. It's about fairness and the right to live one's life free. That's a Constitutional issue, don't you think?"

We all waited out a long pause on the phone line.

"Young man, I believe every person at Middleton Academy and

beyond should be free to live their lives without harassment or discrimination. I had no idea my son had sunk so low as to intimidate others with that language."

Christopher withered in his chair. I wasn't sure what I was seeing, but I hadn't expected him to actually look ashamed.

"I was not aware of any prior incidents between you and Christopher. Nor anything about certain name-calling being involved," Mr. McGovern said. "It wasn't in Mr. Pawlowski's report."

I breathed in some more courage. "I told him the same thing I'm telling you, and that's the truth. And I never saw any report. Mr. Pawlowski didn't write down one thing I told him, so I can't tell you how he came up with a report to start with." I caught Granddaddy looking at me, urging forbearance. I wasn't meaning to be disrespectful, but I was on a roll and I just had to speak my mind.

"Mr. McGovern, don't get me wrong, I come to love this school. But you've got problems here, and you can see and hear them every day. All you've got to do is spend some time in the locker room and walk the halls. Don't I have a right to go to class without people laughing at me and calling me names? What about the teachers who work here? The folks who make our dinners and do our laundry? Should they have to put up with harassment because they're gay?"

"Arizona," my granddaddy muttered.

"What? I ought to know what kind of school I'm going to, shouldn't I?" I turned to Mr. McGovern. "I'm gay. Am I a human being like everyone else?"

Yes, I'd picked up a sense of righteousness from reading about gay activists like Harvey Milk and Frank Kameny, not to mention those kids I'd met at that Boston community center. If they could be brave so could I.

Senator Jennings spoke up from the speaker phone. "Mr. McGovern, I'm going to have to cut this short to get over to the Senate chamber. But I think this young man Arizona makes some good points, and I look forward to hearing how it all gets sorted out. I thank you and Mr. Bondurant for your time. We'll have a car sent over to pick up Christopher."

He hung up, leaving the four of us with nothing to say for a while.

"I guess that does it," Granddaddy said. "I'll be taking Arizona to Boston for the weekend. Thereafter, he can settle up on the terms of his suspension."

"I'll settle up the terms of my suspension. But I want an answer." I looked to Mr. McGovern.

Mr. McGovern gestured to Christopher. "Why don't you go on your way to get packed up."

Christopher stood and drifted from the room leaving the three of us in privacy.

"Now, Arizona, the school takes harassment and discrimination very seriously. It's in our code of conduct that no one should be mistreated based on race, color, religion, national origin, or disability."

"What about sexual orientation?"

"At present, that's not a protected category, neither at the school nor in the state of Massachusetts."

"Brown University has an organization for gay students, and they prohibit sexual orientation discrimination. Yale, too."

I'd done my research.

Mr. McGovern smiled nervously. He stole a glance at my granddaddy. "At Middleton, we've taken the approach of allowing families to handle the subject as a private matter, based on their particular beliefs and values."

I frowned at him. "So, what does that do for my safety and the safety of other gay students?"

He looked at his watch and stood. "I'm afraid we'll have to continue this conversation at another time. I have a faculty meeting to attend." He smiled. "And I'm sure the two of you are eager to head out to Boston for the weekend. I hope you'll have an enjoyable time."

I was still stewing, but what could I do? I got up and left with Granddaddy.

WE TRAVELLED TO Boston separately since Granddaddy had a business meeting in the afternoon. A chauffeur picked me up at two o'clock and loaded my leather valise into a black sedan. About an hour later, he pulled up to the curb of the Ritz Carlton hotel in a swanky part of town right by Boston Commons.

Luckily, I'd worn a shirt and tie and a pair of Oxfords. That fancy hotel had a dress code for the lobby. I was getting used to navigating my granddaddy's world. I didn't even stop to gawp at the fancy lobby with all its blown glass sculptures. I went straight to reception and announced myself. The clerk gave me a key to a suite on the eleventh floor and called over a bellhop to cart my bag.

Granddaddy had gone and booked an entire suite in what had to be the best hotel in all of Boston. We had separate bedrooms and enough living space to entertain a dozen people, never mind it was only going to be the two of us. One side of the living room had floor-to-ceiling windows with a view of the park, and there was a big welcome basket filled with fruit, snacks, and chocolates. I'd been feeling sulky since that meeting with Dean McGovern and Christopher, but it was hard to be unhappy high in the sky in that luxurious suite.

The reception clerk had handed me an envelope with a message. I opened it up and read Granddaddy's instructions to meet him for dinner at eight o'clock at a restaurant called Top of the Hub. There'd be a car picking me at seven forty-five.

So, I kicked off my shoes and spent a few hours lounging around watching HBO on the big screen television. Then I found a clothes iron in one of the closets and tried my hand at ironing my suit jacket and a new pair of trousers and a shirt. I did all right, and then my nerves crept up as I thought about seeing Granddaddy after that meeting at school. I hadn't meant to come out to him like that. I hoped he wasn't sore.

The Top of the Hub was on the fifty-second floor of the tallest building in all of Boston, known as the Prudential Center. All I could do was shake my head. Granddaddy knew good living. He wouldn't settle for anything less than having dinner at the finest restaurant in the city with a king's view of the skyline.

A waiter ushered me to a table right by the window, and I couldn't help giving the man a scowl. How was I supposed to eat my dinner when one look to the side had me feeling like I was in a freefall from fifty-two stories?

I sipped a Coca-Cola, and Granddaddy came along about a quarter past eight. I stood to shake his hand, and he pulled me into a hug and kissed me on the head. He seemed to be in a good mood in spite of the meeting in Dean McGovern's office.

He ordered raw oysters, which I wanted none of. I had my eye on the clam chowder and a lobster. Granddaddy told the waiter that and put in for a strip steak for his main course. When he was settled with his Johnnie Walker, he laid into conversation. "I would've preferred a little advance notice of your announcement earlier today."

I looked down at the table.

"Nonetheless, I have something to say to you, Arizona, and I want you to hear it and remember it."

I snapped to attention.

"I'm proud of you. For who you are and for speaking your mind to Mr. McGovern and Senator Jennings. Nobody ever treats my son...my grandson with disrespect. You've got my full support." His face hardened. "If I ever hear about another boy picking on you about it, you best believe there's going to be hell to pay."

My eyes got misty. I hadn't planned on becoming emotional, though I guess you never do. It meant the world to me Granddaddy accepted me for who I was. Maybe I shouldn't have needed that. Harvey Milk had taught me gay is good, and it didn't matter if the world was against you. Right wins out in the end.

Heck, even before that I hadn't needed anyone's approval to go after what I wanted, first with Preston and then with Nicolas. I guess I'd just been born swimming upriver and ready to fight anyone who said that I was wrong. But that night at the Top of the Hub, I felt grace. I think I'd lied to myself saying Gus Fanning would never get to my head, telling me I was a no-good cocksucker. Part of me had believed that. That's why my sister Dolly calling me the same names had hurt so bad. Well, now I'd been redeemed. Granddaddy loved me. He even loved the ugliest part of me, I mean what the world thought was ugly and unworthy of love. Deep down, that's what was giving me the courage to be myself. I wiped my eyes and drew a breath.

"Thank you, Granddaddy."

He placed his hand on mine and gave it a pat. "You've been working hard at school, and look what you've done. You haven't just fit in. You've gone and made Middleton a better place."

I blushed at that.

Granddaddy took a sip of his whiskey. "I know I haven't been around to help you along, but I'm always just a phone call away." His face darkened. "I don't know, Arizona. I promised I'd do right by you, but sometimes I ask myself if I'm doing right. Maybe you're past the age of wanting to talk to an old man about your troubles. But I'd never mind listening. Might have some advice every now and then."

Now he was getting me emotional again. "You done more for me than anyone ever did. Granddaddy, I was going to tell you. Was warming up to it is all. I told Nicolas. He helped me a lot."

Granddaddy nodded and averted my gaze, looking out of sorts. I guess it had been an emotional day for both of us. He'd barely touched his steak.

"You gonna eat that? 'Cause I could do some work on it."

That got his face brightening a little. "You talk. I'll eat. Now tell me everything you've been up to. I want to hear it all from the chassis to the rooftop."

I told him about my classes, especially Miss Antonelli's English literature class. Then I told him about Jonathan and all the fun we had watching movies and our trip to Boston last Saturday. I kept his ears busy all the way through his big steak. I told him I'd even given some thought to where I'd like to go to college. It was less than two years away, and all the boys were talking about this and that school. For me, I was interested in Columbia or Harvard or a smaller school like Amherst College, which had a nationally renowned English department.

After all that, Granddaddy asked me a funny question. "This Jonathan fellow, is he a friend or something more than a friend?"

I threw down my dinner napkin. "When'd you get nosy? We're just friends, Granddaddy."

"I'm only asking." He looked at me sharply. "I trust you're smart enough to know a young fellow has to be careful these days. I read the papers. There's an epidemic going on in San Francisco and New York City. The doctors don't even know what it is exactly, but you best be safe when it comes to messing around. You know about condoms, young man?"

I scowled at him. "Yes, I do." I suppose he had good intentions, but sex and using condoms were the last things I wanted to talk to him about. I'd read all about that disease they were calling AIDS. I could've said I wasn't messing around with anyone at school, but I couldn't bring that out.

"When you come home for Thanksgiving, I suppose you'll want to stay with your Uncle Nicolas."

That made me feel even more awkward. I remembered that day he'd come by Nicolas's house and peered into the bedroom. I just couldn't have that conversation with Granddaddy yet. I told him yes and put on like it was no big deal.

He looked like he was measuring his words himself. Then a thought occurred to me to change the subject.

"I'd like to see Duke, Dolly, and Little Douglas, too."

Granddaddy's eyes shifted. He got the waiter's attention and ordered another double whiskey. He asked me if I wanted anything else, and I said I'd like a refill of my Coca-Cola.

When the waiter scurried away, Granddaddy leaned a little closer over the table.

"Arizona, I've got some news to tell you, and I'm afraid it's going to be upsetting."

I was as alert as a soldier waiting to hear.

"Your daddy gone and split your brothers and sister up. It couldn't be helped. The Petersons weren't interested in taking them in permanently. But they've got fine homes. Your little brother Douglas is with a married couple in Texas. Dolly, she's living up in Jonesville with a pastor and his wife. That's just north of Alexandria. And Duke, he's with your daddy. They're doing a tour with the Ringling Brothers circus."

I wasn't sure what to feel. I guess in the back of my head, I'd known it was inevitable even though Granddaddy had said he'd told my daddy he better keep everyone together. And Duke and Dolly, well, they'd made their choices. Duke had been talking about going back with Daddy from the start.

But Little Douglas, well, my heart was tore up thinking about him being raised by strangers. I wondered if any of my siblings would accept me as a brother again.

"I can see to it you visit Dolly. It's just a three-and-a-half-hour drive upstate."

"I'd like that."

Granddaddy smiled at me. "Thanksgiving will be here before you know it."

19

GRANDDADDY WAS RIGHT about that. The rest of the term flew by. Schoolwork kept me busy. Then I joined the equestrian club because I missed riding Duchess. I hit the wooded trails around campus every Tuesday and Thursday. They didn't have a thoroughbred like Duchess, but they gave me a roan American quarter horse named Foster who suited me just fine. Added to that, somehow, after the big to-do with Christopher Watts-Jennings, I became just a little bit popular.

Boys who'd never shown any interest in me all of a sudden said hello passing by. Even the snooty crew team and hockey players showed me respect around campus, and the bullies laid off their digs in phys ed. A couple of my classmates quietly approached me, wanting to join my study club with Jonathan. I think people had been whispering about my meeting with Dean McGovern, however that conversation leaked out. A shy, chubby boy named Russell Thorne became part of our clique along with Dale Knox-Levy who was also in our year and could make you laugh until your eyes teared up. Dale was even shorter than me and even brassier than me, a real New England type, and he was crazy about Broadway theater. We all came out to each other and called ourselves Middleton's unofficial Pink Triangle club.

We petitioned the librarian to get a subscription to the *Advocate* magazine, and in the meantime, Dale ordered his own, delivered to a post office box in town. Every week, we'd pore through the magazine and hold discussions about gay rights and fighting homophobia on campus. We made a list of ideas to present to Dean McGovern, but the problem was, Dale and I were the only ones willing to meet with him. Jonathan and Russell were scared about their families finding out. Well, we had some things to work on, but at least our numbers had doubled from two to four.

Then Thanksgiving break came, and I said my goodbyes to everyone and boarded a train and a plane back to Louisiana.

It was strange at first meeting Buck at the airport in New Orleans and driving back to Whittington Manor. It felt like a lifetime had passed while I was away, and meanwhile time stood still for everyone else. The great oaks along the driveway were a little dried up and browner in November, but the mansion house was just the way I'd left it, grand, desolate, and dulled, past its prime. Mr. Wainwright met me with the same aloof, superior manner. I told him I'd be staying with Nicolas, and he gathered my luggage and took me by golf cart to Nicolas's cabin by the lake.

My heart did skips as we approached the house. Nicolas and I had talked just the night before, but we hadn't seen each other in nearly three months. I worried our reunion would be awkward, and what if Nicolas's feelings for me had changed?

We were both a little jumpy around each other while Mr. Wainwright brought my bags into the cabin. Nicolas's face was drawn like he hadn't been sleeping properly, but he looked as earnest and adorable as I'd remembered. Mr. Wainwright left us, and as soon as we heard his golf cart zipping down the road, Nicolas drew up close and held my face.

"How'd you get more beautiful?"

He crushed our lips together, and I knew right then we were back where we'd left off. *Jesus, Mary and Joseph,* how could I have forgotten how good it felt kissing and holding him? The crazy fool lifted me off the floor to carry me over to his bed, and we made love with all the passion of our first time. Maybe with a little extra thrown in. Absence making the heart grow fonder as they say.

That was the Saturday before Thanksgiving. I had a whole week until I had to fly back to school, though I couldn't spend all that time getting reacquainted with Nicolas. Granddaddy had made arrangements for me to visit Dolly in her new home in Jonesville on Wednesday. My teachers had sent us off for break with papers to write and studying to do as well. Plus Granddaddy had a formal dinner planned up at the main house for Thursday.

I spent my days reading and writing while Nicolas sketched and painted. He'd finished that portrait of me and had a couple others in the works. I'd become his new subject, which made me feel really special.

On the other hand, it made me a little sad because I knew how much Sara had meant to him. Truth was, our reunion welled up a sea of complicated feelings. Nicolas was still a man in a cage while I'd gone off and had so many new experiences. He wasn't cross about it, but it didn't seem right to me. Remembering the last time we'd talked about the subject, I was timid to bring it up, and at night, when we made love, all my worries peeled away and I just wanted to be with him like that forever. Maybe our relationship wasn't perfect, but we loved each other so strong, that was bigger than any problems in my head.

Wednesday snuck up on me real fast. I was plenty nervous about seeing my sister, but I knew it was the right thing to do. Before driving upstate, I asked Buck to take me into town to buy something for her, and he suggested Weinstein's boutique on Canal Street in New Orleans, where my grandmother liked to shop.

I knew I'd find something chic and elegant there. The store was in the city's finest neighborhood, just down the block from Ruben-stein's. A saleswoman helped me pick out a fashionable girl's dress in pink taffeta, which was Dolly's favorite color. I had it wrapped up in a box, and then Buck drove up Rte. 10 to Rte. 49 north to the address Granddaddy had given him.

Jonesville was one of those little towns off the highway you passed by and didn't think of stopping to visit. It had an old movie theater on its main strip that was still showing films that had come out nine months ago. The pastor who had taken in Dolly lived about a mile outside of town. Sherman Landry of Paradise Baptist Church. His house was on a two-lane country highway just behind a gray cinderblock church which looked liked it could hold six dozen parishioners. It was one of many hundreds of dilapidated, nondescript churches across the state.

I recall a 1970s Buick was parked in the driveway, and they'd put up a flag by the door that read: Home, Sweet Home. The ranch-style house had mint green aluminum siding, and I guess it was cozy. The pastor and his wife kept up with it a lot better than my daddy did with the house we'd grown up in. Sad thing was the nearest neighbor was a quarter mile down the road.

At the door, I was greeted by Mrs. Landry who was a plain, wide-hipped lady in a modest house dress. Her face didn't seem to have the muscles to put on any kind of expression, smile or frown. After introducing myself, I told her something smelled delicious. Aromas carried from the kitchen where she must've been working on a sweet potato pie for next day's dinner.

Mrs. Landry didn't have anything to say about that. She let me in and walked me over to a living room that didn't look like it got much use. All the pillows on the floral print sofa were perfectly placed, and the room didn't even have a TV. Mrs. Landry told me I could sit, and then she hollered for Dolly to come up to the front of the house.

My heart hung over a blade waiting for my sister. The last time we'd seen each other, she'd said such cruel things. Being the older brother, I know I shouldn't have let that get to me, but my younger sister had always been my conscience. I was supposed to see to taking care of her since my daddy couldn't do it and our mama had died.

I tell you, when Dolly came out to the living room, I might not have recognized her walking down the street. She'd both plumped up and sprouted, looking more like an eighteen-year-old than the girl I'd seen just last summer. I remembered she'd turned thirteen in September. She was becoming a replica of Mama Lou.

Dolly was shy around me at first, but when I called her over and gave her a hug, she hugged me back and a little smile perked up on her face.

"You look real pretty."

She hung her head and blushed.

I gave her the dress box, and we sat down together on the couch while she opened it up. "It's for your birthday."

Dolly pried the box open, and her eyes grew wide when she saw the fancy dress in a bed of tissue paper.

"Go on," I told her.

She lifted the dress out of the box and stretched it out in front of her. Then she threw it down and moped on the couch. "It won't fit. I'm too fat."

She looked like she was going to cry. I eased up closer to her. "All you gotta do is go to Weinstein's and get it altered. You could even have it exchanged if you want something different."

"What's Weinstein's?"

"It's a ladies department store in New Orleans."

"How am I going to get to New Orleans?"

I shrugged, keeping my cool. "You'll just have to have your older brother take you there when he's back for Christmas. We can make a day of it. Have a nice lunch. Ride a trolley car." I thought that might make her happy. But all it did was get Dolly scowling.

"On whose dime?" She snorted. "Your rich granddaddy's, of course."

I didn't answer. I didn't want to get into a scrap like the last time we'd seen each other.

"Did he send you to a fancy boarding school?"

I'll say this about my sister. She'd always been shrewd. I guess I looked like a prep school student in my jacket, shirt and tie. "Yes, he did. I'm going to school in Massachusetts. Middleton Academy."

She made an ugly face. "Well, goody for you. I bet you fit in real well with those Yankee snobs."

"Dolly, let's not fight. What's the point? You gonna go on hating me the rest of your life?"

Dolly crossed her arms in front of her, real bratty. Meanwhile, I could hear Mrs. Landry tinkering in the kitchen. It occurred to me she hadn't mentioned offering me refreshments. Even in John's Island, where nobody had next to nothing, you couldn't pass someone's porch without them offering you cold lemonade or iced tea. That woman either had no sense, or she was tighter than a flea's ass stretched over a rain barrel. We weren't far from the kitchen, and I wondered if Mrs. Landry was listening in on our conversation.

I stood up. "How about you show me around outside?"

Dolly rolled her eyes, but she stood. I followed her out the front door, and we wandered along a path around the house to the backyard. They had a little vegetable garden covered up for the winter and a swing set that looked brand new. We sat down side by side on a pair of swings.

I tried smiling at my sister, but she was giving me the full treatment, pouting and avoiding my glance.

"How you like living here?"

"Fine."

I looked around. They kept the lawn trim. It was quiet. Just the whir of a car speeding by on the two-lane road now and then. I remembered Dolly saying the pastor and his wife couldn't have kids. "It seems like a nice place. I bet you got your own room."

"Oh, it's grand," Dolly drawled. "Just like living in Whittington Manor. You should come by for Sunday tea. We're just dripping in refinement and sophistication."

I grinned. She sure had honed a wicked sense of humor. Dolly made a funny face. I don't think she meant for me to be amused.

"They treat you right—Pastor Landry and his wife?"

"You met her. What do *you* think?"

I chuckled. "I guess she does seem a bit stuffy." I could've said something about Dolly looking well-fed, but I swallowed that down. "You settled in a new school? Made some friends?"

She gazed fiercely into the distance. "They have me going to a Baptist school."

"Well, sounds like you'll get a good education."

"They're all a bunch of stuck-up prissies."

The acid in her voice surprised me. Dolly had always had an easy time making friends, and there'd been plenty of girls from religious families at Le Moyne Central District.

"Is it *that* bad?"

A mirthless smile molded on her face. "They call me Dumb Dolly. Or Dirty Dolly. Bayou trash." She looked at me defiantly. "You think I give a rat's ass? Maybe you care about what people think of you. Prettying yourself up. Taking on fancy manners. But I know who I am and where I come from. And it's the same as you. We're Fannings. White trash. And I don't care if I'm not gonna go to heaven. I wouldn't want to be around anyone who ends up there anyway."

I couldn't say a word at first. "Don't say that Dolly. What's gotten into you? You find yourself some self-respect, young lady."

She scowled and looked away.

"It doesn't matter where we came from," I went on. "Nobody can take away your self-respect unless you let 'em, and that's the truth."

Dolly sucked her thumb and rocked on her swing. Something about that got me hot under the collar.

"Let's get something else straight. You show respect for *me*. You said some ugly things at my birthday party. You look me in the eye and tell me if that's the way it's gonna be."

My sister was as stubborn as a mule, just rocking on that swing, staring off with her thumb in her mouth. Well, she looked ridiculous. Like an overgrown five-year-old instead of thirteen. That got me feeling differently. Something had gone terribly wrong with her. "Dolly, I know things ain't been easy. I've been hurting too since grandma died."

"Oh, you been hurting? How's that? Getting driven around in limousines? Having birthday parties with New Orleans society?"

"Look here. That don't mean I ain't been hurting. I know it's not the same as you, but we all got split up, and none of us had a say about it." I gazed off into the distance like she was doing. "Sometimes it helps to talk. All you gotta do is tell me what's been going on."

Dolly glanced at me but said nothing.

"What is it, Dolly? Are you missing Duke and Little Douglas? You don't like living with the Landrys? Is it the kids at school?"

"I don't care about any of that. I ain't gonna be going to school much longer anyway."

She laid a hand on her stomach. An icy chill clutched my heart.

"I got something," she said. "Something nobody can take away from me. Someone who's gonna want me no matter if nobody else do."

I got up from my swing and stooped down in front of her, grasping her arms. "Dolly," I croaked.

"What?"

I sniffed back tears and looked at her. She didn't try to disguise it, looking back at me with fire in her eyes. I knew. She was pregnant.

"Do the Landrys know?"

She looked away and nodded.

"Wh-what are you going to do?"

"I gonna be a mama."

I eyed her steadily. "You're thirteen. That's too young to be a mama."

"*He* didn't think so."

I couldn't stop myself from breaking out in a sob. My little sister who played with dolls and fought with me over the prize in the Cracker Jack box was having a baby. I was horrified some boy had done that to her. Horrified she was going to give birth at thirteen years old.

"Dolly, you need a mama, not to become one."

She stood up from the swing. "What do you know about what I need? I'm gonna be a mama, Arizona. God wants this for me. You gonna tell me He's wrong?"

She walked lazily around the swing set. I gathered myself and followed her. "This boy who done this to you, he going to help out?"

Dolly got fierce with me again. "It's *God's* child. Pastor Landry told me himself. He chose me."

I glanced at the house, and a terrifying thought hit me. So terrifying, I'm ashamed to say I pushed it away. Dolly just wasn't making sense. Did she even know where babies came from? I was plum dumbfounded, not knowing which way to go.

Then she got hysterical. "Arizona, they sending me away to some house in Mississippi for girls who got in trouble. They say they'll find a good home for my baby, but I'm gonna keep it. I'm telling you, I gonna keep it. You'll help me, won't you? You can't let 'em take away my baby."

I gathered Dolly in my arms. She'd set my mind to thinking the only good I could do was comfort her. So I did, holding her tight like Mama Lou used to do when I was little. I just wanted to take away every pain she was feeling. I brushed her hair while she shuddered against me, weeping.

"It's all right, Dolly. You cry all you need. I'm your big brother, and I'll always help you. You know that, don't you?"

She buried her face against me, weeping out more hurts than any little girl ought to feel.

20

THAT VISIT WITH my sister left me with a lot to think about. I wondered if things would've been different if we'd never left John's Island. Maybe if Grandma Tilly hadn't died, or if I hadn't hit Gus Fanning in the head with that bottle, which had led to the four of us being separated. Or maybe I should've stayed in Louisiana and gone to that Catholic school so I could've looked after Dolly. I could've at least visited her on weekends.

Back at Whittington Manor, I beat myself up. Was I a lousy brother? I'd worked so hard to better myself, I'd forgotten all about Dolly, and who knew what Duke and Little Douglas were going through? Going to a boarding school and a top college—it was hard to figure I'd look back feeling proud of any of that if my sister and my brothers were suffering.

I told Nicolas what was on my mind. He didn't have much to say, but he comforted me and thank God for that. Whoever was to blame, the plain truth was Duke, Dolly, Douglas, and me had gone our separate ways, making new kinds of families. Maybe it was something like God's will as Dolly had said. I couldn't fight against that. Lord knew I'd tried.

Nicolas held me and loved me. He was my family now, along with Granddaddy and the friends I'd made at Middleton. But I was torn in half. Was I wrong feeling that way, making a family without my siblings? I wore myself out trying to come up with answers about what I should do and finally fell asleep in Nicolas' arms.

Then the next day was Thanksgiving dinner.

Nicolas and I came up to the main house, and the first thing I noticed when we went into the dining room was four place settings, which meant my grandmother Virginia was joining us. I had memories of my last dinner with her and memories of catching her with Dan Jolly. You can bet I was queasy about that dinner. Granddaddy came down to join us, and shortly after, Virginia arrived. All three of us were silent, and even my granddaddy looked like he was on guard for trouble.

Well, my grandmother had dressed for an occasion. She had her blonde hair done up and pinned. She was wearing a lovely black velvet holiday dress that complimented her figure, and she was decked with silver bangles, a diamond necklace, and diamond pendant earrings. It made me think of something I'd learned in biology class, how the most beautiful things in the world are often the most poisonous like tropical fish and cherry blossoms. I bowed my head in respect, and Virginia smiled at me. I couldn't tell if it was sincere. She sat down at one end of the table with Granddaddy at the other, and Nicolas and I sat on either side.

One of the servants brought Virginia a gin martini, and she fit one of her skinny cigarettes into her holder and lit up.

"Your grandmother has promised to be on her best behavior," Granddaddy said, watching her carefully. "It's Thanksgiving after all."

"Now, when am I *not* on my best behavior, Poly?" Virginia's eyes twinkled at him. "You talk like I just got my release from a ladies penitentiary."

I smiled. She did have a funny way of putting things.

"How do you do, Ginny?" Nicolas said.

"I do just fine." She gave him wide-eyed glance. "Why Nicolas

Bondurant, how's it possible you get more handsome year after year?"

"I thank you." Nicolas said. "And I must say you're looking as radiant as ever."

"I'm feeling radiant." Virginia sat back in her chair, looking at Nicolas with a flirtatious grin. "Such big green eyes and broad shoulders. Sometimes I think I married the wrong Bondurant." She took a thirsty sip of her martini, daintily patted her painted lips and gave Nicolas a sidelong glance. "Don't make me misbehave."

He chuckled. I could see they had something of a camaraderie, which was curious since Nicolas had told me Virginia didn't like him. Well, it seemed like Nicolas might serve as a buffer to her sharp tongue and save Granddaddy and me some grief.

"Happy Thanksgiving, Virginia," I greeted her.

"Is that you, Indiana?" She put on an amused gape. "I thought Mr. Tom Cruise had gotten his plans mixed up and joined us for dinner."

I blushed, though I had a feeling she was fixing to turn that compliment around. "Virginia, you never will get my name right, will you?"

She exhaled a plume of cigarette smoke and waved me off. "I'm just having some fun."

I played into her routine. "How'd you like it if I called you Mississippi from now on?"

She eyed me sharply. "Buttercup, as long as you don't call me *granny*, we'll do just fine."

The servant brought in the salad course and served each of us a plate.

"Well, no one would believe it anyway, Ginny. You hardly look old enough to be a grandmother," Nicolas told her.

"I was an infant when I had his mother. You know the doctor said it was one of those freak things."

We all had a little chuckle over that.

"Hmm. I think it must've been you sold your soul to the

devil," Nicolas said. "Just like that book by Oscar Wilde, *The Picture of Dorian Gray*."

Virginia smiled at him in delight. Though I picked up something had changed in Nicolas's bearing. Like my grandmother, he had a clever way of getting swipes in with the appearance of blamelessness. I was both fascinated and dreading where their conversation would go.

I watched her drain her first martini. "I *loved* that old movie," she drawled. "Who played the handsome fellow Dorian. Peter Lawford?"

"Hurd Hatfield," Granddaddy corrected her.

A servant drifted over with a silver shaker to refill Virginia's drink.

"Well, they don't make movies like that any more." Virginia peered at Nicolas. "Now that's what I should do. Have you paint a portrait of me. Dredge away all the old age." She put on a petulant face. "In all these years you never once let me sit for you. What's wrong with me, Nicolas? You butter me up, but you never do invite me over to play at your cabin."

"That's because my brother is a gentleman," Granddaddy said.

Virginia rolled her eyes. "That's because your brother is a queer."

Granddaddy glared at her. "Ginny, that's an ugly word."

She threw up one hand. "That's what they're called, isn't it? And it's a crying shame. All those good looks wasted, Nicolas. Why you could've had your pick of girls when you came back from Vietnam. A young, handsome veteran. They'd have been throwing themselves at your feet."

"That's enough, Ginny."

Nicolas spoke up. "It's all right, Poly." He turned to Virginia. "Some of us just don't care to spend our good looks so liberally."

Good God. I was back to sinking in my seat.

Virginia seemed to take it in with good humor. Still, I nearly choked on my salad when she turned her attention to me.

"You've been away at school, haven't you? How you finding living among the Yankees?"

I swallowed and took a drink of water to clear my throat. "Well, as a matter of fact, I'm finding some of them Yankees aren't half bad." I ventured to confess a little more. "I was lonesome the first few weeks. Some boys made fun of the way I talked, and they're not as warm as folks 'round here. But I made some friends. My best friend's from Los Angeles." Because it was irresistible to challenge her prejudices, I said, "And he's a Mexican."

She got a gleeful look on her face and fired up another cigarette. "My, my. So very cosmopolitan of you, Appalachia." She fixed on Granddaddy. "Poly, did you know they're admitting Mexicans to Middleton Academy?"

His face was weary. "Times have changed, Ginny. No one cares about race, colors or creeds."

She frowned thoughtfully. "Is that so? I think that's lovely. We should all be sophisticated like our grandson. Now, what about the Chinese? I hear they do quite well in school."

Nicolas chuckled. "Ginny, you're nothing if you're not consistent."

"Whatever are you implying?"

"I'm implying you were never one for culture beyond Southeast Louisiana. Some folks might say that makes a person downright provincial."

I bit my lip.

Virginia swirled her martini, looking like that spring inside her was winding up. The servant cleared our plates, taking her salad away untouched. She seemed to survive on a diet of gin and nicotine. I guess with an olive thrown in now and then.

"Well, it's true it's been a long time since I travelled," she said. "I married young. Then Philippa came along. But before that, I'd been to New York City and San Francisco and Alcapulco and Cuba. Why, Poly took me to Europe for our honeymoon. Paris, Venice, Rome. You remember, Poly? We saw all the sights."

Granddaddy nodded along, looking proud.

I was happy to see Virginia's face brighten, remembering. But it dimmed as quickly as it had lit up.

She glanced at me. "Your granddaddy loved me then. Treated me like a princess. But it was short-lived on account of your mama."

Nicolas glanced at me protectively then fixed on Virginia. "Good Lord, Ginny. You're talking about the boy's mother and your own daughter. Philippa was a beautiful, big-hearted young woman. God rest her soul."

Virginia gazed off vacantly. "Oh, she had a big heart for Poly."

"We *all* loved her," Nicolas said.

The color had drained from my granddaddy's face. I wasn't sure what I was witnessing, but it made me jumpy seeing it.

"To get back to your point, Nicolas, I suppose some folks would call me provincial. It's been seventeen years since I left Whittington Manor. You know something about being a shut-in. What would you recommend to improve myself under the circumstances?"

She stared at him with her martini glass in her fist.

Nicolas said nothing. Granddaddy eyed her carefully.

Virginia sipped from her glass. "It's been a long time since *you* left Whittington Manor, hasn't it? I guess we've both had our reasons." She chuckled to herself. "But sin finds its way in, doesn't it? You just loved Philippa, and you love my grandson even more."

I don't think I'd ever blushed that hard. It felt like I ought to cover my face with my arms for fear I might blind someone from looking at me. What made it worse was the silence that followed.

Virginia cackled. "Did you sit for your uncle Nicolas, Armadillo? Let him sketch you for one of his nudes? I bet you did. I bet you let him put his pervy hands all over you. I bet you enjoyed that. Your mama sure liked dirty old men when she was your age."

I burst out, "You're a nasty old cunt."

She brayed with laughter. Nicolas pushed back his chair, stood, and threw down his napkin on the table.

"Happy Thanksgiving, Ginny. Looks like it's just going to be you and a bottle of Tanqueray as usual."

I stood up to leave with him.

"Oh, don't be such a stick in the mud," Virginia went on. "I was only making conversation."

I swung toward her. "I don't care that you don't like me. I don't like you, either. But the next time you say something cruel about my mama, I swear you're going to regret it."

Virginia stared at me in amusement. "I won't abide threats of violence in this house. Poly, we best lock up the liquor bottles. The boy's got a mind to bash us all over the head just like he did with Gus Fanning." She laughed. "You can take the boy out of John's Island, but you can't take John's Island out of the boy."

Nicolas took my arm. It was a good thing because I was ready to go at her. But I turned and walked away with Nicolas. She'd always get in the last word, and who cared that she did?

21

NICOLAS AND I had our own Thanksgiving dinner back at his cabin. Chef Boyardee raviolis and Edy's Rocky Road ice cream for dessert, which we ate right out of the tub. It reminded me of dinners with my siblings after Mama Lou died and my daddy was off driving his truck cross-country. I'd throw together whatever was in the larder, and Duke, Dolly, and me would eat in front of the living room TV, one of us with Little Douglas on our lap. I didn't need a big fancy meal to be happy.

I did wish Granddaddy could've joined us, though. He and Nicolas were my family now, and we'd left him with vicious Virginia. I couldn't comprehend why Granddaddy hadn't thrown her out of the house by now, though I supposed I didn't understand some things about marriage. In fact, Virginia had said things I didn't understand either. When we were done eating, I asked Nicolas something I'd questioned him about before.

"Were you and Virginia more than friends when you were younger?"

Nicolas threw back his head with a great big grin. We'd both kicked off our shoes, pulled off our ties and unbuttoned our shirts. I was sitting across his lap on the couch with his arm around my shoulder.

"Your grandmother would've wanted it that way. But no. Besides the fact she was barking up the wrong tree, I'd never have done that to Poly. Ginny never could stand being told no, which is why she likes to spar with me."

I pushed aside the hair from his forehead. "You were sparring with her some yourself, Nicolas Bondurant."

"I suppose I was." He snuck his hand inside my shirt, pricking up sparks across my skin as he slid his palm along my side. "Maybe it's not my place, but I don't like the way she treats you."

I didn't mind him standing up for me. I felt no connection to Virginia. She was my grandmother in name alone the same way Gus Fanning was nothing but a sperm donor like Preston had said. Funny that Gaston Bondurant was only my granddaddy by marriage, but I loved him like he'd raised me all his life.

"I just don't understand why he stays with her."

"Hmm. Obligation, I suppose. I don't recall them getting along so well even before your mama died. But after...well you've seen yourself your grandmother isn't right in the head. Losing your mama changed her. I guess somehow your granddaddy blames himself, and he just can't find his way to doing the right thing."

His hand came to rest under my arm with his thumb brushing against my nipple. He looked into my eyes. "People are complicated, Arizona. They can have all the answers right in front of their face and still manage to go off and make the same mistakes."

I could sense he was talking about himself as much as his brother. He made me think about Dolly as well. "How do you help someone like that?"

"You can't. You either accept them for who they are and love them, or come to terms with walking away."

My heart felt fragile. I didn't want to walk away from Nicolas. I couldn't, even though we'd only see each other on school breaks. I'd like it different. Sometimes my mind would wander, thinking about having a boyfriend up at school who I could see whenever I liked and truly live with in the world. But I always cleared my head of those ideas right quick. Nothing could be better than how Nicolas made me feel. We just fit together.

Thinking about that made me worry about something else. "Am I enough for you?"

He brought his hand out of my shirt to hold my face. "Arizona, you're *too* much for me. But I'll cheat the scales of justice as long as I can."

He wound his hand around the back of my neck and brought me close for a deep kiss. I didn't understand what he'd said exactly, but while we were kissing and touching, I couldn't think about anything else.

THE NEXT DAY, we were lazy like we'd been over the summer. We slept in and barely left Nicolas's bed, just listening to his records, fixing things to eat in the kitchen, and grabbing for each other when that need rashed up.

We were rutting bucks out in the wild. Each time felt like a sweet death with the breath socked from my lungs and Nicolas shuddering against my back. Then, when he was done, I was reborn as he clung to me, heaving hot breaths against my cheek. I was his. I didn't want to be anything else. For a whole day and night, it was just him and me. Anything beyond Nicolas's cabin might as well have disappeared.

Then on Saturday morning, I woke up and found myself alone in his bed. I figured Nicolas had gone out to the kitchen to make breakfast. I stepped into a pair of briefs and threw on a long-sleeved pullover because it was chilly, and I ventured out to the cabin.

Lucky thing I'd put some clothes on. Granddaddy's voice travelled from the deck. He must've come by while I was sleeping, and he and Nicolas were talking. They couldn't see me through the glass door, and I couldn't see them.

I almost went back to the bedroom to throw some pants on.

But by golly, what was the use in pretending? I pushed through my nerves and stepped out to the deck to say hi.

"Morning."

That must've been one heck of a conversation they were having. Neither one looked over my way or even budged. Granddaddy was standing on one side of the picnic table, and Nicolas was sitting down, wearing a sweater and pajama bottoms he must've thrown on before taking a shower. He looked like he'd been hit over the head by a ton of bricks.

Granddaddy swiped his face and greeted me, putting on some cheer. "Good morning, Arizona. I was just talking to Nicolas about loaning you out for the morning. How'd you like to saddle up Bonnie and Duchess and take a ride with me?"

I'd sure been hoping to see Duchess during my visit. I was headed back to school the next day, so there wasn't much time. I looked to Nicolas. Something wasn't right with him, though. I didn't want to leave him. He glanced up and forced a grin.

"Go on. You ought to spend some time with your granddaddy."

Something felt off, but I did what I was told and went to wash up and get dressed. Maybe they'd been talking about that awful dinner with Virginia. I wondered if something else had happened that night after we left. Maybe Granddaddy had decided to leave my grandmother. I rushed through things, curious to find out.

By the time I was ready to go, Nicolas was in the yard, chopping wood for his stove. He still looked awfully dejected. I walked over, waited for him to set aside his axe, and I wrapped my arms around him. Granddaddy was just over by the front door. I was nervous showing so much affection for Nicolas in front of him, and I think Nicolas felt it too. But something happened in their conversation that hurt Nicolas's heart, and I wasn't about to let anything get in the way of saying I loved him.

Nicolas gently tried to break things off, but I held on, getting him flustered and smiling a little. I finally released him and looked him in the eye. I saw love there, which warmed my heart, but I also saw his pain. I kept staring, wanting to make sure he was going to be all right.

"Go on," he told me again. Then he gripped me again and kissed my face. "Why you gotta make me love you so much?"

I smiled at him, hoping he would smile back, but he didn't. One of his moods had come over him. I thought maybe he was sad about me leaving tomorrow.

"I'll be back 'fore dinner. Don't be glum."

I went on my way with Granddaddy, and he drove us in a golf cart to the stables.

I WANTED TO know what he'd said to Nicolas to put him in that mood, but something inside me had me changing my mind before the words came out. I felt like a little kid, too meek to ask questions, just hoping my granddaddy would explain when the time was right. I didn't like feeling that way.

Well, I eased up some when I saw Duchess in the stables, and I gave her long muzzle some strokes to say how do you do. She was as friendly and gentle as ever. I swear she remembered me. I brought her out of the pen and got her geared up while Granddaddy got Bonnie ready.

We loped along side by side for a while, not saying anything but enjoying each other's company all the same. When the trail narrowed, I let Granddaddy go ahead, and I followed along. He picked up the pace for some fun, and we galloped through the wooded grounds, which were damp and thick with the scent of decaying leaves.

Granddaddy brought me along a trail I didn't remember. Until we came up the old, fenced-in family cemetery, which I'd noticed from the distance during my riding lessons with Dan Jolly. The old copper fencing was tarnished green and deeply weathered. The grayed stone headstones were as tall as a man and embellished with gothic sculptures—cherubs, angels, and the like. An ancient weeping willow sheltered the plot, and it was overgrown and unruly, obscuring parts of the yard. I had to presume the private cemetery went back to the 1800s when the plantation was built.

That was where Granddaddy was leading me. I didn't know why, but I was breathless with dread.

We dismounted the horses and found some old pickets by the yard to tie them up.

"I thought it was time for you to see your mama," Granddaddy told me.

At sixteen years old, I'd already been to lots of cemeteries. It shouldn't have spooked me, but it did.

I followed him into the cemetery. I saw lots of Bondurants on the headstones but also a fair share of others, especially Malgrin.

"This plot goes back to 1894. That was four years after your great granddaddy Henri Bondurant bought Whittington Manor from the successors of John Randolph Whittington himself. The houses and the sugar plantation had fallen into disrepair. Your great granddaddy bought it for a song. Ten thousand dollars, if you can believe that. Well, he had to spend ten times as much fixing the main house to make it habitable along with various improvements to the property."

He led me over to one of the smallest headstones. *Charlotte Bondurant. April 3rd, 1894 to July 2nd, 1894.* The little plinth had a sculpture of an angel with a bouquet of roses.

"Your great aunt Charlotte," Granddaddy explained. "The cemetery's first resident. She was your great grandfather and grandmother's first child. Only lived three months."

He took off his riding cap. I did the same, and we stood there for a moment to pay our respects. Then he led me deeper into the yard.

"Your great grandmother's maiden name was Malgrin, and for a time, her parents and brothers and sisters, nephews and nieces lived here, too."

Granddaddy stopped to show me Helena Bondurant's grave. She was my great grandmother, he explained. I felt somber, but truth be told, I didn't know how to feel. I knew since Granddaddy Bondurant had adopted me, it was important to him I knew the family history. But it didn't feel like *my* family history. Not by a mile. The Fannings were all buried in a cemetery for poor people on John's Island. Nicolas had mentioned Virginia's maiden name was Stewart, and she was such a witch, I didn't even want to know about that side of the family.

Granddaddy led me along again, and we came up to the biggest, tallest marker in the cemetery. I couldn't quite believe my eyes. I never would have expected the grandest headstone to be for Philippa Bondurant, my mama. It was beautiful, with carved garlands and flowers in the stone and topped with a winged angel gazing upon the plot with sorrow. *September 1, 1949 to August 12, 1968.* That last date—the day I was born—brought out a lump in my throat. I dropped my head.

I felt my granddaddy's hand on my shoulder. "Your mama," he said softly.

"I should've brought something."

"I should've thought about that, too. But we can come back. Maybe tomorrow morning before your flight to Boston. She loved Morning glories."

I grasped his hand. "I would've liked to know her."

"She would've liked to know you, too. She wanted a boy." He snorted mildly. "Your grandmother was hoping for a boy."

He covered his face with his hand. I was shocked to see tears sprout from his eyes. I squeezed his hand and watched him kindly. He drew a breath, brought out a handkerchief, and wiped his eyes.

Afterward, he glanced timidly at me. "Son, there's something I need to tell you. Something I should have said a long time ago. I been keeping it from you, and there's a reason for that. I don't know if it's the right reason. I just hope you understand." He turned his face from me, but I could see he was quivering, fighting something inside him. "It's my fault, and now that you and Nicolas have gotten so close, I can't keep it from you any longer."

I hung on his last words. The truth was already pressing in on me.

"I'm your daddy, and your step granddaddy." He faced me, gaining some confidence. "Well, it should be a good thing for you to know, shouldn't it?"

I dropped his hand and stepped away from him. I was in a daze, not letting what that meant sink in. I guess I'd had an inkling or an intuition. I had his same coloring and facial features, and it made sense in terms of his age. Though I didn't want to believe it.

"I love you, Arizona," he called after me. "With all my heart and soul. And that's because you're mine. Flesh and blood. My only son."

Anger tore at me. I marched right at him. "Why'd you abandon me then?"

"I was a coward. It was 1968. I had a wife, your grandmother, and I'd gone and fallen in love with her daughter, your mama. Now you have to understand there was but nine years between us. Through my marriage to your grandmother, I adopted Phillipa, but I couldn't be a real father to her. We were lonesome souls, and we found each other and made something beautiful. That's you. But I was young and trying to uphold the family name, and when your grandmother found out we'd been messing around, she swore she'd ruin me if I didn't call things off with Philippa. That's what set your mama to running off and taking up with Gus Fanning. Maybe things would've been different if your mama had survived, but son, I was who I was."

I eyed him fiercely while tears streamed down my face.

"I had to hide you. Virginia wouldn't have survived the scandal. I was twenty-six years old and responsible for my daddy's company and the family estate." He dug his hands into his pockets and slumped a little. "There's nothing I regret more than not marrying your mama. She wanted the three of us to be a family, too. I just couldn't at the time. When she started showing, she told Gus you were his. We fought about it, but she turned me around to thinking it was the best for everyone concerned, namely your grandmother. To this day, Ginny doesn't know any different."

A light phase passed over his face. "Philippa always said if she had a boy, she'd name him Arizona. A strong name, she said. With lots of history. We took a trip cross-country in 1967, and we both fell in love with the Painted Desert. Said we'd go back there and show our son how beautiful the world can be." He shook his head. "I wanted to raise you as my own. I guess I convinced myself when the time was right, I'd do the honorable thing." He looked back at the grave, and his voice turned fragile. "Time just slipped away. You were born, and Philippa was gone. I didn't know how to be a man."

My head was so full, I thought I might keel over. Duke, Dolly, Little Douglas—we weren't even half-siblings. I fought against it. It had to be a lie. I didn't mind that Gus Fanning wasn't my real father, but for the brothers and sisters I'd known all my life to not be real? It was too painful to accept.

"I'm sorry, Arizona. I've been trying to make it up to you."

"I really am a Bondurant." Saying it out loud, the words still seemed paper thin, a charade.

My granddaddy, my daddy held me by the shoulders. "Yes, you are. My son. My blood. My heir."

I shirked away from him and gulped back tears. "You should've told me. You should've come for me. You made me live a lie. Now what am I supposed to do?"

"I can't change the past, Arizona. But I'm telling you here and now, I'm not giving up until you say you'll be my son."

Many things flipped through my head. What was I going to say to Dolly and my two brothers? I'd already let them down, and now they'd have no reason to consider me family at all. Then I was struck by something even more chilling.

"Nicolas didn't know?"

He shook his head. "I had to tell him. He's your uncle." He gasped and wrung his hands. "Nicolas had to know it couldn't be."

A cold, black veil dropped over me. Of all the horrors of his

confession, he'd ruined Nicolas. I remembered how out of sorts
Nicolas had been when I'd left him.

My legs carried me along before my head had thoroughly reckoned the situation. My grandaddy, my daddy was calling after me.
I rushed ahead, untied Duchess, stepped into the saddle, and
whipped her into a gallop back to Nicolas's cabin.

22

TERROR GRIPPED ME as I rode back to Nicolas. He'd given me signs, and I'd been too dumb to pick up on them. Now, everything came into focus, and I cursed myself for leaving him with the news my granddaddy brought him that morning. Duchess couldn't carry me fast enough. I galloped to his cabin and jumped down from the horse, not even taking the time to secure her in place.

As soon as I went inside, I knew he wasn't there. The place was too still. Then, I saw the medicine cabinet ajar in the bathroom. He'd cleaned out all his pill bottles from the veteran's hospital, and he'd left a handwritten note on his work bench addressed to me.

I didn't have the time or the guts to read it. I slammed out the door to the deck. *The lake.* There was a trail down to it from the back of the cabin. I climbed down the stairs and hurried along, hollering through the woods for Nicolas.

At the end of the trail, I came up to the rock ledge where the two of us had gone fishing. I whimpered and bit down on my fist. Nicolas's clothes and all his medicine bottles were scattered near the edge. I scanned the water, crying out for him.

The lake was eerily peaceful. Just some geese and ducks gliding far from the bank. I pulled off my riding cap and swatted myself. Then I wrestled off my boots and couldn't wait to strip down any more before I plunged into the water, crying out for Nicolas while I trudged around.

The water shocked me. We'd had a cold snap that week, and you could see your breath in the morning. But I was so hopped up on desperation I fought through the water's cold deathly grip. Nicolas must've swum out deep. I waded out to where the water was over my head. I dove to the bottom again and again. I held a wild hope I could save him. It took some time for a person to drown, didn't it? I needed to believe I still had a chance to bring him back.

My muscles cramped, and I could barely get air into my lungs. Hard as I fought, my limbs were sluggish to respond, numb in the freezing water, and then all I could do was struggle to keep my head above the surface. I didn't want to die, but I felt death creeping over me.

Then someone grabbed me and dragged me to the shore. Gradually, through my shock and terror, I realized it was my granddaddy. I would've died if he hadn't come along.

He held me as I lay gulping breaths on the mucky bank of the lake. I was frozen to the bone, but I still managed to sob. Nicolas was gone. He was never coming back.

LATER THAT DAY, after I dried off and got warm in Nicolas's cabin, Granddaddy and I read the letter together.

My dear Arizona,

What I've done is mine to answer alone. Don't ever blame yourself. In our short time together, you brought me more joy than I ever thought was possible. You deserve much more than a broken man can give you. I think you know that deep down in your heart.

You also know by now the kind of love we had was never meant to be. I've always been straight with you. If I had known before I was your uncle, I can't say that would've stopped me from loving you in every possible way. I wish I were a stronger man, but when you came into my life, you gave me what I needed so badly. I'd never have been able to stop loving you, and I feared you would feel the same way, which is why I had to leave you, darling.

I'm sorry. I know you've been through more pain than the world has a right to heap on anyone. I can only hope the hurt I left you with will mend in time. You're young, Arizona. I know you don't like hearing that, but it's the truth. You'll go on to be an amazing person, and so many people are going to love you. Thank you for letting me be one of them. I had to do the right thing and let you go.

Please don't blame your daddy, either. He saved us both. He's a good man, Arizona, and he's going to take good care of you.

I have to say goodbye, my love. I couldn't do it unless a little part of believed we'll see each other again someday. Take your time, though. You've got a lot of life to live, so many people to meet, so much of the world to see. And when you're one hundred years old and get to that beautiful world where your Grandma Tilly, Grandpa George, Mama Lou, and your mama Philippa are waiting for you, you promise you'll look for me.

With all my love,
Nicolas

I tore up that letter and cried out with all my soul. It felt like every time I'd gotten ahead, eked out some happiness from the world, someone came along to rip it from my hands. I didn't know if it was God or some curse of my birth. Once again, I'd been shown love and kindness wasn't meant for me.

Granddaddy called my school to explain I wasn't coming back for at least another week. I couldn't think of him as my daddy just yet. Too much had happened too fast, and for the next few days, I just went through the motions of getting out of bed, showering and dressing, eating a little bit here and there, and breaking down and crying in between. I went back to living in my old room up in the main house, and Granddaddy looked in on me three, four times a day. I couldn't talk to him about my grief, but I didn't mind having him close by.

The sheriff never found Nicolas's body. He had a team of divers try for three straight days, and then one night my granddaddy explained they'd given up and we'd have to hold a funeral with an empty casket. He had to restrain me that night. I told him I'd go down to the lake again myself to find Nicolas so he could have a respectful burial. While Granddaddy blocked me from the door and held me firm, I collapsed in tears again.

I was lost. I didn't have much fight left in me. Granddaddy drew me over to my bed and told me the divers would try again when it warmed up in the spring. Meanwhile, the lake was just as fine of a resting place for Nicolas. He loved it, which is why he'd built his cabin by the water.

The Friday next, we held a private funeral at the house. It was just for the family, the household staff, and a handful of people from B&B who had known Nicolas over the years. Father Timothy presided over the service in Whittington Manor's little chapel. Then we all walked over to the cemetery for a ceremonial burial in a freshly dug up plot.

Strange enough, that day I kept it together all the while Father Timothy spoke from an altar surrounded by flowers and a big photo of Nicolas on an easel. Granddaddy had found one of the shots from Nicolas's army service and had it enlarged. I didn't cry neither while Granddaddy delivered the eulogy, and when we stood around the empty grave. I guess I'd cried too many tears already and figured, just like with Grandma Tilly and Grandpa George, Nicolas deserved a respectful remembrance.

But that all changed when the guests departed after a little gathering for coffee and cake. That left just me, Granddaddy, Virginia, and Mr. Wainwright in what they called the Louis Quinze salon. It was the fanciest room in the house, with a gold leaf chandelier and sconces, framed mirrors and antique stuffed chairs. I'd been leaning against a mantle, fatigued and numb, not knowing what to do with myself.

Then Virginia called out to me. "Why don't you come over here and sit down, Arizona? Get something warm into your body. A growing boy needs something to eat."

She was done up in fancy black lace and pearls, sitting on a high-backed divan with Mr. Wainwright. Across a dainty table with the urn of coffee and cake and pastries, Granddaddy sat on a wingback parlor chair. That little comment of hers raised a demon in me.

"Now you're going to call me by my name and be kind to me?"

She raised a gloved hand to her neck. "I'm your grandmother. Why *wouldn't* I be kind to you?" She glanced at Mr. Wainwright as though he was a longtime witness to her grandmotherly affection.

I staggered toward her, pointing my finger. "You never been kind. You never treated me like a grandson. Don't pretend to start now."

I pierced clear through her artful facade. She looked fearfully at Granddaddy. He cleared his throat and told me, "Arizona, son, let's try to get along. We're all hurting today."

My mouth split open in a cruel grin as I stared at Virginia. "Is that right? Are you hurting, Granny? Did you even shed one honest tear?"

Virginia put on her best indignant face. "I don't know what's gotten into you, but I don't like it. And I won't stand for being judged by a boy who's been part of this family for all of six months."

"Six months is plenty of time to understand this family. I pay attention. How 'bout you? You remember your last words to Nicolas at Thanksgiving dinner?"

She turned her head away from me and fussed with the skirting of her dress. "I haven't the foggiest idea what the boy's talking about. But he better watch his tone."

"Arizona," my granddaddy muttered.

I ignored him. "You called him a queer and said our relationship was disgusting."

She swung toward me, defiantly. "You best think about what you're saying. Because if you want to have that conversation, we'll have it. It's the truth, isn't it?"

I mocked her with laughter. "Oh, it's the truth all right. You just love making people feel ashamed of themselves. Makes you feel that much better about yourself, does it? You're a fraud. You couldn't even love your only daughter. How you live with that, Virginia?"

"Oh, I see a lot of your mama in you now. Judging *me*?" She eyed me tauntingly. "How about you take account of yourself? Why, Nicolas would be with us right now if it wasn't for you. Tempting him into sin. He's burning in hell because of you."

I lunged for her. Granddaddy and Mr. Wainwright caught me and held me back. Virginia shrieked and scuttled around the back of the divan.

"You take that back," I shouted at her.

"He's out of his mind," Virginia declared. "Somebody call the hospital to take him away."

"Nicolas loved me. And you couldn't stand it. You can't stand anyone having any happiness because you're so goddamn miserable."

Granddaddy had an arm strapped across my neck and he warned me in a stiff voice, "You take it easy now."

"I know about misery all right," Virginia snarled at me. "Being left with a baby by a man who betrayed his wedding vows. Having that child grow up to hate me. So spiteful she tried to steal my husband. Then dying and leaving me a mother with no child."

I didn't care if the anguish on her face was real or not. I had so much rage inside me, I couldn't keep it in. "She left me too," I shouted at her. "And you know what else? She *did* steal your husband. I'm *his* son. That's why Nicolas killed himself. You go on and think about that."

That shut Virginia up, but only for so long. She couldn't look at Granddaddy, but she gave me an ugly sneer. "I had my suspicions. So, maybe you're not Gus Fanning's son, but you're still a bastard. And you inherited your mama's sinful ways."

I stared grimly at her. "I am a bastard. But you? You're swimming in sin ten times worse than me. Ain't adultery one of them things the good book warns against? You want to tell your husband about that, or should I?"

I felt my granddaddy unhand me, and he stepped away. In that moment, I wished I hadn't taken things that far. I turned to him, but he'd drifted away with his back turned to me, minding his own shame about my revelation. Meanwhile, Virginia looked at Granddaddy, trembling and wringing her hands.

"Poly, it's not true. Poly, now look at me. He's lying. He's a demon spawn. Been conspiring to wreck everything since the day he set foot in Whittington Manor."

I felt like I'd been spawned from a demon. For what I did to my granddaddy, not to her. "You pushed me too far," I told her. I combed through my hair, and another wave of rage came over me. "You made me do it. With every vicious word you've said to me. So, what do you say? *I'm sorry, Arizona?*"

I stepped toward her, and she jumped in the other direction.

"I've got nothing to apologize for." She called out for my granddaddy again. He wouldn't face her, and after a while, he strode out of the room. Virginia whimpered and ran out the opposite door.

I was breathless, sweating, and quivering. Mr. Wainwright stood off with his eyes pointed at me in judgment of what I'd done. That got my blood boiling again.

I strode over and looked Mr. Wainwright in the face. "Let me ask you something. Those letters I wrote to my siblings over the summer, the letters I wrote to Preston Montclair, did you send them?"

His nose twitched. He opened his mouth, and then his gaze shifted, not saying anything.

I grabbed his arm and shook it to make him look at me. "You

never sent them. Why? My people aren't good enough? Or did you just want me to be miserable living here?"

Mr. Wainwright yanked his arm away. "I won't stand for your accusations. Your conduct is entirely inappropriate."

I swayed up in his face. "You mind your own conduct. Things are going to be different now. You're going to respect me, Mr. Wainwright. I'm Gaston Bondurant's son."

His ugly eyes bulged, and then he shrank away and left the room.

I stood there alone for a spell, catching my breath and wiping tears from my face. Then I went to find my daddy.

I HAD TO ask around to the servants to find him in his study. I stood outside the door and couldn't go in at first. I really did feel terrible hurting him. Now I had to answer for it. I took a moment to straighten my shirt and jacket and smooth my hair. Then I stepped in.

Daddy had only turned on one lamp at the far end of the room. I'd been in his study just once when Mr. Wainwright let me make that phone call to Dolly and Little Douglas, but I hadn't done much looking around. The room didn't look much used. Framed portraits, diplomas, and commendations hung from the wood paneled walls, and bookshelves lined one side of the room with his textbooks from school, encyclopedias, and long-neglected hardcover volumes. A seating area took up two thirds of the room, and a long, tidy executive desk and chair sat at one end. Daddy was sitting on the Chesterfield with a cigarette in his hand and a tumbler of whiskey on the coffee table in front of him. He'd thrown off his suit jacket and loosened up his tie.

I'd never seen my daddy smoke. Our glances crossed, and he looked away. I marched over to him nonetheless and took a seat on the couch about an arm's reach away.

"I'm sorry."

Daddy said nothing.

I perched a little closer to him. "I didn't mean for it to come out like that."

He squashed out his cigarette in an ashtray. But he still didn't speak.

My voice shook. "I did wrong, but I'm trying, Daddy. I got so many emotions inside me, it's all I can do not to burst." I swiped my eyes. "Tell me I was out of line. Go on and slap my face. But don't turn away from me, Daddy. I got nobody. I can't lose you."

"What I told you about me and your mama was not yours to share."

My eyes were blurry with tears. "How much longer you planned to keep me a secret?"

"Your grandmother deserved to hear it from my mouth, not yours."

I took that in for a little while. But I was still aching so much, I couldn't control myself. "When, Daddy? When were you going to tell her? You told Nicolas and me almost a week ago."

"It doesn't matter when. It's between me and your grandmother."

"It's about *me*. Who has to live here while you decide if and when anyone knows I belong to you. After the man I loved died because you kept me a secret." I don't know where that boldness came from. I'd come to apologize to him, but things were shifting in my head. Not everything was Virginia's fault. He was part of it, too.

His face trembled. "I lost my brother, Arizona. My little brother. You think you're the only one in pain?"

He broke down in tears. My Lord, it shook me to the core. All week long he'd been strong for me, holding in his own grief. I felt like a fool, then I felt worse because it shamed me that such a strong man let himself bawl like a little child.

Why'd I have to be so hard on him? I didn't judge myself, didn't judge Nicolas when he cried. But somehow I didn't allow my daddy that dignity. Well, that changed that night. I slid over on the couch and took his hand in mine.

"I'm sorry, Daddy. If I could turn back time, I'd never have started up with Nicolas. I'd have sacrificed everything so he'd still be here."

We both gasped with tears. Gradually, he settled, straightened out, and kissed my hand. He looked at me with wide, forlorn eyes. "What are we going to do?"

Something about that brought a little smile to my face. Maybe because I felt the same way, like all the world had turned against me, and I didn't know how I was going to manage even the simplest thing.

"We're going to get by, you and me." I nodded at him. "Don't you doubt it. Ain't nothing gonna stop us."

He took me in his arms and held the side of my face. I hugged him tight to me while he softly gasped and moaned. I guess what you call clarity had settled over me. Nicolas had left my heart hollow, but life goes on, you know? You only got one alternative, and giving up had never been for me. Or I suppose you can become a drunk like Virginia and Gus Fanning or become a shut-in like Nicolas and miss out while life keeps going on around you.

I wasn't going to be that kind of person, and I knew Daddy was stronger than that, too. I'd go back to school. I had good friends back there, and I'd keep studying hard, get good grades, and take the SAT so I could get into a good college.

I'd never give up on my brothers and sister. It didn't matter we weren't blood. We loved each other, and that's what made us family. When summer came, I'd find Duke and Little Douglas and make sure they were doing all right. I'd visit Dolly, too. I'd set aside my allowance in case they needed money and never let them forget who their big brother was.

I'd go on being the best man I could be. I'd make Daddy proud, and I'd be kinder to him too. I was Arizona Bondurant. Let anyone try telling me there was anything I couldn't do.

ABOUT THE AUTHOR

Romeo Preminger has been called the master of the romantic thriller. He's the author of over a dozen books including the Southern Gothic ARIZONA series, the branded romantic thriller series GUILTY PLEASURES EDITIONS, erotic romance stand-alones, and some naughty shorts called STORYBOOK EDITIONS.

Romeo lives on the East Coast with his husband. Beyond writing, some of his favorite jobs on his resume are a brief stint as a zookeeper, an even briefer stint as a hot dog vendor, and a more substantial career as a counselor and advocate for LGBTQ+ youth. For more about Romeo, visit: https://romeopreminger.com or connect with him on Twitter at https://twitter.com/Preminger RomeoSign up for his mailing list and get news on sales and upcoming releases:

https://mailchi.mp/78bc1368af1e/team-romeo

Made in United States
North Haven, CT
01 May 2024

51994317R00135